It was just a simple gold-prospecting trip...after all, how much trouble could Rachel get into with the four of them all there together?

"You know, I can hardly believe your sister is still over there working," JT whispered. "My guess was that she would have quit when the shovels came out."

"You forget that once she latches on to something, she can get pretty obsessive and dig in," Heather replied.

Buddy nodded. "Yeah, like a pit bull."

Heather's eyes twinkled. "Or maybe she really wants that gold jewelry."

"Hmm...okay. Rachel," JT called out to her. "You can quit any time now."

"No way," Rachel called back. "I found a soft area and don't have to dig as hard."

She pushed aside a few big rocks and dug out a couple shovelfuls of lose sand. She stopped and stared down. Something sparkled. It looked like a jewel of some type. *A diamond? Did the mine also have diamonds?*

Heather turned around to watch her. "Rachel, what are you doing?"

"I see something." Rachel flung her shovel aside and reached for the twinkling stone. She tried to lift it and it resisted. She pulled harder and the stone came up attached to something stuck in the ground. It looked like a—

A scream escaped from Rachel's throat when she pulled the hand up, then she dropped it and leaped back as if she had touched fire. Heather jumped up when she heard the cry but could only see her sister's back. Then she watched Rachel fall over on her face in a dead faint.

Young women and girls are disappearing, and bodies start showing up in the desert around the old Blood Mountain hotel...

Sales Director, Rachel Ryan, who never could mind her own business, decides to investigate at the request of an elderly friend of one of the women. And, this time, Deputy Tucker doesn't mind as his case is going nowhere, despite the many and varied suspects. Rachel quickly gets in way over her head, as usual, and Tucker takes her off the case. Undaunted, Rachel charges off on her own, determined to find the killer, especially after she discovers one of the bodies herself. Another body is discovered by Jared Johnson, a retired detective from Detroit, and Rachel immediately enlists his help in solving the cold-case murder of her parents in Grand Rapids more than a decade ago.

To make things even more complicated, Alex Tucker suddenly swoops back into Rachel's life—just as she finds herself falling for Buddy—and Rachel is forced to make a life-changing decision...if she survives the murder investigation.

KUDOS for *Blood Mountain Conspiracy*

In *Blood Mountain Conspiracy* by Joanne Taylor Moore, intrepid Rachel Ryan gets in over her head investigating the disappearance of young women and the bodies that start showing up in the desert around the old Blood Mountain hotel. In addition, Rachel discovers that her parents' death a decade earlier was not what it seemed to be. As Rachael investigates, and gets into trouble, her sister and JT try to keep her under control, while Buddy gives her a shoulder and any help she asks for. Just as she starts to fall for Buddy, Alex Tucker, her old flame, rushes back into her life. As always, Moore's characters are charming, flawed, and very human. Her plot is strong, with plenty of surprising twists and turns to keep you riveted from beginning to end. ~ *Taylor Jones, Reviewer*

With *Blood Mountain Conspiracy* by Joanne Taylor Moore, the third book in the *Blood Mountain* series, we are again treated to another edge-of-your-seat mystery. In this story, Rachel investigates the disappearance of young women from the area and uncovers a human trafficking ring of major proportions. Rachel starts out on her own, but Deputy Tucker admits he needs help and let's Rachel do her thing until she screws up. Even after she's taken off the case, so to speak, Rachel doesn't give up. (This girl is nothing if not tenacious.) Enlisting the help of some residents of the old-folks home, Rachel quickly gets in way over her head. Like Moore's other books, *Blood Mountain Conspiracy* keeps you on your toes and turning pages. I especially like the fact that I couldn't figure who all the bad guys were and some that I thought were, weren't. While the story has lots of twists and turns, Moore adds some additional surprises, which will make you shake your head and say "Huh?" A very intriguing and satisfying read. I highly recommend it. ~ *Regan Murphy, Reviewer*

ACKNOWLEDGEMENTS

This book would not be possible without a little help from my friends and advisors: my husband, Larry, who read my manuscript at least ten times, weeding out my typos; my fellow Yuma writers: Pinkie Paranya, John Coltas, Debbie Lee, and Robin Christiansen, who critiqued my work with a critical eye; my first readers: Valarie, Donnelly, and Gail Thompson, who gave me support from my very first book; Betty Webb, who gave me advice and encouragement; and my mentor Don G. Porter, without whom I would have never published my first book. Thank you.

I also want to thank and acknowledge the people who gave me their time and assistance in getting my facts straight: Angenett Vaill, supervisor, Yuma County Adult Probation Office; and Julio Sanchez, along with Armano Duron, from the Fisher Hyundai Dealership in Yuma. If any of my story is wrong, regarding the work of the probation officers or the malfunction of cars, I am entirely to blame.

And finally, I want to thank the Black Opal Book crew who put it all together for me: perfectionist editors Lauri and Faith, and talented art director Jack, Jackson who designed all my covers. There are many others who play a background role in getting a good book out, and I want to thank all of you, even though I may not know all of your names. You are the nicest group of folks I've ever had the pleasure of working with.

All of you have helped me to make a life-long dream come true.

Blood Mountain CONSPIRACY

To Elaine,
Thanks for being a faithful reader!

Joanne Taylor Moore

Joanne TM 2015

A Black Opal Books Publication

GENRE: MYSTERY-DETECTIVE/SUSPENSE/THRILLER

This is a work of fiction. Names, places, characters and incidents are either the product of the author's imagination or are used fictitiously, and any resemblance to any actual persons, living or dead, businesses, organizations, events or locales is entirely coincidental. All trademarks, service marks, registered trademarks, and registered service marks are the property of their respective owners and are used herein for identification purposes only. The publisher does not have any control over or assume any responsibility for author or third-party websites or their contents.

BLOOD MOUNTAIN CONSPIRACY
Copyright © 2015 by Joanne Taylor Moore
Cover Design by Jackson Cover Designs
All cover art copyright © 2015
All Rights Reserved
Print ISBN: 978-1-626942-47-9

First Publication: MARCH 2015

All rights reserved under the International and Pan-American Copyright Conventions. No part of this book may be reproduced or transmitted in any form or by any means, electronic or mechanical, including photocopying, recording, or by any information storage and retrieval system, without permission in writing from the publisher.

WARNING: The unauthorized reproduction or distribution of this copyrighted work is illegal. Criminal copyright infringement, including infringement without monetary gain, is investigated by the FBI and is punishable by up to 5 years in federal prison and a fine of $250,000.

ABOUT THE PRINT VERSION: If you purchased a print version of this book without a cover, you should be aware that the book is stolen property. It was reported as "unsold and destroyed" to the publisher, and neither the author nor the publisher has received any payment for this "stripped book."

IF YOU FIND AN EBOOK OR PRINT VERSION OF THIS BOOK BEING SOLD OR SHARED ILLEGALLY, PLEASE REPORT IT TO: lpn@blackopalbooks.com

Published by Black Opal Books **http://www.blackopalbooks.com**

DEDICATION

I dedicate this book to my eleven grandchildren: Justin and Jovanni Taylor, Kaden, Kelci, Kole, and Karli Taylor; Evan and Jay Boardman; Scott, Travis, and Tyler Moore. You are all intelligent, and yet each of you is unique with your own special talents. All of you are beautiful on the outside, yet even more loving and beautiful on the inside. Thank you for bringing so much joy into my life.

Prologue

The corridor smelled of dust and cobwebs. Zoe Liddy slipped inside, leaving the door ajar, and paused. A wave of anxiety swept over her and she stood rooted to the spot until it passed. All the residents were asleep, she assured herself and took a deep, calming breath. Enough light flowed in from the nurse's station that she could see the steel fire doors ahead. She clicked on her flashlight, swept it around the hallway, and peered down the dim passageway. The only sign of life was a lone black widow hanging by a thread from her web, the orange hourglass on her underbelly glowing in the light.

The hallway was warm and Zoe felt the sweat bead up above her lip and between her breasts. She was plump, busty, and wearing her favorite pair of Mickey Mouse scrubs that were made of heat-retaining polyester. Feeling around for her pants pocket, she dropped the key in and pulled the door shut. She knew she wasn't supposed to be where she was and, even though she had taken every precaution, there was always the possibility she would get caught.

The possibility was very slim, however. Teresa Espinosa, her CNA on night duty, could come out of the break room, but it was doubtful. She constantly sat in front of the stove's exhaust fan and smoked while she inhaled one of her romance novels, always using up her full allotment of break time. Sometimes she'd even stay a couple minutes longer if she was at a real juicy part of the book.

Then there was the managing partner, Bricknell Krutzer. He popped in at night once a month, but only on the weekend. His mother and partner, Hester, rarely showed her face after five, no matter what day it was.

So that left the residents of Golden Vista—who were all drugged up and happily awaiting their turn at the pearly gates—as the only possible witnesses. Unless one of them woke up and yanked the emergency cord, no one would know Zoe had unlocked the door to the old wing of the home and had entered forbidden territory.

Forbidden territory. It was one of the things that made it enticing for her, she realized. That, and the money she'd get if her instincts were correct.

Zoe approached the set of fire doors, hit the open button, and angled left down the corridor. The air smelled of old plaster walls and brand new wood.

She looked down and stopped, flashing the light back and forth in front of her. Yeah, there was something weird going on inside this part of the building, all right.

Closed up tighter than a tick on an old dog, it was. Boarded up, walled in, and written in the employees rules as off limits. Yet fresh footprints were scattered in the layer of dust at her feet.

She came to a door on her left and pressed her ear to it. Nothing. She turned the knob, the door opening with a pop, and shined her light into the dark room. Her flashlight revealed a room full of empty shelves and the smell of stale air greeted her. She closed the door with a feeling of relief and trepidation. If she got caught now, getting fired might be the least of her problems, especially if her hunch was right.

Zoe swung the flashlight around and illuminated her watch. Five minutes had passed. She advanced a few more yards and the light hit another door. It looked strong, solid, with brand-new wood that had never been painted. At the very bottom, a red glow seeped out between it and the threshold.

Zoe watched her hand move to the knob as if everything was moving in slow motion. The door was locked. She dug in her pocket and retrieved the key. If the key fit, she could check out the room for ten minutes. That would leave her with five minutes to get back to the nurse's station, barely enough time.

She put the key in the lock, heard it settle in place, and felt the key move. A rush of adrenaline blazed across her chest and up to her ears. She turned the knob and opened the door.

The horror scene in the red-lit room exploded in her brain, and then the smell hit her. Her flashlight tumbled to the concrete floor. She stood frozen, her mouth gaped open, her thoughts frozen in her mind.

"Oh, Zoe," a voice behind her softly admonished. "What have you done?"

Zoe winced, and her heart sank. She recognized the voice. She turned to face her questioner, but only saw a flash of light and heard the crack of metal against her skull.

She crumbled to the ground like a stuffed doll and never felt a thing.

Chapter 1

Rachel Ryan left the hotel lobby and walked through the courtyard to her casita. The April sun felt good after spending the day behind the desk in her air conditioned office. She eagerly climbed the steps to her suite, unlocked the door, and glanced around the southwest-themed living room. Slanted rays of light glinted off the copper lamp shade, bathing the room in a golden glow.

She kicked off her red Jimmy Choos when her feet hit the carpet and removed her designer jacket on the way to the bedroom.

At five-feet-eight, she was a tall woman and looked even more so because of her long, slim legs.

She'd hung up her office wear and pulled out a T-shirt and jeans when her cell phone rang. She glanced at the caller ID. It was her sister.

"Hey, Heather, what's going on?"

"Not a whole lot. What are you doing?"

Rachel frowned. "I'm standing here, looking in the bedroom mirror, wishing I had bigger boobs."

"Oh, for Pete's sake, Rachel. Get off that. Women would give their right arms to look like you."

"Easy for you to say, Mrs. 'C-Cup' Carpenter." Rachel posed in front of the mirror, flipping her pale hair back, letting it flow down over her shoulders like a stream of chardonnay.

"Rachel, stop it. You know I was practically flat-chested until the twins were born and it never bothered JT one bit. God made me the way he wanted to, and I was fine with that."

"Okay," Rachel conceded, not wanting to go there. "You win. I totally renounce my sin of covetousness and I'll even throw in a couple of Hail Marys." She could hear Heather trying to suppress a laugh and glanced at her watch. "You called, remember?"

"Yes. You want to meet JT and me for dinner later? In the Plantation Room? Chef Henri just received a shipment of prime filets."

"Ah, the perks of living at the Mesquite Mountain Inn." Not having a domestic bone in her body, Rachel loved the hotel life, especially the part about eating there three times a day and not having to cook or wash a dish. She paused to think about the JT part. "Um…how is my favorite brother-in-law doing?"

"He's fine. Why?"

"Oh, no reason," she hedged.

A note of caution crept into Heather's voice. "You two didn't have a fight, did you?"

"No, we did not have a fight," Rachel reassured her sister. "However, we could not agree as to why the sales and catering department's first quarter financials did not come in according to budget, nor could we agree on a marketing budget for the summer months." She decided to leave off the part about the raised voices.

"Sweetie, it wasn't your fault about March. JT knows that. He also knows we're very fortunate to have someone with your background and expertise as our sales director."

"So you say."

Rachel's mind skipped back to the time JT hired her. She'd practically begged for the job, knowing she could help her sister—and herself—since she was unemployed and had no place to live. But dealing with JT every day…well, that was the downside of the deal.

"So, are you coming or not?"

Rachel was tugged back to the present and pictured herself consuming a filet mignon covered with a thick layer of mushrooms sautéed in a butter-wine reduction. Then the vision disappeared. "I can't. I'd love to but I'm afraid I have a hot date I better not cancel," she reluctantly replied.

"A hot date? Hmm. Let me guess. You're visiting Hank at the rest home."

"You guessed right, but it's not a rest home. It's called assisted living."

"Oops. Sorry. So much for my political correctness.

Tell him we miss him and bring him a lemon meringue pie for me."

"I already have one set aside, my dear." Rachel would have preferred to bring the whole meal from the hotel kitchen instead of dining on what she was afraid might be pureed chicken and prunes, but Hank insisted he host their meal. "And I really would love to join you and JT for dinner, but Hank sounded pretty worried when he called."

"Worried? That doesn't sound like Hank Levinson. Did he say why?"

"No. He just seemed anxious about needing to see me as soon as I could get there."

"Oh, dear."

Rachel could almost see the frown on her sister's forehead, the freckles popping up on her nose.

"I hope everything is okay at Golden Vista," Heather continued. "I've read stories about awful things that go on in old folk's homes."

"You mean like sex orgies?"

Heather gasped. "Rachel Ryan, you're incorrigible!" She tried to sound annoyed, but she was laughing.

"Yeah, I know. It's part of my charm."

Rachel dropped the phone into her purse, finished dressing, and skipped down the stairs from her suite. She stopped and looked back at the two-story casita that sat along the hill with the others. *Did the door click shut?* She had to think a minute. *Too many things on my mind.* But the truth was, she, too, was worried about Hank.

Deciding the door had locked after all, Rachel jogged

on ahead and made a quick stop at the cafe for the pie. She drove the Hummer down the winding mountain road toward town. The sun was setting, a fiery gold sphere in a clear blue sky. She glanced in her rear view mirror at Blood Mountain and could already see the magic happening. The sunset was turning the mountain's rock face into a dark shade of red, like the color of blood. *Montana de la Sangre,* Rachel mused. *They really couldn't have called Blood Mountain by any other name and been honest about it.* Her body heaved in a deep sigh. *And to think, this is where I've ended up working—in a dry gulch little town on the Mexican border.*

She reached the bottom of the mountain in a cloud of dust and drove through the valley on the blacktopped road that led to town. Miles of farmland stretched out on either side. fields that were covered with checkerboard squares of vibrant greens and golds. Not that she cared. Rachel much preferred living with tile and carpet under her feet, surfaces she'd rather navigate in a pair of her designer shoes.

Noticing the town limit sign of Mesquite, Arizona, looming ahead, Rachel slowed her speed. Her eyes searched around for signs of the old sheriff's deputy that slapped a speeding ticket on her shortly after she moved to Blood Mountain.

She recalled Deputy Tucker was an amusing sight with his gray walrus mustache and bowed legs that particular day, but their ensuing relationship was hardly comical. It seemed like they were always on the opposite side of any opinion or disagreement. She also appeared to be a constant source of irritation to him because he *claimed* she was always butting into business she shouldn't be butting into. Maybe a *little* of that was true, Rachel admitted to herself, but only because Tucker acted like a bumbling idiot at times and needed her help solving cases. So she considered it an even exchange.

She drove across Main Street to the historic section of town and turned onto River Street, the surface of which was old, cracked, and looked like alligator hide. It felt like it, too. The street led past historic adobe houses that still stood with their stucco coatings partly chipped away, while their interiors had been converted into shops and artists' studios. Many of the houses were attractively landscaped with *Agavero licor* ficus and palm trees and so much greenery, it almost made a person forget they were in the middle of the Sonoran Desert.

She braked when she arrived at Golden Vista where a large sign above the porch boasted: *Home of Gracious Assisted Living.* Hank had complained that, with most of the residents in wheelchairs or using walkers, it seemed more like a nursing home than assisted living—and that was only one of Hank Levinson's complaints.

He was waiting just inside the foyer when Rachel arrived, sitting tall and upright in a wheelchair, wearing a western shirt, Wranglers, and a pair of cowboy boots. His hair was thick and white as cotton.

At eighty-two, Hank was still handsome in a distinguished kind of way, with prominent cheekbones and a chiseled jaw that went back a few generations to an Apache heritage.

Rachel leaned over and kissed him on the cheek. "You need a haircut," she teased, roughing up his hair.

"Yeah, and who's gonna make me get one?" he said, squinting and trying to look tough.

"Uh—well—" Rachel stammered, pretending to be afraid. "I guess not me." She shot him a quick smile and pulled the pie out of a bag. "Peace offering—your favorite, lemon meringue."

"Ah, now we're talkin'!" Hank's eyes lit up and so did the smile on his face. "Follow me to my place. I don't want any of these old people spotting my pie. They'll be hounding me for slices if they suspect it's from the Hibiscus Cafe."

Hank scooted down the foyer, which smelled faintly of disinfectant and roasted chicken. Rachel stayed at his side, her arm securely latched onto the pie. As they passed by the dining room, she glanced through the columned doorway and noticed the room was nearly filled with elderly residents. A lofty cathedral ceiling arched over the room, and crystal chandeliers hung high above the tables, casting a warm, luxurious glow.

Golden Vista had emerged from a year-long remodeling project of the Krutzer family and it was the only facility of its type existing in town. Bricknell Krutzer and his mother, Hester, had reclaimed the town's first hospital, renovated most of it, and turned it into a facility that housed the elderly with varying degrees of disability. Overseen by a couple of nurses and their certified assistants, forty residents lived in private studio apartments and shared common dining and recreation areas.

Rachel and Hank were viewing the pictorial history of the renovation that lined the entire hallway when a huge man in gray scrubs came barreling toward them with a scowl on his face. She stepped back as the man charged past without a smile or greeting and rushed out the main entrance.

"Who was that?" Rachel asked, turning to look at the man who had already disappeared.

Hank's smile was gone. "Ron Emmett. He helps out around here."

"Not with the residents, I hope."

"No, he's Brick's right hand man. I'm not really sure what his position is, he just kind of hangs around, doing whatever needs to be done."

Rachel shivered. "I can't imagine Brick Krutzer hiring someone like him to work here. I mean, I never met the man, but he seems too smart for that."

"Oh, Emmett's an old high school buddy of his. They used to play football together." Hank paused at the nurses' station and turned a sharp right.

"Well, that explains it. But he still gives me the creeps."

"Yeah, he has that effect on quite a few people." Hank stopped and turned his chair in front of a doorway. "Here we are. I'm lucky to have the first room next to the nurse's station," he said with a smile back on his face. "I get to check out the action."

Rachel gave him a sly look. "You mean check out the babes, don't you?" She laughed. "Oh, Hank, you haven't changed a bit."

"No, and I don't intend to, either."

He cocked his head, indicating Rachel should enter his apartment. She stepped in on the taupe carpet. It was new and smelled faintly of formaldehyde. The paint job on the walls, a bland shade of beige, was also new. The studio itself was L-shaped with a small kitchenette located near the entrance. It contained a sink, a counter with a microwave on it, and a small, but sufficient, refrigerator.

"They completely redid the place before I moved in," he said. "The old guy who lived here before me must have really torn it up."

"It's lovely." Rachel looked around. "No stove, huh?"

"Too dangerous for us old people." Hank's tone dripped with sarcasm.

Rachel had sympathy in her eyes when she turned to look at him. "I'm so sorry. I know it must be hard for you to adjust to this kind of life."

"Hey, it could be worse."

By the sound of his voice, Rachel didn't believe he meant a word of it.

A small table with two chairs sat adjacent to a comfortable looking sofa. A flat-screen TV hung near the opposite corner, enabling Hank to see it from both the sofa and the bed, which was tucked into the end of the "L."

"This is actually quite nice," Rachel said, studying the simple decor. "I guess I won't have to call Heather in for decorating advice after all," she teased then glanced back at the table. It was set with flatware, napkins, and goblets filled with ice water and lemon wedges. A basket of corn chips sat in the center. "I assume we're eating here today?"

"You assume correctly." Hank extended his arm. "Please sit down and allow me to serve you."

"Thank you. Now this is a treat," she said, slipping into the chair that faced the window. "You have a nice view from here."

"Yeah, it's not bad. I get to see a lot of what goes on around here." Hank opened the refrigerator and pulled out a tray with two bowls. Holding it in one hand, he wheeled himself to the table, set down the tray, and maneuvered himself into the chair across from Rachel.

"Looks like you're doing better," Rachel said, noticing how easily Hank accomplished getting the meal set up and seating himself.

"Only physically," came the curt reply.

"Okay, Hank," Rachel huffed, dropped her hands to her lap, and looked at him. "It's obvious you're upset. Are you going to tell me what's going on?"

"Yes, but try the salad first. This is one of the best things they make."

Rachel looked down at the crispy chicken lying on the bed of greens. It was sprinkled with black beans, chopped tomatoes, corn, cheese, and pieces of red and green pepper. "It looks delicious." She took a small bite. "It tastes good, too." She put her fork down. "So, now, tell me what happened."

Hank's head and shoulders drooped, and he raised his eyes to look at her. "Zoe's gone."

"What?"

"Zoe's gone. Disappeared."

Rachel blinked. "You mean, Zoe, the nurse? The cute little redhead with the ponytail you keep proposing to?"

"Well, she's not exactly little. She's got a big, lovely set—"

"Okay, okay. I know who you mean. She quit?"

"No, she didn't quit. She just disappeared."

"What do you mean, she just disappeared? She just walked off the job?"

"No!" Hank raised his voice and pounded his fist on the table, nearly sloshing the water out of his glass. "She just disappeared. Like into thin air. One minute here. Next minute gone."

Rachel looked at Hank, dumbfounded, and wondered if there was something going on with his head. Maybe all of this was too much.

"No, I'm not going crazy," he said calmly, reading her mind. "I talked to Zoe shortly after she came on night duty last night. Everything was fine. I'm telling you, she just disappeared."

"Now, Hank," Rachel began, a little condescendingly, "I'm sure she just didn't disappear. Maybe she got sick and went home. Something must have happened."

"Something happened all right, but I know she wasn't sick. There was nothing wrong with her when she handed out the night meds. That's when she told me she'd come back to see me. But no one's seen hide nor hair of her since." He looked at her and frowned. "And you don't have to patronize me, Rachel. I'm not senile."

"Oh, Hank, I'm sorry. I didn't mean it that way." Her ivory skin flushed with embarrassment. She felt like she was making one faux pas after another. "Did you ask around?"

"Of course I asked around," he snapped, then dropped his voice, embarrassed. "Ah, I'm sorry Rachel. I'm just so dang upset. Nobody around here knows anything. And if they do, they ain't talking."

"Hey, it's okay. I want to help. Do you want me to call Zoe at home?"

"I already did. No answer. Nothing."

"What about family?"

"None. The only thing I know is that she was seeing Long John."

"Long John? The locksmith?" She remembered seeing him around the hotel before.

"Yeah, the locksmith. And he hung up on me when I called."

Rachel's eyes teased. "Did he know you were his competition?" She took another bite of salad.

Hank grinned a little cockeyed smile. "Aw, Rachel, it wasn't really nothin' with me and Zoe. I'm old enough to be her grand pappy. And she flirts with all us old guys."

"But she really cares," Rachel said, softening.

"I suppose." He then dropped his head and turned pink.

"What?"

"I gave her a ring."

Rachel gulped down the salad she had in her mouth. "You gave her a ring? As in diamond ring?"

Hank shook his head. "Naw, it was a big, fake stone, one of those man-made diamonds. It was like a joke, Rachel. I asked her to marry me, like I do nearly every night when she comes by to hand out the meds, and I gave her this ring I bought at the outlet store."

"Then what happened?"

"Zoe liked it. It was fake, but it was pretty. She put it on her finger and wore it."

Rachel laughed and shook her head. "Hank Levinson, you are quite the romantic."

She gazed out past the window. The sunset was casting a reddish glow over the garden, and a white panel truck was headed down the driveway to the rear of the home.

"So do you think Long John came by, saw the ring on Zoe's hand, got jealous, and bopped her one?"

"Aw, Rachel, no. He could have come by, though. He often does after he locks up the shop. I've seen him pull up the driveway, there, and knock on the side door."

He started poking at his salad and Rachel thought a minute. "So what's the official word from Golden Vista?"

"Well, Teresa Espinoza was the CNA on duty, and she said that when she came out of the break room, Zoe was gone. Just gone. She'd been on break fifteen minutes. She said she sets the timer on the stove because she likes to read and would probably forget about work if the buzzer didn't go off."

"And Teresa said Zoe was just gone?"

"Yup. Like she disappeared into thin air, like one of

them alien abductions. She said she looked all around and then called Brick."

"Then what happened?"

"Brick called his momma, they both showed up, looked around. Nobody saw nothin'."

"Did anyone think to call the Deputy Sheriff?"

"Yeah, I finally did. Everybody else had their fingers up their noses. But Deputy Tucker said we had to wait 24 hours to file a missing person's report, 'cause she was an adult."

Rachel glanced at her watch, knowing what Hank said was true. "It's almost twenty-four hours now."

"Yeah. Tucker said he'd come back tonight. I imagine he's probably already here. He don't seem to have too much to do lately."

Rachel wasn't about to get into a discussion of Deputy Tucker. "What about Zoe's car? Does she drive to work?"

"Her car's still sittin' out in the lot right where she left it."

"Oh, boy." Rachel looked down at her salad and moved it around with her fork. She was afraid to raise her eyes. "So, what do want me to do?"

Hank suddenly grabbed Rachel's wrist. "I want you to find her."

She jerked her head up when she felt his rough hand grip her.

Hank quickly let go of her wrist. "Aw, Rachel, I'm so sorry. I didn't mean to grab you like that." He shook his head, humiliated. "I'm such a jerk."

Rachel rubbed her wrist. "You know, you're still pretty strong for an old dude." She wasn't smiling and, for a minute, neither one of them said anything. Finally, she spoke. "If I leave now, I can probably catch Long John before he closes up his shop. He might be willing to share some information with me."

Hank raised his head. His eyes were wet. "Aw, would you do that, Rachel? At least somebody around here would be doing something."

Rachel saw raw pain in his eyes. *Funny,* she thought. *Even at his age, love hurts.*

"You know, you don't have to."

Rachel thought his eyes said otherwise. "I know I don't have to." She rose from the table. "But Zoe Liddy isn't the only one around here who cares about you."

॰೨॰

Only a few blocks away from Golden Vista, the sign for Long John's Lock and Key stretched across the front of a small stucco building that sat on the edge of the sidewalk. The sign was new and replaced the "Long and Sons Locksmith" sign that had hung above the door for twenty-six years.

Long John's name was actually John Long. The twist on his name started back in John's grade school years. When his teachers called the roll, they'd always call the last name first, hence, "Long, John." Even in grade school John was always the tallest in his class, so the name, Long John, stuck.

John was also wire thin, which made him look even taller than his six-six frame. His hair was a dark brown, and he had learned to keep it long enough to hide his ears, which stuck out from his head like little wings. When Rachel parked in front of the lock shop, twilight still clung to the sky. She glanced around the area, glad for the little bit of light. Old Town wasn't the best place to be after dark. She opened the door to the shop, and a little bell on the back of it announced her entrance.

"We're about to close," Long John called out. He stood behind a counter at the back of the room, sorting through papers.

The shop smelled of metal and dust and old linoleum. A big gray area was worn into the floor in front of the counter where people had stood over the years. A rack of key blanks in a myriad of colorful designs sat off to one side of where Long John stood. On the other side of the room, a group of safes and metal lock boxes appeared to have been plunked down on the floor without any thought to artistic arrangement.

Rachel walked up to the counter. "I won't be but a minute," she said.

He continued to sort through papers that looked like the receipts of the day. "What can I help you with?"

"I'm looking for Zoe Liddy, and I was hoping you could help me find her."

Long John snapped his head up. "What do you want with her?"

"She was my friend Hank's favorite nurse at Golden Vista, and he's heartbroken because she seems to have disappeared." Rachel came closer. "I understand you two dated and I was hoping you might have some idea of where she could be."

"I'd like to know myself," he said, obviously miffed, and then went back to his work.

"Hank said he called the Deputy Sheriff."

Long John glanced up and made a face. "I'm sure that was a big, fat waste of time. I already tried that. When Zoe didn't answer her phone, I called Golden Vista and then drove over there to look for her myself. Her car was still there. Nobody could tell me anything, so I called Deputy Tucker."

"And he said you needed to wait 24 hours to file a missing person's report."

"Yeah. Exactly. He said someone had already called in and reported her missing, that he had already gone over there and made an initial report. He said he'd go by Golden Vista tonight to make it official."

"It was a resident who first called Tucker—my friend, Hank," Rachel offered. "I guess the Krutzer's weren't all that worried about her."

She watched Long John attack the pile of papers again. This time she was close enough to see he had bitten his nails down to the quick.

"When did you see her last?"

"Last night." His eyes shifted over to the side. "Last night, just before she went on duty."

"But you spoke to her after that."

Long John leaped out from behind the counter. "No, and I don't need to talk to you about it." His voice boomed out at her. "You just tell that Hank guy to butt out of Zoe's life or I'll tell him myself."

Rachel stepped back, feeling intimidated by the angry man towering over her, even though she was five-feet-eight in her stocking feet.

Before she could reply, Long John walked right past her and yanked the door open, the little bell clanging against the back of it. "I know all about the ring and his fantasy marriage. Zoe is never going to marry him. Heck, she wouldn't even marry *me* and I'm—"

"You're what?"

He glowered at her. "Look, just go, whoever you are."

"Rachel Ryan," she said, holding out her hand. "And I'm really sorry I've upset you. I hardly know Zoe, but she means a great deal to my friend Hank. He's old, he's crippled, and she makes living at Golden Vista bearable for him."

Long John regarded her hand, turned his head, and looked away.

It was dark by the time Rachel left the lock shop and headed back to the Mesquite Mountain Inn. She leaned on the accelerator when she hit the valley. A thin crescent of moon, glowing like an evil grin, rose in the east sky over the mountains.

Irrigation water was flowing into the cotton fields, pushing away the heat of the day. Rachel rolled down the windows to feel the rush of wind on her face. It tossed her hair, but did little to diminish the thoughts that clung to her with angry tentacles.

For every mile she drove, the more she felt her anger build.

She glanced at the clock. Surely Buddy would be back from LA by now. If he wasn't too tired from his day, he might be willing to give her a drink and a sympathetic ear.

Buddy was JT and Heather's partner in the Mesquite Mountain Inn, and Rachel could always depend on him to soften the tension between her and JT. Tonight she was hoping he could…well, she wasn't sure *what* she was hoping he could do and didn't want to think about it either.

Rachel turned on the radio. It irritated her. She popped the music off and began to mentally remind herself that Zoe was not her problem.

She was still telling herself that when she reached the hotel, pulled up in front of her casita, and pulled out her cell phone. She punched in the private number of Byron Edward McCain.

"Okay, Buddy, you can kick all the other girls out. I'm on my way over," she said, hung up, and tramped two doors over.

Buddy studied her face a moment when he opened the door. "Will that be a single or double margarita?" he asked.

She stomped in past him. "Just give me the whole dang bottle of tequila and a glass of ice."

Buddy stood his ground and watched Rachel plop down on the sofa, his eyes soft and sympathetic behind gold rimmed glasses. "I picked up something new you might like," he said matter-of-factly, pretending to be totally oblivious to the storm she blew in on. He set off for the kitchenette and returned with a bottle of *Agavero licor* and two small glasses filled with ice.

"What's that?" Rachel asked, eyeing the bottle.

"Tequila liqueur." Buddy poured the two glasses full and gave her one.

She took a large sip, tilted her head back, and let the sweet liqueur float down her throat. She finally looked at him. Buddy was still standing in front of her, smiling. He was wearing gray slacks, pleated in the front, the cuffs brushing the tops of his loafers.

His Ralph Lauren shirt was the exact shade of blue as his eyes, open at the collar, and it fit him closely, as if it had been custom made for him. He had a trim, athletic body, and moved with grace.

"You look good," she said, checking him out from top to bottom. "Still playing tennis, I see." She picked up the fat-bottomed green bottle to read the label. "And this is good, too."

Buddy sat down beside her. "It's yours."

"Why, thank you. That was unexpected." She held out her empty glass. "But don't mention it to JT. He'll be on your butt about enabling me."

"I think I can handle JT." Buddy laughed an easy laugh. "And I hardly think I'm enabling you." He refilled the glass.

She took another big sip, felt a little click in her brain, leaned back against the sofa, and studied her friend. His bushy, sandy-colored hair was slightly mussed, as usual, and his teeth gleamed in a million dollar smile. "You know, one thing I like about you, Buddy—you don't have a tense bone in your body. It's so easy to relax around you."

"I know. I keep telling you, you need to marry me," he teased. "But instead, you're off having dinner with some other guy named Hank."

Rachel tried her best to look annoyed, but a smile pulled at the corners of her lips. "That Heather Carpenter is such a little tattle-tale. I was hoping you wouldn't find out I was two-timing you."

When Buddy laughed, his whole face lit up. Rachel never thought of him as handsome, in the classical sense, that is. His jaw was a little too narrow and his nose had been broken once by an irate husband. But he was attractive. His eyes were vibrant, and his breath always smelled of peppermint.

Even more important, he was totally charming, a trait that caused women to fall madly in love with him. Rachel suspected, deep down inside, she was probably the only woman alive who resisted that urge with every fiber of her being.

"Have you eaten?" he asked.

"Hardly."

"Why don't we go over to the Plantation Room and get a couple of those filets, a good bottle of wine, and talk for a while. Then you can tell me why you blew in here like a hurricane."

Rachel cast her eyes toward Buddy but her thoughts zigzagged past him. He was so accommodating as far as her temper and her moods were concerned. Her tantrums just rolled off him like rain off tile roofs. She wondered, *maybe, just maybe...*

"Hey, it's only dinner," he teased, bringing her back. "A simple yes would be okay."

၈၅၄

When they arrived at the Plantation Room, the dining room was quiet. It had been that way the last few weeks since a competitor had opened up a fancier place downtown. Rachel looked around, thinking it felt like her own personal dining room. In a way it was, since Buddy and the Carpenters owned the place and their personal imprints were everywhere.

Heather had painted the mural that covered the back wall, a balcony view of a tropical beach. JT had built the rock waterfall that flowed down to a small pool surrounded by tropical plants, and Buddy had inherited the whole place—including Blood Mountain—to begin with. With the soft background music and a fruited drink, it never took much for Rachel, or anyone else for that matter, to mentally transport themselves to the Mexican Riviera.

"This was definitely a good idea," Rachel said, sliding into one of the booths that lined the room, feeling more like herself again. "But it looks like our competition is hurting us more than I thought."

Buddy motioned for a waiter to bring their usual drinks and then turned to Rachel. "Give it a little time.

Right now, Anna Venkman is pouring on the charm, the cheap meals, and the fancy service. She can't keep it up forever. Even with Pappa Hans bankrolling her, there's a limit. He'll have to cut her off eventually. She's already gone through one chef, half her silver-plated flatware has been stolen, and most of the fancy crystal is either smashed or missing. She even had to replace her beloved Domino dummy."

"Mannequin."

"Whatever. The point is, once she has to make it on her own, she'll have to cut back on the fancy stuff and raise her prices. Her customers won't take kindly to that. We did things right the first time. You and Chef put together a great package. We've never raised our prices and until two weeks ago, we were in the black. The people will tire of Queen Anna's shenanigans and come back. Trust me."

Manuel arrived at the table with a tray of drinks: ice water with lemon slices and golden margaritas. He set them out and Buddy ordered the prime filets along with baked stuffed crab for the both of them. "We have a new Cabernet Sauvignon," Manuel offered. "A French import. Would you like to try it?"

"Yes, bring us a bottle."

Manuel stood a moment and shifted his weight from one leg to the other.

"Is there anything else?"

"Um—I thought you and Miss Rachel might want to know, two of our people who left to go to Domino's came back in this afternoon to ask for their old jobs back."

Buddy turned to Rachel with a told-you-so look in his eyes. "Thank you, Manuel."

They were well into their salads and had thoroughly dissected Anna Venkman's attributes and her restaurant when Buddy asked, "You do remember we're all going on a gold hunting expedition tomorrow, right?"

"Are you kidding? Of course, I remember." Rachel looked at him like he was crazy. "I was ready the last time, when we had to cancel. I've got my clothes picked out. I mean, I've never gone panning for gold in my entire *life*. I'm not about to miss it. What if we discover a rich vein right here on Blood Mountain?" She shifted her eyes away from him. "Besides, Heather and I are already designing the jewelry we're going to have made with our share of the gold."

"Well, I'm happy to hear that," Buddy said, relief in his voice. "I was afraid this problem you're dealing with might have initiated a change in plans."

"No, not at all, but I have to admit I *am* worried." Rachel slouched back in the booth and looked around the room. "You *do* remember Hank Levinson, don't you Buddy?"

"The old white-haired guy that used to sit in the first booth in the Hibiscus Cafe who ended up going to the old folk's home?"

"Yes," Rachel said, smiling sweetly. "Only now it's called assisted living."

"Oops. Sorry."

"Well, his sort-of girlfriend has disappeared."

"His sort-of girlfriend?"

"More like one-way, I suspect. He had a crush on one of the RNs. She's probably thirty-something, young enough to be his granddaughter. She simply disappeared in the middle of her shift."

"And Hank chose you to investigate the great mystery," Buddy teased.

"This isn't funny," Rachel said, pulling herself up, frowning. "He's a nice old man who lost his wife, never had children, and then had a stroke and lost the use of his legs. He had to sell his farm and move into assisted living."

Buddy's demeanor suddenly changed. "I'm sorry Rachel. That really is a sad story."

Manuel appeared at their table with their entrées and more wine. After he left, the couple ate while Rachel gave Buddy her play-by-play account of Hank Levinson and the missing girlfriend.

Buddy put down his fork and asked, "Do you think Long John has something to do with Zoe's disappearance?"

"I'm not sure. But he's hiding something. He said the last time he'd seen or heard from Zoe was last night before she went on duty."

"Which makes Hank the last person to see her that evening, correct?" Buddy glanced at the Rolex peeking out from under his sleeve. "Actually, she's only been missing about twenty-seven hours."

Rachel put down her fork. "That's not the point. It's

the way she disappeared. Poof!" She jerked up a hand. "One minute here, next minute gone. And her car never left the parking lot."

She picked up her wine glass and drained the rest of it.

"And you're saying Long John never talked to her after she went to work."

"No." Rachel shook her head. "I told you Long John *said* he never talked to her after that. But he knew about the ring that Hank gave Zoe. And Hank didn't give it to Zoe until around eight-thirty last night, just before Teresa Espinosa went on break."

Buddy swallowed the last of his wine and worked through the scenario in his mind. "So you think—"

"Yes, of course. Long John is *lying*." She pointed a pink fingernail at Buddy. "But the question is why?"

Chapter 2

That same evening, Long John closed down the lock shop, drove a few blocks over to the Hotel Rios Apartments, and parked in the back. The historic Hotel Rios rose four stories above the other buildings on River Street. Built in nineteen-twenty-nine, it was designed in the art deco style of the times, with a long green canopy over the entrance, and topped with a flat roof, edged with a parapet. In those days, under the moonlight, the roof top was the scene of many dances and parties.

The hotel was located in Old Town, across Third Street from Golden Vista, and had been plucked from its abandoned state, remodeled, refurbished, and given a whole new identity.

The Albarran family had transformed the entire hotel into apartments.

Casa Blanca style fans twirled in the lobby and the

floor sparkled with the white octagon tiles original to the building. Modern furniture in black and turquoise occupied most of the room except for the sectioned-off corner office from where Jesse Albarran managed the apartments. A grandson of the original owner, Jesse was a quirky guy, skinny, funny, with a black goatee and a soul patch under his lip. He acted a little loony at times, but anyone who knew him wasn't fooled. He was as sharp as a brand-new razor blade.

Jesse was still shuffling papers in his office at seven that evening when Long John strolled in. "*Que pasa, Amigo?*" he asked, glad to see his friend. He spun around in his chair, opened the small refrigerator door, and pulled out two Coronas.

"I need a favor, Jesse," Long John said softly and sat down. Reaching for the beer Jesse offered him, he popped it open.

"I was gonna call you," Jesse said, now with a frown. "I heard Zoe disappeared off the job yesterday."

"No. Zoe disappeared *on* the job yesterday." Without looking at his friend, Long John quickly chugged down half the beer.

Jesse stopped midway through uncapping his own bottle. "What? What do you mean?"

"I wish I knew." Long John slumped in his chair and put his fist up against his face. "She's gone. Disappeared. Without a trace." He began chewing on his thumb.

Jesse took off his glasses, thick-framed black ones, and stared at him. His friend looked sick. "You gotta be kidding. How could that happen?"

"I'm telling you, Jesse, I don't have a clue." Long John's gaze dropped to the desk. "I called her, talked to her, I dunno, it was around six-thirty last night. When I called later, around nine, she didn't answer her cell, and didn't return my call. When she didn't answer after a couple more tries, I drove over to Golden Vista, and her car was still in the lot. The owners were there, looking for her, but no one had seen her. They tried to say she just took off, but her purse was still locked up. It was like she vanished into thin air."

Jesse sat there, puzzled. "Man."

"Yeah, that's what I say, too."

"You think something bad happened to her? Like somebody kidnapped her? I thought they locked down the place at six."

"They do."

"Man, this is so freaky." Jesse pinched the spot between his eyes. "How can something like this happen?"

"I don't know." Long John shook his head slowly. "Zoe was afraid something weird was going on at work."

"What do you mean, man? Weird like what?"

Long John wouldn't look at him and shrugged it off. "Just some weird stuff."

Jesse's eyes narrowed, focused on his friend. He got up from behind the desk, stepped over to the window, then waited until Long John raised his head and looked at him. "How long we been friends, John?"

Long John was taken aback. "I dunno. Middle school, I guess."

"Right. We've been friends since middle school. And now you're scamming me."

"Believe me, man, I can't tell you everything," Long John whined. "And, trust me, you don't want to know."

Jesse stared at his friend, his mouth set in a thin line.

Long John let out a breath, defeated. "Okay, okay. Zoe suspected something illegal was going down at Golden Vista. With Brick. I think maybe she might have wanted to check it out."

"What?" Jesse dropped his jaw, aghast. "I can't believe this. Zoe thinks something illegal was going on with Brick Krutzer and you don't tell her to back off? Are you crazy?" His eyes were bugged out. "What the hell were you thinking, man? Don't you remember what happened in high school?"

"Yeah, I remember," Long John said in a dull monotone and looked off. "That won't help me now, though. You mind easing up just a bit?"

Jesse exhaled with a deep growl. He walked back to the desk, punched the fist of one hand into the other, and stared at his friend. "How much trouble are you in?" he asked.

"Me? Right now, none. But that could change, real fast."

"Does your brother know about this?"

"No. Forget Danny. We don't talk much these days."

Jesse squinted at him. "I thought he was working with you. What happened?" He didn't wait for an answer. "Never mind, I think I know. Danny went to school with Zoe. He probably tried to tell you she was trouble."

"Shut up, Jesse!" Long John sprang from his chair, stared at his friend, and then slumped back. "Look, you gonna help me or not?"

Jesse gazed up at the ceiling, discerning the popcorn texture like his mother read tea leaves. He turned. "I'll help you any way I can, John, but only if you trust me enough to tell me the truth."

ಬಡಬ

At nine o'clock that same night, Jackson Thomas Carpenter crossed the lobby of the Mesquite Mountain Inn with long, confident strides. He was a tall man, big-boned, with dark, steady eyes and a strong jaw. JT, as he preferred to be called, was Buddy McCain's partner in Blood Mountain and the hotel that sat on it. A natural leader and building contractor by profession, he had abandoned his hectic, paperwork-filled life in LA to embrace a quiet and peaceful one in southwest Arizona. Although his new life hadn't always been as tranquil as he had planned, he never regretted his decision and was resigned to accept his sister-in-law, Rachel Ryan, as part of the package.

One of his self-imposed duties as general manager was to make a nightly check of the hotel before heading back to the casita he shared with Heather. He had just completed this and was about to turn toward the back exit when he noticed the burned-out bulb in one of the ceiling lights.

That reminded him of the loose sconce he had detected in the ballroom earlier. *Better write it down before I forget.*

He turned at the front desk, greeted Paulina, and opened his office. When he sat down, he noticed the envelope right away.

His name and "personal and confidential" was typed on the front. He picked it up, grunted an inquisitive "huh," and opened it. When he unfolded the paper he read the small poem.

> *Roses are red,*
> *Violets are blue.*
> *Start counting to twenty,*
> *Your days are through.*

What? What is this? JT stared at the paper, re-read the poem. It sounded like a threat, sort of, but what kind? And from whom?

He was at his office door in three seconds. "Paulina. Did you put this letter on my desk?"

The young Hispanic woman jumped at the sound of his deep voice. "Yes, sir. I found it on the front desk. I had to go the rest room for just a minute, and when I got back, the letter was on the counter. I put it in your office." She frowned. "Did I do wrong?"

"No, no. You're fine. Thanks."

JT turned back to his desk, leaned against it, read the poem again. *Start counting to twenty? What in the world did that mean? Twenty days? Certainly not twenty* minutes. *And my days are through? Through with what? My life? My business?*

He looked at the type. It was Times New Roman, a computer generated font every electronic gadget used. The paper looked like ordinary copy paper, and the letter came in a common number ten envelope. Ninety-nine per cent of the population could have left the letter. Even so, was it really a threat? He didn't have an answer and stared at it another minute. He would have assumed it was someone's idea of a joke if it hadn't sounded so sinister.

JT finally folded the paper and put it back in the envelope, refusing to let it worry him. He had a big day ahead tomorrow. They were all taking a day off to pan for gold. He wasn't going to let a stupid letter from some jerk ruin his night, his sleep, or his plans. He folded the envelope and put it in his pants pocket, left the office, and went home.

༺༻

At eleven p.m. Long John drove back to the Hotel Rios Apartments. He quietly unlocked the front door of the building, crossed the lobby, and took the elevator to the sixth floor. At the other end of the hall he entered through the door marked "stairs" and found himself inside the fire exit. Quickly locating the door that led to the roof, he unlocked it, climbed the stairs, and stepped into the dark, moonless night. It smelled of roof tar and river water and a little of his own sweat.

He set down the loaded backpack he had been carrying, pulled the camp chair out of the nylon bag, and set it up. Even with his height, when he sat in the chair, he couldn't see over the top of the parapet down to street level. He pulled over a picnic table that seemed to be a recent addition to the roof top, set the chair on top of it, and climbed up. The view from there was perfect.

He looped the binoculars around his neck and held them up to his eyes, adjusting the sites. He scanned the town. There was no traffic. The Mexican restaurant had shut down at nine and even Cooper's had closed its doors at ten. *So much for life in the big city.*

Other than an occasional car driving by, it was quiet. He dropped the binoculars and reached into his cooler for a can of Pepsi. He popped it open, held it upright between his knees, and pulled out a bag of chips.

When he pulled the binoculars back up, he focused on Golden Vista across the street. From his vantage point he could see the old part of the home, the part that never had been renovated.

Although the old annex was totally dark, the street lights lit the eight-foot, slump-block wall that surrounded the entire back property, along with a large section of the yard and outbuildings. The top of the wall was trimmed out in a gold toned, high-quality brick. The brick matched the ones that were used to construct the facade that covered the renovated part of the building up to where the wall started. The result was an illusion. Golden Vista looked three times the size it was and twice what it cost to renovate.

Long John reached for another Pepsi and was grateful he remembered to bring an empty gallon water jug. He couldn't afford to lose even the ten minutes it would take to go all the way to the lobby to use the rest room, although he wouldn't have minded a change of scenery. The pink-tinted sodium vapor lights glowed on tirelessly through the night, but not Long John. Twice he caught himself nodding off.

Just as he was about to give it up, he heard a truck drive down River Street. He walked to the parapet to get a better look and saw a white panel truck turn down Third Street. Fully awake now, he followed it with the binoculars, and watched the truck stop at the back gate to Golden Vista. A fat man jumped out of the passenger side and opened the gate, long enough to let the Ford through.

Once inside the enclosure, the truck backed in toward the rear of the building before Long John could make note of the license number. The fat man disappeared behind the truck, and in a moment, Long John saw the door to the building swing open.

The driver, a scruffy-looking thinner man, came out of the truck and walked around to the back of it, disappearing from view momentarily. When he flashed back into John's sight, he was helping the fat man haul something into the building. Long John caught his breath and blinked several times to clear his vision. He couldn't believe what he saw. The blood began to leave his head and he sank to his knees, shaking.

He sagged against the parapet and the binoculars dropped against his chest as he thought about how much trouble he could be in. "Zoe," he cried softly to no one. *If she talks, I am a dead man.*

℘℘℘

An hour later, Danny Long pulled the pillow over his head when he heard the phone ring. After seven rings, it stopped, and he rolled back over on his side. The phone rang again. After three more rings, Danny whacked it with the pillow, knocking it off the table. Then someone pounded on the door. Danny screamed a few profane words, kicked the covers off the bed, jumped up, and kicked the bed. He stomped through the house, slipped on the neck of a beer bottle—one of many in several shades of green and brown that littered the house—caught himself, and arrived at the front door cursing. He stood there barefoot and naked except for the striped shorts that gaped open at the fly.

"This better be good!" he hollered when he flung open the door, fumes of beer and cheese curls flowing outward into the night.

Long John stood in the darkness.

"What are *you* doing here?" Danny demanded and gawked at his watch. "At four in the morning?"

"I'm in big trouble." Long John spoke so softly, it took a few seconds for his answer to register in Danny's brain.

Danny stared at his brother a moment and then stepped aside to let him in.

"I'm leaving town for a little while, then I'll be

back," Long John said. "Here's the keys to the lock shop," he said, handing over a ring with several keys. "Everything you need to know is on the desk, in back. I never took your name off the checking account so just do what you need to do. I put the last deposit in the night drop and everything's accounted for."

Danny scratched his head, his brain still fuzzy. "What are you talking about?"

"Go back to bed. We don't open until ten on Saturday. We close at two. It's a short day."

Danny stood there, rubbing his face, trying to wake up. "It's Zoe, isn't it? I heard she was missing."

"I can't tell you about it." Long John stood there, shaking his head. "Don't ask me. There's enough trouble as it is, and you don't need to be involved in it."

"I knew she was trouble." Danny narrowed his eyes. "Was she stealing from Brick?"

Long John shook his head. "No. But it's complicated. I did leave you a letter though, explaining everything, just in case something happens to me."

Danny started to say something, but Long John cut him off. "I gotta go. Don't tell anybody you saw me. I'll be in touch."

Danny stood in the doorway with his mouth still open as his brother shot off into the dark.

Chapter 3

The morning air was crisp with a lingering coolness when the Hummer and Ford 4x4 pulled up to the north side of Blood Mountain. Heather slid out of the truck and looked up. "The sky's as clear as crystal. I bet it'll hit ninety-five today."

JT walked around to the back of the truck and dropped the tailgate. "It may get hotter than that. I talked to Dewey Tucker yesterday and he said it sometimes hits a hundred by the end of April in town."

Rachel stood with her hands out. "It feels pretty nice here in the shade."

"Yeah, and lucky for you pale-faced, Irish-Swedish lassies, the mountain should shade us most of the day," Buddy said. He hauled a large metal contraption from the back of the Hummer with a loud grunt and glanced over at JT. "You need a hand with that sluice box, big guy?"

"Nah, this baby is only eleven pounds. It's mostly

aluminum." JT pulled a rectangular-shaped box over five feet long from the back of the truck. It had seven riffles, or raised dividers, that sectioned off the inside of the box, and a fan-shaped piece of aluminum attached to the end of it.

"I take it this piece of equipment is going to help us find the gold," Rachel said, giving it a rather dubious look.

"No, it's going to help us separate the gold from the all the gravel that we are going to be digging up and throwing on it," JT said, carrying the sluice box in one hand.

"We're going to be digging?" Rachel held up at her newly polished nails for inspection. "With shovels?"

Buddy reached down and pulled out some gloves from the cardboard box he had just set on the ground. "Here you go, my darling, delicate flower," he said, handing a pair to Rachel. "Put these on."

Rachel held them up and inspected the sturdy leather gloves. "Well, at least they're new and clean." She slipped her long fingers inside.

"Come on, Rachel," Heather said, taking the second small pair of gloves and grabbing her arm. "Let's go set up the refreshment station."

Rachel followed her to the Hummer and they unloaded a couple of large coolers and a folding table. "How about over there?" She pointed to a flat area east of them.

They set up the station in less than fifteen minutes, complete with chairs and shade umbrella. Heather looked up at the north side of Blood Mountain, her freckles shining across her nose. "We may not even need the umbrella. I think Buddy's right. We're going to be in the shade of the mountain for most of the morning, anyway."

She looked down at the box containing the sun hats and instinctively reached up and touched her hair, the color of tea. "I don't think we'll need the hats, either."

Rachel twisted her pale hair and knotted it up with a band to keep it out of her face. Together they watched JT and Buddy set up the re-circulating water system that would wash the gravel through the sluice.

"Can we get the gold now?" Rachel asked, checking her watch. JT and Buddy looked at each other.

"Okay," JT said, straightening up. "You ladies remember where the old gold mine was?" He pointed up the hill to Blood Mountain where a level mesa jutted out from the north face.

"Like we could forget?" Rachel mumbled, remembering an earlier, scarier adventure.

"That was a rhetorical question, Rachel." He turned and pointed again. "Notice the small wash that runs down the mountain. It's about where the mine meets the old air field, over on the right. You see it?" As everyone turned their heads to look, JT continued, "I think that little nugget I found flowed down from the area of the old mine during that last big rain. In fact, I found it right about here." He moved over a few steps and pointed to the ground.

"So then we just walk along the wash and pick up the gold?" Rachel asked.

"Ah, well, not exactly." JT took a few long strides to the pick-up and came back with two shovels. He handed them to Heather and Rachel. "Go grab one of those buckets over there and have at it."

Rachel looked at Heather. "Does he mean he expects us to walk over, dig up the wash, put it in the buckets, and walk back?"

"I believe he does," Heather said, heading out. "Come on. I suggest we think in terms of calorie depletion. Say fifty calories per bucket emptied?"

"Yeah, that sounds about right to me," Rachel said, her voice trailing behind, "except we need to add an extra few for walking back and forth."

Four hours later, the sun was hot and directly south. Its rays reached over the mountain top and reflected off the chrome bumper on JT's pick-up. Three of the gold prospectors were still working behind the shade line, filling buckets with gravel and dragging them over to the sluice.

JT stood under the large umbrella, gradually feeding the gravel into the sluice and picking out any large rocks threatening to clog it up. Feeling his stomach rumble, he looked at his watch. "Lunch time!" he called.

Everyone's gloves came off and a liquid hand soap that smelled like grapefruit came out. After they all cleaned up, JT brought a pan to the table that held the few offerings of gold the wash had given up.

"Is that it?" Heather asked, studying the shiny grains of gold. She looked up and noticed JT's fallen face. "Why, I think it's just wonderful, "she suddenly exclaimed. "I'll bet that's enough to melt down for an earring. Don't you think so, Rachel?" she added, kicking her sister's shin under the table.

Rachel blinked then brightened. "Oh, definitely. Definitely an earring," she said, "but even if we didn't get *any* gold, we burned up bunches of calories, didn't we Heather?"

"Right. We certainly did and—"

"Okay, ladies, you can quit now," JT said, reaching for a piece of cold fried chicken. "You know, you can't expect to hit the mother lode the first poke in the potato patch."

Buddy piled a scoop of potato salad on his plate and then passed it to his left. "It's pretty labor intensive, but it's a fun pastime, and if you're willing to put in the effort, it can prove to be pretty profitable, too. Especially with the price of gold today."

"All right, we get it," Rachel said. "It's a 'treasure hunt.'" She held up her fingers and made little quote marks. "You never know what you're going to find."

"True," Buddy said, "and speaking of find, I noticed you were on the phone a little earlier, Rachel. That wasn't about finding Zoe, was it?"

"Yes, but the news wasn't good. She's still missing."

"Someone's missing?" JT asked and put a forkful of coleslaw in his mouth.

"I'm afraid so," Rachel said and told JT and Heather about the events of the prior evening. When she finished, everyone was silent for a couple minutes, thinking their own thoughts.

"That's really, really weird," Heather finally said. She looked down at her plate, poking at her gelatin salad. "How can someone just disappear like that?"

"That's what everyone is asking," Rachel said. "But at least now Dewey Tucker has filled out the missing person's report and put it in the system. He said he'd go to Zoe's house and look for anything that might indicate what happened."

"Well, maybe something will come of that," JT said. He was about to bite into a drumstick, but stopped cold. He stared hard at Rachel. "You aren't thinking of getting involved in this, are you?"

Rachel's eyebrows shot up in bewilderment. "What? Who me? Get involved?"

JT dropped his head into his hands. "Oh, boy."

છ્ય

Two hours of work, a pound of sweat, and a few more flakes of gold later, Heather pulled over a chair by the sluice where Buddy had gravel-washing duty.

"I'm done," she said, plopping down, stretching her legs out in front of her. "I don't care if I die poor. I'm not prospecting for any more gold today." She lifted up an arm and sniffed. "Besides, I think I need another shower."

"Yeah, I think we all might as well quit," JT said, dropping his bucket. "It's going to take us some time to get all the equipment cleaned up and put back."

"Okay for you sissies," Rachel said. "I think I'm going to try a different place and a few more shovelfuls. Maybe I'll have better luck."

She picked up her bucket and moved further west to the area that was leveled out.

"Can I help with the clean-up?" Heather asked.

"No, just sit," JT said and glanced over at Rachel. He leaned back toward Heather. "You know, I can hardly believe your sister is still over there working," he whispered. "My guess was that she would have quit when the shovels came out."

"You forget that once she latches on to something, she can get pretty obsessive and dig in."

Buddy nodded. "Yeah, like a pit bull."

Heather's eyes twinkled. "Or maybe she really wants that gold jewelry."

"Hmm…okay. Rachel," JT called out to her. "You can quit any time now."

"No way," Rachel called back. "I found a soft area and don't have to dig as hard."

She pushed aside a few big rocks and dug out a couple shovelfuls of lose sand. She stopped and stared down. Something sparkled. It looked like a jewel of some type. *A diamond? Did the mine also have diamonds?*

Heather turned around to watch her. "Rachel, what are you doing?"

"I see something." Rachel flung her shovel aside and reached for the twinkling stone. She tried to lift it and it resisted. She pulled harder and the stone came up attached to something stuck in the ground. It looked like a—

A scream escaped from Rachel's throat when she pulled the hand up, then she dropped it and leaped back as if she had touched fire. Heather jumped up when she heard the cry but could only see her sister's back. Then she watched Rachel fall over on her face in a dead faint.

൞

The lock shop was quiet when Danny Long glanced at the clock behind him. Only ten minutes left before he could close up. He was cleaning the counter area and gathering up the sales receipts when the door popped open and the bell announced another customer.

A big, fat man with long brown hair shuffled in.

Danny felt a chill when he saw him. "Hey, Ron, how ya doing?" he asked, hoping to sound friendly.

Ron Emmett looked around, ignoring the question. "Where's your brother?"

Danny's heart skipped a beat. Ron outweighed him by a hundred pounds and could crush him if he chose to. "Out of town."

Emmett kept looking around the room as if Long John would suddenly appear out of the woodwork.

"What'ya need?" Danny asked, wanting to be rid of him.

"Nothin' really," Ron said, skulking up to the counter. "He's out of town? Where'd he go?"

"San Diego," Danny lied. "He had to go to a workshop." It sounded better to him than if he admitted that he didn't know. "How's it going over at Golden Vista?"

"Okay." For the first time since Ron walked in the shop, he looked at Danny. "I suppose you heard Zoe disappeared."

"Like I care?" Danny shrugged. "I could never stand her to begin with."

"Yeah, well," Emmett said. He rubbed the back of his hand across his mustache and started looking around the room again. "You tell Long John I need to talk to him as soon as he gets back."

When the door slammed behind Emmett, Danny felt a strong sense of relief. The last thing he needed was to have Emmett on his back for some stupid trouble his brother was in.

As soon as Danny went back to the pile of receipts, Jesse Albarran came through the doorway.

"We're closed," Danny said, glancing up.

"Danny," Albarran said, taken aback. "I expected to see John. Is he here?"

"Nope."

"Do you know where he is? He doesn't answer his cell and I've left four messages."

Danny went back to stacking sales slips. "You're his friend. You probably know more than I do."

"Well, I *don't,* and I need to talk to him."

Danny didn't bother looking up. "He told me he was going out of town."

"You think he really did? Or is he just hiding out?"

Danny jerked up his head. "What do you mean?"

"I mean I need to talk to him, *now.*"

Danny grunted. "You and a bunch of other people."

Albarran slammed his hand on the papers in front of Danny. "Like who?"

Danny pulled back, startled. "Ron Emmett was in here a while ago looking for him."

Albarran cursed under his breath. "What did you tell him?"

Danny pushed Albarran's hand away. "What is this, the Inquisition?"

"It might be worse than that. I was just on the phone talking to one of the guys at the clinic. We were talking about getting together for a beer later when he gets off duty. In the middle of the conversation, he gets a 911 call, and I could hear the radio in the background. Some people out behind Blood Mountain found a woman's body."

"Zoe?"

"Don't know yet."

Danny picked up the keys to the shop. "Sorry, I can't help you." Danny's face became hard. "I really don't know where he is."

∽∾∽

Rachel was lying on the sand when she opened her eyes. "What happened?" She could see Heather, JT, and Buddy staring at her with anxious looks and nothing but blue sky behind them. "What happened?" she asked again.

"You just fainted and hit your head on the rocks, sweetie. You'll be okay." Heather was smiling, patting

Rachel's shoulder, trying to make light of it. "Just lie there and be still."

"But—" Rachel asked and then closed her eyes. She felt warm sand under her but was confused, as if she were floating around in a fog. Off in the distance, she heard the sound of sirens, two different types, and they were getting louder. She suddenly remembered finding the ring and the hand of a woman attached to it. She opened her eyes. "Zoe?" she asked and tried to move, the sand shifting under her.

"Shhh," Heather said and pressed an ice pack gently against her forehead.

The ambulance pulled up along with the deputy sheriff; the sirens stopped.

"Ow," Rachel said and put a hand to her cheek. "I fell on my face," she said, tasting the blood in her mouth. She looked at her sister. "Is it bad?"

"I think you'll be fine, but don't expect to look too pretty tomorrow."

Heather pulled the cloth away and Rachel saw the blood on it. "Is that from my nose or my face?"

"A little of both, but your nose isn't broken."

A door slammed. Then another. "That's got to be Deputy Tucker," Rachel said, now fully awake and alert. "Help me up. I need to talk to him."

"No, wait," Heather said. "Right now he's going over to look at the girl."

While Deputy Tucker did some initial work with the emergency crew, Heather helped Rachel over to a chair, far enough away from the body so that Rachel couldn't see much of what was going on. They sat for a few minutes before Tucker plodded over to them. He scrutinized Rachel's face and frowned, his long walrus mustache drooping. "You okay, missy?"

"I think I'm better than I look," Rachel said. "I need to know if the girl is Zoe."

"Well, I can't tell for sure, but I don't think so. Hair's blonde, not red, and if she's Zoe, she lost thirty pounds and a good fifteen years."

"Oh, that's a relief," Rachel said, melting into the chair.

Tucker turned his head. "The ME's pullin' up now. Anythin' you need to tell me that JT didn't?"

"Only that it was the ring that caught my attention. The big fake stone. Zoe had one. But if I think of anything, I still have you on my speed dial."

Tucker turned to walk away. "Deputy?" Rachel called out. "About Zoe. Did you find anything at her house?"

Tucker looked back at her and shook his head. *So much for his help on finding her,* Rachel thought. "Okay," she said, turning back to Heather. "I'm ready to go to the clinic. From the feel of my head I'm afraid I might have another concussion."

༺༻

Heather insisted Rachel take a couple days off work. The first day, Rachel lay around, reading and eating pain pills. The next day she was done resting, period. She needed to get out. After a shower and a try at covering up her bruises, she slipped out of the hotel unnoticed and drove down to old town.

When she entered the Lock and Key shop, she did a double take. The tall man behind the counter looked somewhat like the man she had met before, but he was shorter by four inches and was probably a couple years younger. "You're not Long John," Rachel said, walking up to him.

"No, I'm Danny, his brother."

She could see that. He had the same nose and the same European look about him John had. "Is John okay? I haven't talked to him in a couple days," she said. It was the truth, but it erroneously implied she was on a friendly basis with John.

"Yeah, he's fine, but he had to go out of town." He squinted at Rachel. "Are you…"

"Rachel Ryan," she said, now close to the counter. "I'm the sales director at the Mesquite Mountain Inn."

He nodded and flashed her a winning smile. "That's why you look familiar." He was studying her face. "John and I went to the open house party you had last year."

Rachel tried to recall the meeting.

"We never met each other personally," he continued. "Nice party, though, except for the part about Venkman." He walked around the counter to where she stood and studied her face some more. "I bet you're the one who found the woman's body the other day. I heard you fell on your face in the rocks."

Rachel was no longer surprised by how quickly news

spread around the small town. "Yeah, that was a fun day."

"Did they find out who the girl is?"

"Not yet. But she's definitely not Zoe." Rachel watched him for his reaction.

Danny muttered something with a toss of his head.

"What?"

"Nothing."

"You said, 'too bad.' Apparently you and your brother don't share the same taste in women."

Danny moved within Rachel's personal space. "Not where Zoe is concerned."

"I've seen her at Golden Vista and spoke to her once." Rachel took a step back and leaned casually against the counter. "She seemed nice, kind of cute and perky."

"Just goes to show looks can be deceiving," Danny quipped. "Zoe Liddy was a user and a liar. And those were two of her better qualities."

His bluntness surprised her, but Rachel tried not to react and looked down at her feet. She had on a new pair of high-heeled sandals and they hurt her toes.

She knew the shoes were tight when she bought them, but they were covered with sequins and turquoise beads and were a perfect color match for the shorts she was wearing.

"Would you like to sit down?" Danny asked. "I've got a couple chairs in the back."

Rachel was now aware of male vibrations she was getting off him and didn't want that kind of complication.

"Thanks, but I've got to get back to the hotel," she replied and then asked when Long John would return.

"I have no idea," Danny admitted, "but I'll be happy to call you when he comes back. Do you want to give me your number?"

Rachel smiled and said she'd stop by again in a day or two. When she walked to the door, she could feel Danny staring at her legs. She called out good-bye and pulled the door shut without looking back.

ಊಬಿ

The following afternoon ushered in a few breezes, and flat-bottomed clouds floated over the sky. Rachel slid into the passenger seat of Heather's new Hyundai and inhaled the smell of new leather.

"Are you sure you're up for this, Rachel?" Heather turned the key in the ignition. "You could meet Miss Emma some other time."

"I'm fine, although I don't plan on entering any beauty contests today." Rachel pulled the visor down and looked in the mirror. The swelling had disappeared but spots on her face were still looking a bit green in spite of the make-up. "On the other hand," she said, "I might go for the Miss Mesquite pageant if the other women are really ugly."

Heather failed to suppress a laugh and drove down the mountain. A minute later she couldn't resist the urge to ask again, "Are you sure you're doing okay?"

"Pul-eeze, Mother! I'm fine," Rachel bellowed. Then

she dropped her head in shame. "I'm sorry, sis. I know you love me and worry about me. It's just that sometimes—"

"I know, I know—I'm smothering." Heather's shoulder's sagged, and so did her jaw. "Sometimes people forget I lost my parents, too, when you lost yours. But we all deal with loss in our own ways. You pushed away, but I needed my family closer. You were all I had left."

"I know. I learned that in therapy. And I acted out in anger while you held yours in."

"So does that mean you suffered more than I did?"

Rachel turned thoughtfully to her sister. "You're right. In fact, in some ways it was worse for you, wasn't it? Being six years older, you felt like you had to take over Mother's job at a critical time in my life. You were newly married and yet you took me in, rather than have me go to foster care."

"I could have never let that happen!"

"You're right. *You* could never send me away, even if it nearly broke up your marriage. And I'm really sorry for that, by the way. You know that. If I could take those years back, I would in a heartbeat."

"Well, that's all behind us now. We're all together as a family again. Justin and Joseph love you and so does JT."

Rachel was tempted to say something about JT, but her recent argument with him was too fresh in her mind, and she was afraid she might let her mouth overload her brain.

"And you know I love them all, too," she said, nervously pulling down the visor again. She touched the still-sore spots on her face. "So tell me again where you met Miss Emma."

"She comes to my fibromyalgia support group."

"Oh, yeah, I remember now. Well, it's awfully nice of you to take her to the beauty parlor."

"It's no big deal," Heather answered, as she crossed Main Street. "She's a sweet old lady and doesn't really have anyone else to help her. Her daughter works two jobs on the other end of town from Golden Vista."

"No grandkids?"

"Just one, but he's got MS."

"Oh, boy," Rachel said. "Even more reason for me not to get all bent out of shape about my face." She flipped the visor back up.

"That's the spirit, Rachel. The Bible tells us to be thankful in all things."

Rachel looked out the side window, wanting to change the subject before Heather launched into a pitch about religion or finding a husband. "I hope Miss Emma has some information about Zoe."

"Me, too, but even if she doesn't, we'll have a fun night out. I'm due for a change of scenery."

"This already is a change of scenery," she said as they passed by the old city hall. "I just love these old buildings from the early nineteen-hundreds."

When Heather pulled into the Golden Vista parking lot, Miss Emma Hornsby was already waiting for them out on the porch, asleep in a transport chair. She woke up when the doors on the Hyundai slammed shut.

"Oh, Heather, how nice to see you," Miss Emma beamed. Her hair was fine and white, like Christmas angel hair, and it was so thin you could see right through it to her scalp. She had a touch of pink make-up on her cheeks and lips. "And you must be Rachel," she said, reaching out a thin, pale arm.

Rachel gently clasped her hand. It was freckled and wrinkled and felt like all the bones were hollow. "I've really been looking forward to meeting you, Miss Emma."

"Likewise for me, my dear." Emma's face crinkled up with a smile that showed worn, but natural, teeth. "I understand you want to talk to me about Golden Vista."

Rachel helped her navigate her way down the ramp to the car. "Yes, I have a friend that lives at Golden Vista, and he's really concerned about Zoe Liddy."

"Ah, yes." Miss Emma nodded knowingly. "Zoe Liddy."

As Heather drove back out to Main Street and headed east through the center of Mesquite, Rachel turned to Miss Emma. "Do you know Zoe pretty well?"

"As well as any resident, I suppose," Emma said. "She was already working there when I arrived. And I think I was the third resident to move in."

"I see." Rachel nodded. "Is she a nice person?"

Miss Emma raised her eyebrows and looked at Rachel over narrow, wire-framed bifocals. "Not really."

Rachel was surprised at Emma's bluntness. "What do you mean?"

"She's an opportunist and a thief," Miss Emma said

matter-of-factly, as if she were reciting a grocery list.

Rachel blinked, not expecting that strong of an answer.

Miss Emma smiled. "When you get as old as I am, Rachel, you seem to acquire more courage to be truthful and direct."

Rachel nodded. "I'm afraid I've been told I have the same trait, but at my age it's called a lack of diplomacy." She laughed at herself. "But I assume what you said is fact and not just your opinion of her."

"You bet it is. When I suspected she stole my ring, I set a trap for her with some cash. She stole forty dollars. I think she's stolen from others, too, but I can't prove that."

"Oh boy." Rachel sighed. Things were getting more complicated on a daily basis. "What about the opportunist part?"

"Oh, that," Emma said. "It's the way Zoe plays up to the men at the home. She accepts gifts from them, and I'm pretty sure that's against the rules. But it isn't just that she accepts the gifts..." She paused, trying to chase a thought. "She appears to actually *solicit* them."

Before Rachel could think of a reply, Heather broke in to announce they had arrived at Miss Lulu's House of Beauty.

The waiting area was lined with white wicker chairs and smelled of hair chemicals, permanents, and hair spray. Miss Lulu, a middle-aged beauty with thick, blonde hair and a thin waist, ushered Miss Emma into the back room. Heather dived into the pile of gossip magazines on a near-by table. Rachel sat beside her and quietly pondered the ramifications of the information she learned about Zoe and then, after getting nowhere with that, pulled a paperback mystery out of her purse.

When Miss Emma came out of the back room an hour-and-a-half later, Rachel and Heather didn't know what to say. Emma's hair had been permed into tiny, tight, silver-white curls cut close to her head. She looked like a poodle.

"Relax, ladies," Emma said, a big smile wrinkling up her face. "It will loosen up in a day or two."

ℯ⁓ℯ⁓

JT Carpenter and Buddy McCain were sitting in the Hibiscus Cafe drinking coffee when Deputy Tucker hobbled through the door. JT waved him over to their booth.

"He's not looking too good," Buddy noted, watching Tucker limp toward them.

"What happened to your leg?" JT asked, looking down at the deputy's tan pants and red lizard-skin boots.

Tucker hiked up his pant leg to reveal a bandaged knee and several abrasions. "Slipped on the darn rocks at the crime scene and wrenched my knee. Nearly busted my butt."

JT eyed the boots. "I see you went shopping, too."

"Oh, the boots." Tucker turned his leg to display a black lizard superimposed on the red leather. The lizard was sporting two fake diamonds for eyes. "Like 'em?"

JT managed not to laugh. He rubbed his hairline, a

little nervous tic he picked up a while back, and tried to formulate an honest response. "Why, I think they're just perfect for you, Dewey," he answered, quite pleased that he didn't have to lie or insult his friend.

Tucker removed his Stetson. "Well, ya gonna move over? I gotta get off my feet and I ain't sittin' in your lap." JT slid farther in and Dewey sat down with a groan. "Didja order?"

Like magic, Dolly suddenly appeared at their booth with a tall glass of ice water. "Hi, honey," she murmured seductively. "Want coffee?" Dolly was obviously past retirement age, but looked coyly from behind a long wave of bleached-blonde hair that fell over an eye.

"Coffee, yeah. And I'll have whatever he's havin'." Tucker flipped his thumb at JT.

Dolly tucked the loose strand of hair back up into her top knot and bent over close to Tucker's ear. "I set a piece of that caramel cream pie aside for you in case you came in."

Tucker caught a whiff of her perfume. "That's my girl," he said with a wink.

Dolly left the table with a sway of her hips. Buddy looked down at his coffee cup and had to bite his lip to keep from laughing. If Dolly were twenty years younger, he'd probably have to fire her for her outrageous flirtations with all the café's patrons. But at her age, her behavior charmed the customers, male and female alike, and Dewey Tucker was no exception.

"You look like you had a bad day, Deputy," Buddy said.

"Been rode hard and put up wet," Tucker complained and launched into a description of his activities.

Dolly silently appeared with Tucker's coffee, and the deputy immediately drank a half-cup before she made it back to the kitchen.

"Any more news about the woman's body?" Buddy asked.

"Yeah," Tucker answered, wiping his mouth with the back of his hand. "It definitely ain't Zoe."

JT let out a sigh of relief and looked up. The lights hanging above the tables had just flickered on and the recessed lamps dimmed to their evening ambience. He studied the ceiling fans. The paddles, in the shape of palm fronds, turned on the slowest setting.

"So have they identified her?" Buddy asked.

Tucker leaned forward and tossed a paper onto the table. He dropped his face against his fist, crushing his walrus mustache. His eyes were half-way closed, as if he couldn't bear to look. "This is her. The dead girl."

They all stared at the "child missing" poster. It was a duplicate of the one hanging in the employees' lounge Tucker had brought in just a few weeks earlier. A picture of a pretty young girl with long blonde hair smiled up at them. "She was 14 years old, walkin' home from school when she was abducted," Tucker said, his voice cracking.

"Aw, man," JT said. "Fourteen years old? It makes me sick." He had to turn away.

"From here?" Buddy asked.

"No. Casa Grande."

"Man, what is going on in this world?" JT flipped the

paper over, slamming on it with his fist. "How can this happen?"

Buddy shook his head. "And why would somebody bury her in our back yard?"

"That, Mr. McCain," Tucker said, picking up the paper, "is what I'm aimin' to find out. The state's gonna bring over one of them body finders to check around the whole dang area."

"Oh man," JT said.

"In the meantime, I'll be questioning the eight sex offenders we got in this end of the county," Tucker continued. "I gotta start with somethin'."

"So she was—" JT paused, not able to say the word.

"Yeah, she was. And then she was strangled."

Dolly stepped up to the table with a tray loaded with fried catfish, French fries, and deep-fried corn fritters, causing a much-welcomed break from the conversation that had been going around the table. The three men broke into smiles when the smell of all that wonderful grease wafted by their noses.

"Now, Dolly, you better not squeal to Heather that I've been eating all this fried stuff," JT teased.

"What fried stuff, boss?" she asked, handing out the plates. "I never saw any fried stuff."

"Don't look at me," Buddy said, turning to JT. "I never saw any fried stuff either."

The deputy took his napkin and tucked it in around his neck. "Hey, speakin' of the missus," he said, "where are the girls tonight?"

JT dug into his fish. "Oh, Heather and Rachel are

taking Emma Hornsby to the beauty salon and then going out to Cooper's to eat."

"Emma, huh?" Tucker dipped a fritter in maple syrup and popped it in his mouth. "And how's Rachel doin'?"

"Rachel thinks she's just fine. She refused counseling and went back to work."

Tucker grunted as a drop of syrup leaked down his mustache. "And one of these days, she'll just spazz out, right?"

"Yup." JT looked at Tucker out of the corner of his eye. "You want us to call you when she does?"

಄಄಄

Heather was trolling by Cooper's Bar and Grill, searching for a parking space. The popular hang-out was located in Old Town, a couple of blocks east of Golden Vista, and had been dispensing beer and wine at that location for over sixty years. The place looked it, too. A U-shaped bar sat in the center of the room, surrounded by red swivel stools with chrome legs straight out of the fifties—which could have been the last time the place had been painted. Black and white movie posters from the early-to-middle twentieth century were now aged to a dull yellow. They filled most of the available wall space along with an eclectic assortment of art work.

The place smelled of grilled hamburgers and French fries, and it was packed with people sitting at tables or standing around the bar, drinking. The three women wound their way through the crowd, walking in single file on the worn vinyl tiles, finally finding an empty table toward the back of the room.

After getting seated, Rachel took a quick look around at the odd assortment of paraphernalia that hung from the pressed-tin ceiling. "I don't know if the food is any good, but just getting a look at all this old junk is worth the price of a drink."

"Oh, but the food *is* good," Miss Emma crowed. "I've been craving their potato tacos for two weeks."

Rachel and Heather pulled up the menus that were tucked in between the hot sauce bottles and one of those old-fashioned answer boxes that took a quarter to give you a yes, no, or maybe answer to your question.

A blonde waitress with rough skin and a great smile took their drink orders. Heather and Rachel continued to study the room.

A two-wheeled bike, strung with tiny red lights, was suspended from the ceiling over the bar. "I had a bike like that once," Heather said, nodding in its direction.

"If you look around long enough," Miss Emma said, "you'll find most anything you've ever—uh, oh."

Rachel and Heather followed her eyes.

"It's Bricknell Krutzer," Emma said, jerking her face away from him. "I think he spotted us." She suddenly found her place mat consuming her total attention and pretended not to notice Brick's arrival.

"Well, well, Miss Emma Hornsby." Brick flashed a full set of big, square, capped teeth. "How nice to see you." Rachel and Heather turned toward their visitor. Brick towered over them with massive upper body weight, a big square head, and a thick neck. "Aren't you going to introduce me to your lovely friends?"

Miss Emma made the introductions but made no pretense of enjoying it. Rachel, however, jumped at the chance to engage him in conversation. "Have you heard from Zoe Liddy yet?" she asked.

"Not a word," Brick said, his smile ebbing away. His voice became soft and conspiratorial. "No one can understand what happened. We're all just thunderstruck." He shook his head sadly. His blue eyes darted to Rachel's left hand and then took in the bruises on Rachel's face before they rested on her eyes.

"I can understand that," Rachel said. "My friend, Hank Levinson, is just broken-hearted."

"Ah, yes, Hank…" Brick's voice trailed off, cheerless and pensive.

"He wants me to help find her," Rachel added, a little embarrassed.

"Oh, does he now?" Brick raised an eyebrow and Rachel would have sworn she saw a look of skepticism or something equally unpleasant, flash across his face. He stepped back from the table when the waitress approached with a large tray. "Well, next time you visit Golden Vista, come say hello to me, and I'll give you a personal tour."

The waitress set the plates down and Brick walked back to his friends. Rachel watched him out of the corner of her eye. He stood next to a big, fat man with long hair tied back in a ponytail.

Rachel recognized him as the man who nearly

knocked her over in the hall the day she visited Hank.

"Who's the other guy, Emma, the smaller one with the stringy, reddish hair?" she asked.

Emma glanced over with a look of disgust. "That's Adam Tackett."

"I gather you're not too fond of him, either."

"Oh, Rachel, all three of them together aren't worth a bucket of warm spit."

Heather tried to keep a straight face at Emma's outspokenness. "That sounds pretty worthless to me." She pulled out a French fry from the huge pile on the plate.

"Not to mention discourteous," Emma added. "Downright rude, really—and that Tackett? Why, he's so stupid he couldn't pour piss out of a boot."

Heather almost choked on her fry.

"But Brick won't fire them?" Rachel asked.

"Fire them?" Emma held up her fork for emphasis. "Why, those two have never held any other jobs outside of working for the Krutzer family. If Brick fired them, they'd be on welfare forever. Lord knows what kind of trouble they'd get into then."

Heather looked at her warily. "I hope they don't make things difficult for you at Golden Vista."

Emma shook her head. "They don't. They don't have much contact with the residents at all except for moving furniture and big fat people and stuff like that. They're kind of like vampires and mostly come out at night."

"Oh, Emma." Heather laughed. "You are the master of metaphors. I never knew you had such a sense of humor."

Emma looked a little sheepish. "I do try to keep it down in the support group, Heather. You know they're such a prissy bunch of old ladies."

When they finished eating, Heather drove back to Golden Vista, and she and Rachel waited with Miss Emma after ringing the bell for evening entry. In a couple of minutes, the thinnest woman Rachel had ever seen—outside pictures of the Holocaust—appeared. She was probably sixty, but she looked like she was pushing seventy because of her deeply lined, leathery face. She wore no bra and didn't need to. In the thin top she wore, the front of her body looked like two pimples on a washboard.

When she opened the door, Rachel smelled smoke on her clothes and skin.

"Why, Mrs. Krutzer, what a surprise to see you here," Miss Emma crooned and introduced her friends.

Hester Krutzer greeted them cordially, showing the square, yellowed teeth of a long-time smoker, and extended a boney hand to Rachel and Heather. It was ice cold. "With Zoe gone, I've had to pull nursing duty," she complained. "It's a good thing I've always kept up my license."

She turned her attention to Miss Emma. "Will your friends be staying long?"

"No, they're just seeing me to my apartment and want to say hi to Hank Levinson, if he's up."

Hester looked the two sisters up and down. "Very well," she said. "Just be sure to pull the door closed on your way out so that it locks behind you. We don't want anyone else turning up missing. I've had enough grief over that Zoe business as it is."

When she strode away, Rachel couldn't help wondering how Hester could have given birth to Brick. Other than the blond hair and square teeth, they didn't seem to have any other physical trait in common.

Emma invited Heather and Rachel in to see her apartment. It was designed like Hank's, but the furnishings were Victorian style antiques and the place smelled of English lavender instead of testosterone. Photographs and shelves of knick-knacks covered most of the wall space, a definite contrast to Hank's sparsely furnished unit.

"Oh, look, Hester's already put out the evening meds." Emma picked up a saucer with four pills on it and then held up a small, red-coated one. She tossed it into the toilet from the hallway. "Two points," she quipped.

"What are you doing?" Heather asked. Miss Emma was certainly full of surprises.

"I don't need a sleeping pill. My doctor said I don't have to take one." Emma jutted out her chin in total defiance. "And just because they want to put all us old folks out in la-la land for the night doesn't mean I have to go."

"What? What do you mean?" Rachel looked doubtful and traded glances with Heather.

"I can see you don't believe me," Emma said. "But it's true. Ask your friend, whats-his-name. There's a lot that goes on here at night; a lot of noises for an old folks home. You can find out quite a bit if you don't let them knock you out."

Rachel traded glances with Heather again, but this time she looked worried.

After a little more small talk, the sisters made sure Miss Emma was secure in her room and then headed down the hall to the men's wing.

The door to Hank Levinson's room was half-way open and the lights were out. Rachel straddled the threshold and noticed Hank's legs stretched out on the sofa. "I think he's sleeping," Rachel whispered.

"Come in and shut the door," Hank said roughly, startling Rachel.

Once she and Heather went inside, Rachel flipped on the light switch by the door. "Hank, what in the world were you doing in the dark, pretending to be sleeping?"

Hank sat up, ignored the question, and waved the women in. "Come sit down. Grab a soda if you want one."

"No, we're full. We just got back from Cooper's."

"Well, I'm glad to see you, ladies, especially you, Rachel. I heard about you finding that body." He studied her face. "But you don't look too bad."

"I think I'll live," Rachel quipped.

She and Heather seated themselves, and Heather looked around, studying Hank's choice of decor.

"So, what's the deal on the pretend nap?" Rachel frowned. "Considering what's going on around here, shouldn't you keep your door locked?"

"All the more reason to keep it open." Hank took a sip from the glass of water on the table. "I want old Hester to walk by and think I took her darned sleeping pill."

Rachel's eyes darted over to her sister's then back to Hank. "Hester's giving you sleeping pills? I thought that falling asleep was the only problem you *didn't* have," Rachel said.

"You're right. I'm lucky to get both feet in bed before I nod off. But Hester insists we take 'em, and she watches us until we do." He stuck his hand in his pocket and fished around until he pulled out a small pill. "See? They're coated to make you sleep all night. I jus' pretend to swallow mine and spit it out after she leaves. Then I pretend to sleep and listen for anythin' that goes on by the nurses' station." He pulled something out from another pocket that looked like an ear phone and showed her. "I've even got one of these ear things that can pick up sounds from far away."

Rachel's mouth dropped open. "Hank, just what the heck do you think you're doing?"

"I'm just tryin' to find out what's goin' on around the place, that's all."

She met Heather's eyes then turned back to Hank. "How long has this sleeping pill business been going on?"

"Hester came in the night Zoe disappeared and finished out her shift. She gave a sleeping pill to anyone who was still awake at the time. I took one but figured out the next day what it was. I spit out the rest of 'em."

Rachel let out a deep sigh. "Okay, Hank, so what do you think is going on?"

"I'm not sure yet. But whatever it is, I'm willin' to bet it's something illegal."

Rachel studied his face. "Like what?"

Hank made a face. "Who knows? With Brick runnin' the place it could be anything."

Rachel felt like her brain was spinning in circles. "Well, do you think maybe Zoe might have found out what they were doing, whatever it is they *are* doing, and that's why she disappeared?"

"Maybe." He jutted out his chin. "But I don't care about her anymore."

"What?" Rachel's eyes snapped open. "What happened? I thought you were in love with her."

Hank looked away, sullen. "Not anymore."

"So are you going to tell us why, or are you going to make us guess?"

"She was usin' me, plain and simple."

"Oh, Hank, I'm so sorry," Rachel said.

"Not as sorry as I am," Hank said, his words tinged with anger. "She played me like an old fiddle—me and all the other men in the place. Why, I even gave her money to get her car fixed."

Rachel's mouth dropped open again and she looked at her sister. Heather's lips were pressed tightly together and she was slowly shaking her head back and forth, taking it all in.

"How much money?" Rachel asked.

"Three hundred bucks." Hank finally looked at Rachel. "But it wasn't the money that hurt. Heck, I've given a lot more than that away."

"I know, Hank. It was the deceitfulness of it all." Rachel put her hand on his shoulder. "Betrayal hurts more than anything." She felt the pain in her own heart, leaned over, and pressed her cheek against his. "One more quick question," she said. "That ring you gave Zoe, do you remember what it looked like?"

"Course I remember what it looked like. I bought it, didn't I?"

"Well, could you describe it to me?"

"I can do better than that." Hank rolled over to a dresser and opened the top drawer. He rolled back and handed Rachel a little square of cardboard with a picture of a ring on it along with a description of it and the price, seventy-five dollars.

"I got it on sale," he said proudly. "Genuine cubic zirconium."

"And this is the size? A six?"

"Yeah. I guess I thought her hands were smaller. But it fit perfect on her little finger. She just loved it."

"Hank, would you mind if I borrowed this little card for a couple days? I'd return it to you."

"Heck, you can throw it away for all I care. Don't want it now."

Rachel glanced over at Heather who was discretely pointing at her watch. She leaned over and gave Hank a warm hug. "Hank, it's going to hurt for a while. But you still have friends. I'll be by in the next day or so and have lunch with you."

"In the dining room?"

"Sure, in the dining room."

"Good. Then when the other guys see you, they won't think I'm such a loser."

Rachel took a long look at her old friend. "Oh, Hank, men don't change, do they? No matter how old they get, it's still a game of King of the Hill."

☙❦❧

After Heather came home and settled in, JT told her what he had learned from Deputy Tucker about the dead girl. After they discussed it for a few minutes, Heather deliberately changed the subject to a more pleasant topic and shared all the details of her evening out with the girls.

JT looked pensive. "So now that Zoe is out of the picture, do you think Rachel is going to let go of this thing with Hank?" he asked.

"I don't really know," Heather said, getting up from the sofa. "I never know what Rachel's going to do. I think she may end up talking to Dewey about it, though. She kept that little card that came with ring Hank bought." She moved over to the kitchenette and placed two cups of water in the microwave. "What worries me are the sleeping pills. That's just not right. Both Emma and Hank told us about them, but I suspect it would be their word against Hester's, at this point. And as far as the so-called illegal activity is concerned, we have no idea what that could be."

"Hmm." JT rubbed his hairline, trying to think of a solution. "I suppose Hank and Emma don't want to move."

"No they don't. They'd have nowhere else to go that's anywhere near as nice, unless they moved to Yuma or Casa Grande. Then they'd really be alone. I know Emma would never consider it." She spooned instant cappuccino into the mugs and stirred.

"It's a tough deal all the way around."

"I know. But in spite of what's going on, they do like the place and the other residents," Heather said, bringing the mugs back with her. "It's really quite lovely, sweetie. The Krutzer's did a great job of remodeling that old building. They hung up some before-and-after pictures in the lobby. I found it quite interesting, and I bet you would, too."

JT nodded, expecting he would, and his mind slipped back to his pre-hotel days and the construction business he left behind in LA. Heather handed him his mug and he took a quick sip.

"Do you miss it?" Heather asked, as if reading his mind.

"The construction business?" JT patted his lap, his signal for her to sit. "Never once."

Heather sat in his lap, snuggled up against him, and rested her head on his chest. "JT? Do you remember how we promised we would never keep secrets from each other?"

"Of course." A pang hit JT's chest as he silently worried what secret Heather was going to confess.

"I found this when I went through the laundry." She handed him a folded piece of paper that looked vaguely familiar.

JT took another sip of cappuccino then set the mug down. He took the note and unfolded it.

It was the anonymous poem he had received. "Ah, man."

"And you were going to tell me about this when?"

JT was trapped. "I was going to wait and see if anything else happened."

"And did it?"

"Not yet."

A quick knock on the door interrupted their conversation. *Saved by the bell.* JT went to the door. A bellman handed him an envelope and he walked back to the sofa studying it. "To JT Carpenter, URGENT" was typed in large bold print across the front. JT ran back to the door and called to the bellman, who was already at the bottom of the steps. "Where did you find this?" he asked.

"Someone left it on the bell stand," the young man answered.

"What is it?" Heather asked when JT headed back her way.

"I'm not sure." JT sat down next to his wife and studied the type style. It was Times New Roman. He flipped the envelope over and tore it open. Heather stared, wide-eyed, while JT read the poem.

"'I'm coming for you;
Don't think you'll be fine.
Trouble will follow
The end of the line.'"

Chapter 4

The sun was already up four fingers when a late-model motor home rolled down a road at the east edge of Yuma County.

"It's a perfect spring morning, just like Paradise," one of the occupants remarked.

After driving for the last two hours, Jared Johnson glanced at his wife and chuckled to himself.

"What's so funny?" Lily asked, tipping her head, looking out over her reading glasses.

"Nothing, really." His eyes looked back at the road through the giant windshield, his hands solidly on the steering wheel. "I was just thinking about what a great idea this was, taking the grandkids to Arizona. This is best time I've had since I retired. We should have done this ten years ago."

"Uh, huh," Lily said, nodding, giving him the eye. "Ten years ago you wouldn't have taken the time off, the

Browns didn't have a motor home to rent us, and we didn't even *have* grandkids."

Jared let out a big belly laugh. "Ah Lily, that's what I love about you. You do have a way of bringing me back down to earth."

"Well, somebody sure needs to," Lily teased. "But you're right. It's been a wonderful trip. We've been on the road for only two weeks and I've already seen more of the USA than I have in my entire lifetime. That's one of the great things about home schooling, you know? We can take the grandkids wherever we want and not have to worry about getting back at any special time."

Jared nodded, his mind flashing back to the family and friends they left behind. "Not to mention, when we left Detroit, there was still snow on the ground."

The motor home whizzed by a vast expanse of desert dotted with creosote bushes, ocotillos, and an occasional saguaro cactus. At a much closer range, mounds of brittle bush covered with bright gold blossoms lined the edge of the road.

"Hey, Grandpa?" Thomas called from the captain's chair behind him. He had a hand-drawn map in his lap. "I think the next right turn is Dead Cow Road."

"Okay, navigator," Jared said, slowing the RV down to fifteen miles an hour.

Six-year-old Willie leaned forward in his seat. "Nana, why do they call it Dead Cow Road?"

"Why do *you* think, Thomas?" Lily asked the older brother.

"Because there are dead cows on it?"

"Very good, Thomas," Lily said. "Now you boys keep your eyes peeled out the windows and let me know when you find one."

Perked up with more enthusiasm, the boys swiveled in their chairs and pressed their faces to the windows.

Dead Cow Road veered off the main road toward denser vegetation. Farther off in the distance, rock-covered mountains were dotted with yellow and green flora. Jared kept a slow pace so they wouldn't miss anything while the old road undulated and curved through a couple of miles of desert marigolds, purple verbena, and dazzling brittle bush.

"Jared, stop ahead," Lily said. "Just look at that tree!" A large Palo Verde was covered with a cloud of sulfur-colored blossoms. "Wouldn't that make a great photo for the boys' scrapbook?"

He slowed the motor home to a stop at the edge of a wash, crushing gravel and river rock under the big tires. After unbuckling his seat belt, he stood up in the aisle, the top of his head nearly brushing the ceiling. "Now boys," he admonished. "Remember what we learned about snakes and Gila monsters. And if you turn over any stones, make sure you use your walking sticks."

Jared barely finished speaking before Thomas and Willie grabbed their sticks and jumped out of the RV, eager to expend their pent-up energy. Each boy had a digital camera hung around his neck and began taking photos of the cactus and flowers that lined the wash.

A buzzard flew by low in the sky, and Jared watched it drop over the next hill. The sun was hot by Michigan standards, and it felt good on his brown, muscular arms.

Something suddenly whirred by his ear. Startled, he spun around, and a ruby-throated humming bird zipped away.

Lily laughed and pointed at him. "It's your shirt!"

Jared looked down at his Hawaiian shirt, its fabric printed with red hibiscus flowers and green leaves.

Willie ran along the wash, dragging his stick. "A lizard!" he suddenly cried, spotting the sand-colored reptile doing push-ups on a rock. The lizard zigzagged off into the desert. Willie dropped his stick and chased after it, his camera in his hands.

Lily cocked her head in his direction and said to Thomas, "Don't let your brother get too far."

Thomas climbed out of the wash to go after Willie, when a dust devil appeared out of nowhere and swerved toward them, spinning wildly. Lily squeezed her eyes shut against the spitting sand, waiting for it to pass. When she opened her eyes, both boys were gone from sight. She headed off after them while Jared called for them to come.

Over the crest of the hill, Thomas called to his brother. He caught up with him and grabbed him by the shirt. "We need to go back."

Willie tried to twist himself away, but Thomas held on tightly to his charge and noticed movement out of the corner of his eye. A large, brown-and-black bird with a white head landed twenty feet away.

Thomas turned to watch and did a double take. Vomit rose up in his throat, and he turned away quickly, yanking his brother with him. "Quick, let's go!" he said, tugging Willie by the arm and running with him back to the wash. "Grandpa!" he cried at the sight of his grandparents. "You need to go over there. Go look! There's something awful!"

Willie jerked his head around, trying to get free of his brother's grasp. "Where?"

Jared was already striding toward them.

At that moment the wind picked up, blew toward them from over the hill. Lily lifted her nose in the air. "Oh, mercy! What's that?" she asked, reeling back.

Jared stopped dead and Lily caught his eyes, now dark. Jared recognized the smell: it was one you never got used to, one you never forgot.

"Lily, take the boys to the motor home. Now." It was a command. Lily didn't stop to question him and herded the boys back to the RV. Jared unlocked the glove box and removed a handgun. "Lock the door," he said, already headed in the direction the boys had been.

He climbed up the edge of the wash, the revolver following the direction of his eyes. The stink got worse. When he crested the hill, he scanned the area before dropping the barrel of his Smith and Wesson.

Jared waved his arm and shouted. Three turkey vultures flew off something they had been eating—something an animal had dug up from a putrid, shallow grave.

Chapter 5

Deputy Tucker and Buddy were sitting in the Hibiscus Cafe drinking coffee when Rachel walked in, desperate for her morning cup of caffeine.

Dolly immediately spotted her. "You want coffee, honey?"

"Please. And one of those cinnamon buns."

Buddy waved her over and she slid into the booth, giving Buddy an affectionate squeeze on the arm. She looked across at Tucker. "You're just the man I need to talk to."

Tucker was chewing on a toothpick. He pulled it out of his mouth and squinted at her. "Yeah? 'Bout what?"

"First, coffee," Rachel said, holding up a finger. She grabbed the carafe on the table and poured herself a mugful, added two creamers, and gulped down half the cup. Dolly sashayed up to the table with a smile and set down

Rachel's roll and a fresh carafe. After giving Tucker a quick wink, she waggled off.

Rachel stabbed her bun with a fork and caught Tucker's look. "What?"

Tucker gave her a shrug and shake of his head.

"What?" she asked louder, with attitude.

"Nothing, I was jus' thinkin'."

"Thinking *what,* Dewey?"

Tucker scratched his head. "I believe I never seen a girl, skinny as you, eat so much."

Rachel turned to give Buddy an incredulous look and then stared back at Tucker. The man was rude beyond comprehension. "Is that so," she demanded. "Well, it just so happens I inherited my mother's metabolism. She was a model, much thinner than I ever was, and put herself through Harvard with her earnings. She ate whatever she wanted and never gained an ounce." Rachel cut off a huge chunk of her bun and stuffed it boldly into her mouth.

Tucker studied her. "Heather have the same mama?"

Rachel's eyes popped open and she almost choked on the bun. She took a sip from her coffee and resisted the urge to pick up the rest of her roll and squash it into Tucker's face. Then she remembered she needed a favor from him and smiled sweetly, somehow managing to control her temper. "Yes she did, and our father was Irish, as you can no doubt tell from the Ryan name. Heather got all her genes from his side of the family. I took after my mother."

Tucker nodded. "Makes sense, her red hair an' all."

"Anything else you want to know about my family?" Rachel asked, sarcasm dripping off her words.

Tucker raised his eyebrows in a "Who me?" look and didn't say anything.

"I noticed both you and Heather are left-handed," Buddy said cheerfully, trying to break the tension. "I find that quite interesting, since only ten percent of the population has that trait."

Rachel looked up, her mouth again full of cinnamon bun. Buddy reached over with a napkin and removed a bit of icing from her cheek. He gave her a smile and his blue eyes twinkled.

"That's true," she finally said, softening. "Both my parents were left-handed. Now, if it's okay with the two of you, I'd like to drop the discussion of my family tree and ask Dewey a couple of questions."

Tucker shrugged. "Shoot."

Rachel told her version of the Golden Vista story starting with Hank's visit, detailing her meeting with Long John, Danny Long, Emma Hornsby, and ending with her worries about Hester's pill-pushing.

When she was finished, Tucker scrunched up his face and scratched behind his ear.

"Well?" Rachel asked.

"Well what?" Tucker asked back.

"Well, is it illegal for Hester Krutzer to be handing out sleeping pills or not?"

Tucker swallowed the rest of his coffee, leaned back against the booth, and stroked his walrus mustache. "I got a young woman, kidnapped from Casa Grande, sexually violated, and turned up dead on Blood Mountain; a bunch more sex offenders I gotta round up and check out; a nurse that disappeared in the middle of a shift; and you want me to arrest Hester Krutzer for handin' out sleepin' pills to two old folks, that right?"

Rachel felt like a big balloon with a fast leak, and she sank back into the booth. "I was kind of thinking that maybe the whole thing was all tied together."

"I'm not sayin' it ain't, Rachel."

"But?"

"But it's kinda like a jigsaw puzzle without the box. You gotta get enough pieces put together before you can even get an idea about what the picture looks like."

Rachel looked at him intently, refusing to give up. "Well, what about—"

Tucker held up his hand to her and, with the other, dug down in his pocket. He pulled up his cell phone which was buzzing like a tarantula wasp.

Rachel and Buddy watched Tucker's face. From the look of it, the news wasn't good.

"I'm on my way," the deputy said and snapped the phone shut. He reached for his Stetson. "It's been fun, kids."

"Wait, Dewey," Rachel cried. "At least tell us what happened."

Tucker heaved his body out of the booth. "A family out on Dead Cow Road just found a body."

Rachel jumped up. "Dead Cow Road? Can we come?"

Tucker spun around and pointed at her, his face hard.

"No. You stay!" He rushed by Dolly, squashing a ten dollar bill in her hand, and was out the door.

Within seconds Rachel and Buddy heard the siren on Tucker's truck as he rushed down the mountain.

"No. You stay!" Rachel mimicked Tucker in a deep voice, her green eyes angry little slits. "What does he think? That I'm a dog?" She took a long swig of her coffee. "That family probably just stumbled over one of those old dead cows on the side of the road and thought it was a person."

Buddy tried to suppress a laugh at Rachel's response. Not at all successful, he just rested his head in his hand and let it out. He finally looked up. "Rachel, seriously, have you ever thought about talking to your psychiatrist about your anger toward authority figures?"

Rachel looked at him like he was crazy. "What? And stop having all this fun?"

A little later, when Buddy and Rachel strolled across the lobby, her mood was subdued. "Do you think there's really a body?" she asked him. She was standing in front of her office, looking earnestly into his eyes.

"I wouldn't be surprised." Buddy looked down at his English shoes. They had been professionally polished. "A person would really have to be dense to confuse a cow with a human."

"Yeah, I know." She said it softly. "I was just showing off my Irish temper back there. I—I hope it's not Zoe."

"Me, too."

Rachel unlocked the French doors to her office and

drifted inside. Buddy followed, took Rachel's hand, and looked at her with tenderness. "I really was serious about the counseling, Rachel. I have another friend in LA who is very good with trauma. I understand about your problem with the police. I think he could help you with that."

Rachel leaned against her desk and slowly moved her head from side to side. "I already tried therapy, remember? I went to your friend, what's-his-name."

"One time. You went one time."

"True, but he can't change history. He can't make wrong into right." Her eyes skipped around the room, finally settling on a distant spot outside the office doors. "If I could just prove that my father..." she said, her voice trailing off.

"Maybe you could."

"What?"

"You know, prove it about your parents. You're not thirteen anymore, Rachel. You have knowledge, experience, and friends. Maybe you *could* prove it."

Rachel's mouth opened slightly, but Buddy touched his finger tips to her lips. "Just think about it," he said, leaving her with that thought.

Rachel watched him walk away. *Could it be possible? Could I actually prove it?* The horrific events from years ago flashed through her mind. She pressed her hand to her forehead, said aloud, "No! Stop," and turned away from the door. She sat down at her desk and immersed herself in her work.

By the middle of the afternoon Rachel felt restless. She scanned the papers on her desk but didn't want to deal with any of them. She wondered about the call Deputy Tucker received and wondered what was keeping him from coming back to finish his meal at the cafe. It surely must be a body—almost nothing could keep that man away from the feeding trough. Rachel considered calling him, but decided against it. She wouldn't give him the satisfaction. Still, she suspected he must have found *something.*

She left her office and headed toward the café for a cold drink, the clicking of her Jimmy Choo heels echoing across the lobby. She heard a loud *whump,* turned her head, and saw the wind pushing the lobby doors apart and banging them together. Wondering about the sudden change in the weather, she headed toward the entrance for a closer look and heard the sound of something hitting against the building. She stepped outside. A gust of wind out of the west hurled against her, sounding like a waterfall as it roared through the palm trees. She squeezed her eyes shut against the dust and sand. *Where in the world did this come from? The weather was perfect a couple of hours ago.* When she opened her eyes, a tall brown cloud covered the southern sky and she saw Dewey Tucker heading toward her, holding down his Stetson.

Walking beside Tucker was a man she'd never seen before, but one who looked familiar. The two men had similar builds: big boned, full bodied, filled out with muscle and fat. But the man with Tucker was younger and had skin the color of fine mahogany.

Dewey uses this place a lot to meet with people, Rachel thought and, a moment later, remembered why.

She'd been inside the deputy's office twice and had seen what it looked like. *I wouldn't take anyone in there, either.* As the men walked closer, Rachel noticed the man with Tucker had a shaved head and aviator glasses and began looking more and more familiar.

"Hey, Dewey," she said, greeting him, and then turned to the other man, finally placing him. "I'm Rachel. Are you Randy Jackson?"

The man burst into a melodic laugh, deep from his belly. "No, I'm not," he said, "but I sure wouldn't mind having his money."

A puff of wind blew Rachel's hair over her face but she couldn't take her eyes off the man. "You look just like him. It's uncanny. You could be his twin."

"Yeah, I've been told that. Especially after my wife insisted I get glasses."

"Rachel," Tucker said, breaking in, still holding on to his Stetson. "How 'bout lettin' us in before we all blow away."

Rachel quickly pulled the door open and, once inside, Tucker introduced her to Jared Johnson, adding that Jared was the man who found the body on Dead Cow Road.

Rachel extended her hand. "Well, Mr. Johnson, that actually makes you a lot more interesting than Randy Jackson." She turned to Tucker. "Do you mind if I join you?"

Tucker cocked his head toward the cafe. "Come in and take a load off. I was just tellin' Jared about you findin' the first body."

As soon as they sat in the reserved corner booth, Dolly appeared and handed them menus.

Rachel held her hand up and said she just wanted iced tea. "I'm still stuffed from lunch." She gave Tucker a sideways glance. "On the other hand, I just might have a piece of pie." After Dolly glided away, Rachel turned to Tucker. "So any ideas about the body you just found? I'm hoping it wasn't Zoe."

"Nope, wasn't Zoe." Tucker shook his head. "From what we could tell, it was her boyfriend."

"What? It was Long John? The locksmith?" Rachel's eyes widened and her hand flew up to her face. "Are you sure?"

Tucker cast his eyes down at the table and fiddled with the end of his mustache. "He weren't all there, Rachel, with the vultures and all, but not many men are six-foot-six and that skinny. And he was wearin' one of them company shirts with their logo."

"Was he…was he…"

"Shot in the back of the head, close range."

Rachel hugged herself and rocked back and forth in her seat. "I can't believe it. I just saw him the other day. The day after Zoe disappeared." She lifted her head and said almost to herself, "So he didn't go out of town after all." She turned to Tucker. "Have you talked to his brother? Danny said Long John was out of town."

"We're goin' over to the lock shop after lunch."

"We?" Rachel asked, looking from one man to the other.

"Yeah, I didn't tell you. Johnson here is a recently retired chief detective from the Detroit, PD."

Rachel jerked her head toward Johnson. "Detroit, Michigan?"

Johnson smiled and nodded. "None other."

"I grew up in Grand Rapids. I lived there until I was thirteen." Rachel's mind was spinning. She needed to talk to this man. "Will you be staying a couple of days?"

Johnson cocked his head toward Tucker. "Your deputy sheriff here asked me if I'd hang out with him a while, kind of like an advisor. I know he's shorthanded, and my wife's gonna take the grandsons over to Yuma for a few days. She wants to give them time away from what happened."

"Besides, he's had his fill of lookin' at flowers," Tucker added.

Before Rachel could respond, Dolly was at their table with everyone's drinks, Rachel's pie, and her order pad out.

Rachel stood up, beverage and the mile-high lemon meringue pie in hand. "I need to get back to work, gentlemen, but I'd really love to talk with you, Jared, about something that happened in Grand Rapids a while back."

"Be happy to," Johnson said. "I imagine I'll be hanging around here with Tucker quite a bit. He already told me about the pies, and Lily's not around to remind me about my cholesterol."

Tucker had a sheepish grin on his face.

She narrowed her eyes at him. "And the cinnamon rolls aren't bad either."

It was nearly time for happy hour when Buddy stepped through the door of Rachel's office. "You have a few minutes?" he asked.

Rachel invited him in and told him the latest news from Tucker. When she finished with the story of Long John, and they got caught up on hotel business, the day was pretty well shot. Buddy suggested they grab a drink, but Rachel had a few loose ends to clean up and a couple of phone calls she needed to make before she could quit for the day. One of those calls was to Hank. She didn't know if he had heard about the discovery of Long John's body, but if Hank hadn't, she wanted to be the one to tell him.

Hank was happy to hear from Rachel and even happier that she agreed to have dinner with him at Golden Vista. "Get us a table on the edge, as far away from the others as we can get, unless they're stone deaf," Rachel suggested.

"What? What'd ya say?" Hank teased. "I can't hear you."

"I'll be there at five." Rachel's voice was definitive. "I'll be wearing a red dress and a rose between my teeth. Look decent, will you?" Rachel hung up the phone and smiled to herself. It was good to hear Hank sounding like his old self.

She tidied up a few papers and freshened up before she drove down the mountain to Golden Vista. As usual, Hank was waiting for her in the lobby, but this time, in what looked like a better mood. He led her to a table at the edge of the dining room.

"The rehab's been payin' off," Hank said, after they were seated. "I was able to walk a little bit with a walker today. They think I might be out of the wheel chair in a couple weeks, if I keep workin' at it."

"That's wonderful, Hank, I'm really happy for you."

The rolls and salad were already on the table, and Hank and Rachel made small talk while they ate. After the staff served ham and corn chowder, Rachel told him about the discovery of Long John's body.

"You don't seem too upset," Rachel said, watching her friend.

"I'm not. The guy was a jerk."

"But what about him being shot in the back of the head?"

"Yeah, I've been thinking about that. It makes me wonder a lot about Zoe—if she met a similar fate, somewhere, maybe way out there in the desert." Hank's eyes shifted beyond Rachel, a sadness flowing into them.

"It seems kind of odd to me," she continued. "First Zoe disappearing, then Long John turning up dead." She pushed her empty bowl away. "There's got to be some kind of connection."

"Yeah, like she found out there was weird stuff going on, and let her boyfriend in on it. Or maybe it was somethin' *they* were doing."

"Like what?"

"How the heck would I know? Like I said, there's a lot of stuff that goes on here late at night. Lots of noises, people comin' and goin'. That Emmett and his sidekick, Tackett, wandering around at two in the morning. No need of them doin' that."

Hank stopped talking and pulled back. The server came up to their table with the dessert cart. "We have a choice of white cake or lemon meringue pie," she said, tiredly.

Rachel looked over at the small and pathetic looking portions. "No thank you," she said politely.

"Me, neither," Hank said, remembering the caramel pie Rachel brought with her. When the server was out of hearing range, Rachel took a sip of coffee. "What else have you seen?" she asked casually, continuing the conversation. She stared down at her coffee cup.

Hank waited until she lifted her head. "Don't go messing around in this, Rachel."

"What? What do you mean?"

"You know what I mean. Zoe disappearin' was one thing. But Long John was *murdered.* You need to back off." He leaned in close to her. "That Brick's been in trouble since he's been a teenager." His eye caught a movement, and he muttered under his breath, "Aw, crap."

Bricknell Krutzer was beside their table. "Why, Rachel Ryan, how nice to see you again," he said, extending his hand. He exhibited a slow smile with lidded eyes.

Rachel shook his hand firmly. "It's nice to see you, too. I just had a lovely meal with Hank."

"I'm glad you enjoyed it. We're really proud of our chef here. Now, if I remember correctly, I promised you a tour of the place."

After a bit more small talk, Rachel rose to leave with Brick. Hank glared at her, but she smiled sweetly at him. "I'll come by your apartment before I leave," she said and gave him a quick kiss on the cheek.

"You better, or I'll have to call the deputy to tell him you're missin'" Hank smiled, but he had an edge to his voice and looked directly at Brick.

It was a half-hour later when Rachel and Brick stood in front of the nurses' station, the tour of the building completed.

"So what do you think?" Brick asked, leaning casually against the counter, his eyes intently on her face.

She looked into his eyes and shivered inwardly. Was he mentally undressing her? No. It was more the look of a predator, like an animal, stalking his prey.

"Brick, you've done an amazing job with the renovation," she said, focusing her thoughts toward his question.

As he murmured appreciation, Rachel's eyes flicked to the door behind him. "What's that over there?" she asked, pretending she didn't know what it was.

Brick turned his head to glance at the heavily secured door. "Oh, that," he said. "That's part of the old annex, what's left of the original building. We may develop that wing one of these days, if the demand keeps up." He turned back to her. "You know how it goes. One month you're full. The next month you got six vacancies and the same number of employees to pay."

"I know *exactly* how that goes. I'm the one that gets chewed out if there are too many vacancies at our place." They laughed a bit, chatted, and finally Rachel said, "By the way, did you hear that Zoe's boyfriend was found out in the desert today, shot in the back of the head?"

Brick flinched, the thin-lipped smile freezing on his face. "Long John? No kidding. What happened?"

Rachel told him the story while she watched Brick's face change. The charming Brick had disappeared. He was no longer looking at her; he was looking *through* her. His mind appeared to be elsewhere, his lips pressed together, his jaw set tight, forcing his square-looking face to look even more so. Like a block, Rachel thought, and he was reminding her more and more of those figures in those old, 'knock-'em, sock-'em' robot games.

༺༻

Later, when Rachel arrived at Hank's apartment, she could tell he was still a little miffed. "You want pie?" he offered, frost in his voice.

"No, thanks," she said, sitting on the sofa next to him. "I better head on out."

"Well, did you learn anythin'?"

"Depends." She propped her elbow on the back of the sofa and leaned into him. "Are you still angry?"

Hank looked down at his lap. "No. I was just worried something might happen to you. You know, I just don't trust that man."

"Well, that's understandable," Rachel nodded and patted his shoulder. "I don't trust him a whole lot, either. But tell me, the entrance to the old annex—did it always have that huge hasp and padlock on it? I don't remember seeing it the last time I was here."

"Wasn't there. Ron Tackett just put it on a few nights ago, the night before we had dinner together."

"That was the night after Zoe disappeared."

"Yeah, that's right. I heard him workin' on it and peeked out. That was just about five minutes before the sleeping pill kicked in. Made me wonder."

Rachel looked thoughtful. "Makes me wonder, too." She turned her face away from Hank and stared off in the direction of the hallway. "I'm curious why an old, empty annex needs to have a huge padlock on it, in addition to a dead bolt."

Chapter 6

The next day Rachel slapped a file down on her desk in frustration and muttered an obscenity. She quickly looked around to make sure no one heard, particularly JT, who had acute hearing and wouldn't allow the least slip of profanity from employees.

She sat immobile, staring at her desk, with anxiety gnawing at the pit of her stomach. She couldn't concentrate on her job and felt nausea flowing through her. She was just sick over Long John. True, she hardly knew him. In fact, her one experience with him wasn't all that pleasant. She remembered how visibly upset he was that day she had talked to him, how he lied, and how he had bitten his fingernails nearly down to the bone. He knew something, but he wouldn't be telling anyone now.

Yet, he might have told someone *something*. His brother perhaps? A friend?

Stop! Stop! Rachel scolded herself. *This is not my*

problem. I don't have to be involved. She dropped her head in her hands and grabbed clumps of hair by the roots.

It was of no use. Thoughts of everything except work buzzed around her brain like citrus gnats. She looked at her watch. It was still an hour before lunch. But she wasn't able to function, so why should she sit there?

When Rachel finally gave up and stepped outdoors, a few cumulus clouds were popping up along the horizon and a gentle breeze stirred. It was ninety-one degrees and too lovely to sit behind a desk. When she opened the door to the Hummer, a wave of heat hit her in the face. Time to buy sun shields, she thought, happy to use any excuse to justify a trip into town.

Rachel drove directly to Long John's Lock and Key.

The sign on the door of the lock shop read, *Closed temporarily for family emergency*, but when Rachel looked inside she could see Danny Long unpacking some shipping boxes toward the back of the store. She knocked as loud as she dared on the glass window.

"Hey!" Danny said, seeing her. He let her in, a forced smile on his face, and locked the door behind her.

"How are you doing, Danny?"

"Okay." He nodded, but Rachel easily saw through him.

"No. How are you *really* doing?" She took a step closer. No stranger to death, she could sense its defiling pain so easily in others.

Danny's smile disappeared. "I think I'm still in shock." He lowered his gaze to the floor. "Truthfully, it's hard. Our father died three years ago, from a heart attack. But this…this…" He bit his lip and shook his head.

Rachel reached out and touched his arm. "I am so sorry," she said. Danny looked up at her and she could feel the familiar knife-like stab in her gut. "I understand the pain, believe me." She paused, not sure she should continue. "Not many people know this, but both of my parents were killed when I was thirteen."

Danny looked into the eyes of the lovely, poised woman standing in front of him. "Oh, no," he breathed. "That must have been horrible."

Rachel nodded. "More than you could ever know. I've had therapy, but, truthfully, I'm not sure I'll ever really be over it." She saw the distress in Danny's eyes. "But you're older than I was. You're what, twenty-five?"

"Twenty-six."

Rachel nodded. "You'll be okay. It will take a while. But eventually…"

"Yeah," Danny agreed. "Eventually…" He looked around, a thought suddenly occurring to him. "You know, I haven't eaten anything at all today. Do you think we could continue this over a couple of fish tacos?"

Rachel hesitated.

"A little taco joint just opened across the street, and the food is great."

She glanced out the window at the restaurant. Several people were sitting outside on rustic furniture with misters above them pumping cooling moisture into the air. "Sounds good," she said, giving Danny a reassuring smile.

Baja Tacos smelled like its name—deep fried fish and warm tortillas. After ordering at the counter, Danny and Rachel carried their trays to a salsa bar and filled little cups with salsa, pickled onions, and guacamole. All the inside tables were occupied so they went outside and sat at a table under a wooden umbrella covered with palm fronds. "Cute place," Rachel said, looking around.

"Yeah, and pretty handy for me, too." Danny took a long swig of his Coke. "So how long did you know John?"

"Not very long," Rachel answered honestly, deciding she needed to be up front with Danny if she was ever going to get any help from him. "In fact, I don't think he even liked me."

Danny broke out in a laugh. "Don't worry. John was the kind of guy that didn't like a whole lot of people. Most of the time he didn't even like me."

A server walked up to their table and delivered their tacos, still hot and nestled in baskets. When he left, Rachel continued, "Well, then, maybe I should just start at the beginning of how and why I met him," Rachel said.

"That would be perfect. You talk. I'll eat." Danny slathered his tacos with condiments and took a big, juicy bite.

Rachel took her time telling him the whole story of Hank and Zoe, all the way through her visit with Long John, and finally, her conversation with Jared Johnson.

"So you think this retired chief detective will do some good in finding the person who murdered my brother?" Danny asked.

"Truthfully, I don't know. I only talked to him once. But I grew up in a town not that far away from Detroit. Detroit was a tough town, even then. If you were a cop, you'd have to be pretty smart just to survive there." She took a small sip of her iced tea while Danny watched her, a small spark of hope in his eyes. "And let's face it, any help Deputy Tucker gets from the outside is bound to help him more than what he could do alone."

"That's the truth."

Rachel nibbled at her taco, trying to keep everything from falling out. "But *we* could help find the killer, Danny. Maybe there was something John told you, something he said that may not have seemed significant at the time, which would help."

"Everything I know, I already told Tucker. John came to my house in the middle of the night, woke me up from a sound sleep. He said he was leaving town, that there was some kind of trouble, and he left me in charge of the shop."

"What kind of trouble?"

Danny scratched the side of his head. "I don't know. My brain was fuzzy. Like I said, John just woke me up from a sound sleep. It was like four in the morning. I remember asking him if Zoe was involved because I'd heard she'd disappeared. I actually asked him if she'd done something, if she stole from Brick."

"You asked him if Zoe stole from Brick? Why would you ask that?"

"If you knew what kind of person she was, you wouldn't need to ask me that question."

"I see." Rachel nodded. She didn't really understand, but she was beginning to get a more complete picture of Zoe Liddy. "So what did John say?"

"He said no, but that it was complicated. He didn't want to explain, didn't want me to be involved. He said he left me a letter."

"He did? What did it say?"

"Have no idea. I never found it. I looked through the whole office. Nothing.

"What about his house?"

"That's a whole 'nother story."

"What do you mean?"

"Well, I went over there earlier today. The place had been ransacked."

"Did you call Deputy Tucker?"

"Sure did. He said he'd check it out, but I can't imagine it doing much good."

Rachel tossed that over in her mind while she finished her tacos. "Maybe whoever killed your brother was looking for something, something John didn't have on him at the time. The letter?" She looked at Danny quizzically. "No, it couldn't be that. Maybe some kind of clue as to what was going on?"

Danny hunched his shoulders. "I have no idea. Nothing. *Nada.* And if Zoe was involved, who knows what he could have been doing?"

Rachel pushed her taco basket aside and sipped her drink. "What about friends? Did he have any friends he might have confided in?"

Danny chewed on the last remnants of his taco before he spoke. "You know, a friend of his did come in looking for him. He was pretty upset, too. He needed to see him right away."

"Who?"

"Jesse Albarran."

Rachel frowned, trying to remember. "The name sounds familiar."

"He runs the apartment building downtown, the Hotel Rios."

"Yes, now I remember. He was with you guys at our open house party." She looked off, trying to formulate a picture in her mind. "He's dark, with a goatee and a soul patch, big black glasses."

"Right. He and John were friends for years. If he told anybody anything, he would have told Jesse."

"I'll look him up," Rachel said. "Anybody else?"

"Well, just before Jesse showed up, Ron Emmet had come by, looking for John. Didn't say why, just that he wanted to see him."

"He's the big, fat guy who works for Brick Krutzer, right?"

"Right."

"I never really met the man, but he seems really nasty."

"He *is* really nasty. I could tell you stories..."

"What kind of stories?"

Danny glanced at his watch. "Interesting stories. But they'll have to wait for another time. I need to get back. I'm expecting a shipment I need to sign for."

"Okay, another time. Maybe you can come to the hotel and have lunch with me."

Danny's eyes lit up. "Let me give you my cell phone number."

They left the table, threw the remnants of their lunch in the trash can by the door, and walked back through the restaurant and across the street to where the Hummer was parked. Danny held the truck door open and Rachel climbed into the driver's seat.

"You know, there is something else," Danny said. "But it's probably nothing."

"What is it?"

"That day, when Ron Emmett came over? He asked about John but kept looking around the shop, like he was looking for something, checking the place out. He just acted kind of weird, that's all."

Rachel looked up at the puzzled expression on his face. "Huh. Interesting. I'll keep that in mind." She turned the key in the ignition.

"One other thing."

"What?"

"Why are you even getting involved in all this?"

Rachel stared at the steering wheel a moment and then turned to Danny. "I don't quite know. I started out trying to help a friend find Zoe, and now I'm just kind of…kind of…"

Danny gently put his hand on top of hers. "Look, I'm happy you want to help find out who killed my brother, but I don't want you taking any kind of personal risk. You don't have any stake in this, but I do. If Brick is involved in any type of illegal activity or knows anything about my brother's murder, then believe me when I tell you that you need to drop this whole thing."

Rachel nodded and worked at painting a sincere expression on her face. "Okay. If I find out anything that points to Brick's involvement, I'll just back off and let Deputy Tucker handle it."

Danny studied her for several seconds. "Why is it I really don't believe you?"

※※※

The rest of the day was uneventful. Rachel spent all of it in her office going over previous contacts to see who might be a prospect for summer business. When she heard sounds of country music coming from the lounge she lifted her head and noticed Heather heading toward her.

"Hey, sweetie, you want to have an early dinner with just me?"

"Sure, but what's wrong?"

"Who says something's wrong?"

"Ah, geez, Heather, I can see it in your face."

"Okay, okay. I was going to tell you about it, anyway."

"Sure you were. So sit down and tell me about it now." She pointed at the chair in front of her.

Heather promptly sat. "JT's been getting some unsigned threatening notes. They're poems."

"Threatening poems? Really?" Rachel let it sink in a

minute. "Did he talk to Dewey Tucker about them?"

"You're not serious, are you?"

Rachel slapped her own face. "What was I thinking? Mr. Macho asking for help with a personal problem?" She turned back to Heather. "Tell me what the letters said."

Heather handed her sister a small piece of paper.

Rachel read the two poems. "This is it?"

"Those are my copies. JT wouldn't let me have the originals. I suspect he thought I'd show them to you, so I memorized what they said and put them in the computer."

"Good. I'd like to see the originals, but my guess is the person sending these seems somewhat educated. He knows how to use a semi-colon. And he knows how to use a computer. Let's think about this a while and talk about it again." Rachel slipped her feet into her favorite Jimmy Choo's under the desk. "I'm ready. Will it be the Hibiscus Café or the Plantation Room?"

"Mmm. I'm thinking the Plantation Room tonight. Let's go for the star treatment."

"Oh, Heather, we always get the star treatment." Rachel laughed. "You own the darn place."

As they navigated through the lobby toward the dining room, the two women spotted Dewey Tucker and Jared Johnson coming in the front door. They met up with the men in front of the Plantation Room.

"Do you gentlemen have dates for tonight?" Rachel asked.

"No such luck there, young lady," Jared answered.

"Well then, why don't you join us? We were just going in to have dinner and would love to have you as our guests," she said graciously, extending her arm toward the restaurant door.

After the four of them had settled in and ordered drinks, Heather answered the obvious question as to the whereabouts of JT and Buddy. She then asked Jared about his wife and grandsons.

"I think they'll be coming back next week," he said. "I guess there's quite a bit to do around Yuma, and they're taking it all in. You know—historical sites and touristy things. They went to the old Territorial Prison today and saw a re-enactment of an old western shootout."

After a bit more small talk, Heather turned toward Dewey Tucker. "Deputy, I hate to bring this up, but I need to tell you something that JT would never mention to you." She glanced over at Rachel then handed Tucker the poems. As he read them, she related the story of the anonymous notes. "That's not the original. JT kept it. We've had our hands all over it so you might not be able to get any prints off it, anyway."

Just then, Manuel came to the table with their salads. Tucker nodded, folded the papers, and said he would talk to JT about it soon.

Manuel left and there was a lull in the conversation. Rachel brought up the subject of Long John's murder.

"We ain't come up with nothin' worthwhile so far," Deputy Tucker admitted.

"What about Long John's apartment? I heard it had been ransacked."

The deputy narrowed his eyes at her. "You knew about that?"

"Yes. Danny told me. He and I are good friends," Rachel said, mentally wondering if the "good friends" part was an exaggeration or an out-right lie."

"Yeah, somebody went through and tore it up pretty bad. It looks like the person who killed Long John was lookin' for somethin', but we have no idea what."

"Do you think it had anything to do with Zoe's disappearance?"

"We'd *like* to think so, but again, we have nothin' to go on," he said, tugging at his gray, walrus mustache. "We don't know if she's alive or dead, left town in a hurry, or what."

"Well, I can assure you of one thing, Deputy," Heather said, "Zoe did not leave Golden Vista of her own volition. Rachel said she left her purse behind in the locker. No woman would ever go anywhere without her purse. Not just because of the money. A woman has a thing about her purse. Her whole *life* is in there."

Deputy Tucker and Jared Johnson looked at each other. "She's got a point there," Johnson said.

"Dewey, didn't you indicate once that Zoe had a rather murky background?" Rachel asked. "Maybe she was involved with the wrong kind of people and got in trouble with them."

"Yep, I been considerin' that possibility myself. In fact, it kinda complicates the whole thing. You see, if a gal wanted to fake an abduction, the simple act of leavin' her purse behind would make it a little more convincin'."

"You can't be serious," Rachel said.

"That so? Even if she were runnin' out on a huge debt and a couple bad check charges?"

Rachel was stunned. This was something new, but before she could speak she noticed Manuel coming up toward the table with a large tray filled with dinner plates.

When the group was nearly through with their steaks and sipping the last of the bottle of wine Heather ordered, Chef Henri appeared at their table. He wore a clean white apron around his wiry frame, and a few black dreadlocks hung down below his chef's cap. He often came by, particularly on slower nights, to talk to the patrons and make sure they were completely satisfied with their meals.

Heather introduced Chef Henri to Jared who immediately assured the young chef that his steak was the finest he had ever eaten. As they made small talk, Rachel revealed that the retired Detective Johnson was working with Deputy Tucker on the recent murder. She added they still had no new information about Long John or Zoe.

Chef Henri suddenly appeared uncomfortable. His smile left his face and he shifted from foot to foot.

"What's wrong?" Rachel asked, reading him.

The chef dropped his face. "Ah, I don't know if I should say this. It's probably nothing." He looked from Rachel to the deputy.

"Let me be the one to decide if it's nothin', Henri," Deputy Tucker replied in a gruff voice, determined to assert his authority. "If you have any information, you need to tell us."

Chef Henri glanced around to make sure no one was within hearing distance. "Manuel said Long John and Zoe were in here for dinner on Thursday afternoon at four, right when we opened. They had prime rib. I was too busy to come out that day, so I didn't actually see it myself."

"Fine, fine, but what happened?" Tucker asked impatiently.

"Well, Manuel said Long John and Zoe were having some kind of argument. The only reason he mentioned it to me today is because everyone's been talking about the murder ever since it happened."

As soon as Chef Henri left, Rachel turned to Tucker. "We need to talk to Manuel. Please let me ask him about it. I think it will be less intimidating if I do it."

In a minute or so, Manuel was back at their table to clear away the dishes. Everyone murmured their appreciation of his attentive service and declined dessert. Manuel appeared to be relaxed and happy as he loaded up the large tray.

"Hey, Manuel?" Rachel asked casually. "Remember when Zoe and Long John were in here last Thursday and they had that argument?"

The server suddenly straightened and looked at her. Rachel was looking cheerful, along with everyone else at the table, hoping to convince Manuel he wasn't in trouble. He nodded warily.

Rachel continued. "Do you remember what they were arguing about?"

Manuel shrugged. "I think they were fighting over a

key, some key Zoe wanted. I don't think Long John wanted to give it to her," he said, in a heavy Mexican accent.

"Do you know if he gave her the key after all?"

A half-smile formed on Manuel's lips. "I think so, Miss Rachel. You know how women are. They get what they want." He shrugged again and left with the tray.

Rachel turned to the two men. "So what do you think? That Long John the locksmith made Zoe a key he really didn't want to give her?"

"That's better than we've been able to come up with," the retired detective said.

"Yeah, and if the key is important," Deputy Tucker said, pulling on one side of his mustache, "I'm wondering what the durn thing opens."

Chapter 7

It was the first call of the morning when Deputy Dewey Tucker drove his truck past the small stucco house on Second Street. The house looked neglected and forlorn, with a shutter hanging at an angle from one of the front windows, its peeling paint revealing a wash of blue beneath a dirty dark red.

Tucker parked a few houses over, but out of sight of the house, and shut off the engine. He leaned as far back as he could in his seat, reached under his Kevlar vest and slipped the key into his pants pocket. He turned to the muscular, clean-cut probation officer beside him. "You ready, Pete?"

Pete Diaz instinctively reached below his bulletproof vest and touched the butt of his gun. "Let's do it."

The two men slowly emerged from the Ford. Their eyes carefully scanned the house, the windows, the roof, and what they could see of the backyard before closing the truck doors and walking toward the chain link fence that surrounded the property and separated it from the neighbors. Pete jiggled the latch and watched to see if dogs came bounding out of hiding. When none did, he opened the gate, allowing the deputy to go through first.

The concrete walkway was fractured and had been for a while. Weeds grew in the cracks in several places. The men never noticed. They were busy watching the door and windows, alert for a possible ambush.

The men stepped to the side of the door opposite the hinge. Tucker leaned over and pounded on it with his fist. "Open up. Sheriff."

A dog barked inside, and they heard movement, a man shouting to the dog to shut up. In a minute, the door opened inward and the smell of old grease and cat urine assaulted the officers.

An older man with thinning gray hair and bushy, gray eyebrows stood in the doorway appearing to wear the clothes he'd slept in. "Yeah, yeah, what'd ya want?"

"Hey, Jimmy, may we come in?" Diaz asked. "We just need to talk."

Jimmy shrugged. "Suit yourself." The man turned back into the house. "Have a seat," he said, extending his hand toward the sofa.

The fabric, once a dull green color, was torn, punctuated with holes, and covered with stains of questionable origin. The two men scanned the inside as they stepped into the living room but declined the offer to sit.

"Anybody here with you today?" Tucker asked.

"Nobody but the dog and cat."

Tucker eyed the pup crouched by the sofa and the old cat curled up on one of the cushions. "We ain't gonna stay long. Just need you to answer a couple questions."

"Where were you all last week?" Diaz asked.

"Here."

"You never left to go anywhere?"

"Does it look like I got the money to take a trip?" Jimmy asked sarcastically.

"Never mind the lip. Just answer the question."

"No. I never left Mesquite. Never left the area. Never had the money for gas. Happy?"

"So you never went anywhere, even with a friend.

"Right. I never went nowhere." Jimmy crossed his fleshy arms over his chest. "This about that girl that got killed?"

"Yeah. How'd you hear about that?"

"I got a land line, I still got friends."

"Any ideas about it?"

Jimmy turned away and kneaded his bulbous chin for a minute.

"You don't wanna be withholdin' information from us," Tucker chimed in.

"Yeah, yeah, just let me think a minute. Seems like I heard somethin' about somebody."

Tucker and Diaz stood patiently, still with an eye on the hallway at the end of the living room.

"Yeah. Now I remember." Jimmy turned to them. "Pete Cervantes told me he ran into Shorty Baker at a yard sale a couple weeks ago. I'm pretty sure it was Pete that told me. He said Shorty was buying a stack of old

Penthouse magazines. He said he also saw Shorty hanging around the bus depot in Yuma about a week or so ago. He went to pick up his brother coming in from LA, but he said Shorty wasn't waitin' for anybody. He was just hangin' around."

Diaz and Tucker exchanged glances.

"I heard Shorty Baker really likes them young blondes," Jimmy said, a hint of a sneer on his face.

"Okay, thanks, Jimmy," Tucker said. He gave the room a last look and turned to leave, sidestepping a dirty cat toy and a dusting of litter.

ഔഔ

Back at the hotel, JT Carpenter was glued to his chair, hunched over a pile of bills sitting on his desktop, totally ignoring the ring of the telephone. Within seconds, his cell phone rang. Finally giving in, he clicked it on to hear the voice of his maintenance manager.

"Hey, Mr. JT, it's Toro. I'm stuck in front of the hardware store and the truck won't start."

JT groaned inwardly. "Did you check the battery?"

"Yup. And the cables."

"Did you try jiggling the key in the ignition?" There was hope.

"That, too. Even checked the gas."

JT let out a sigh of resignation. "Okay. Hold on. I'll be right there." He clicked off the phone and muttered, "If it's not one thing, it's another."

He swung by the front desk and told Amalia he was

off to rescue Toro at the hardware store. "I'll be right back," he said, rushing off.

JT jumped into his Ford F250 and started it up. At least something worked, he thought and patted Tommy-Boy's dashboard. He'd always given his trucks names. Somehow, they each seemed to have a distinct personality.

He slipped Tommy-Boy into gear and rolled forward out of his parking space. No need to get frustrated, he assured himself. He'd get to take a break from hotel problems and writing checks. Now he had a chance to enjoy a quick ride through some of the newly planted fields in Venkman's Farms.

Still, JT drove too fast through the parking lot, which was now quiet, the hustle and bustle of the daily checkouts finished. At the end of the lot, he put Tommy-Boy in fourth gear and stepped on the accelerator and sped down the dirt road that led to town. *I may need to pave this track someday. There are so many things I need to do it hurts my head to think about it.*

Suddenly aware of his speed, he glanced at his speedometer and stepped on the brake. The truck didn't slow.

He pumped the brake again, and then again. He realized something was wrong and Tommy-Boy was up to forty-five. He yanked the wheel to the left to avoid the outcropping of rocks on a curve and then quickly pulled it to the right as his vehicle careened across the road. *What the heck?* Even his power steering seemed to be failing. He quickly tried to jam the transmission into third gear, but he missed it and the transmission slipped into neutral. The truck began to race even faster down the steep hill. He yanked the truck to the left to avoid running into the outcropping, kicking up dirt and gravel. At the same time he realized he had to stop the truck immediately before another vehicle came up the hill.

He saw his opportunity in a flash when he caught a glimpse of the clear road ahead. He jerked the wheel sharply to the left again and spun the truck into the hill, where it came to a hard stop. The bumper, now dented, sat up against a jagged boulder and the butt end of Tommy-Boy jutted out into the road.

When JT's adrenaline stopped pumping, he pulled out his cell phone and made a call.

"Good morning. This is Rachel Ryan. How may I help you?"

"You can jump in the Hummer right now and come meet me half way down the hill and give me a ride into town."

JT's voice had enough anger in it that Rachel knew to drop everything. "Okay. I'll be right there."

It was less than three minutes later when Rachel pulled over on the right side of the road.

She observed Tommy-Boy's blinking emergency lights and his dented front end while JT sat behind the wheel finishing a phone call to the insurance company.

"The tow truck should be here within fifteen minutes," he said, after exiting the Ford, and gave Rachel a quick explanation about what had happened.

Rachel looked up at him. "Do you think somebody cut your brake line?"

"What? Why would you think that?"

"I don't know," Rachel said. "Just guessing."

JT gave her a disgusted look and shook his head. "We might as well wait in the Hummer." He opened the door to the truck and then stopped. "Aw, what the heck." He pulled out a small rug from behind the driver's seat and laid it on the ground halfway under the truck. He got down and eased himself under Tommy-Boy.

"What?" Rachel asked. "Did I hear you say the word 'damn'?"

"No! I said, aw, *man!*"

He pulled himself up looking more disgusted than before. "What made you ask if it was the brake line?"

"I told you. It was a guess."

"Why would you guess that?"

"I don't know. I read a story about a person cutting someone's brake line to try to injure them. You know—like in that cheesy poem that ends with 'and trouble will follow the end of the line.'"

JT stared at Rachel for several seconds. "So Heather told you. I should have known she would."

She smiled ever so sweetly at him. "Yeah, so are you going to call Deputy Tucker or shall I?"

Tucker arrived first, followed by the tow truck about five minutes later.

JT was silent the rest of the way into town. Rachel had enough sense to remain silent, too. They found Toro sitting in the company truck in front of the hardware store. The huge Indian jumped out, looking distraught. Perspiration glowed on his dark skin, highlighting the vertical scar that ran down the length of his face. The scar—a souvenir from a bar fight that sent him to prison for killing a man—was a constant reminder of the changed life he now led.

"If Rachel will get behind the wheel, I can push this next door to the service station," the muscular Indian offered.

JT surveyed the parking lot and the entrance to the service station next to it. "Piece of cake. Let's both do it."

After moving the truck and asking the service manager to call him about the damage as quickly as possible, everyone climbed into the Hummer and JT drove back to the inn. JT turned to Toro who was looking particularly troubled. "Hey, don't worry; it's not your fault."

"Maybe it is."

"What do you mean?"

Toro just looked down at his lap. "I parked on the end, a little ways away from everybody else so nobody would whack the paint on the new truck and this kid comes running up and sits in one of them lawn chairs they got for sale. I get out and he doesn't look at me, just keeps his eyes down. He's got a paper bag in his hand. I get a funny feeling and keep looking at him but he never looks up. I felt a bad spirit around the kid and shoulda gone to talk to him, but I didn't. I went to the store."

"Yeah. And then what?"

"I get the parts I need and come back out, maybe five or six minutes later. The kid is gone. I get in the truck and crank it. It starts up and just before I start to back out, it just dies. I try to start it again, but it won't even turn over. A brand-new truck and it doesn't start. I check the gas tank and there are scratches around the gas cap I never saw before."

"How old was the kid?"

"Ten, maybe twelve years old."

"Doesn't matter. It's not your fault, Toro. You can't sit around and watch a truck twenty-four hours a day. I mean, what's the worst that could happen?" JT turned back in his seat and didn't say another word all the way back to the hotel.

Rachel, wisely, never said a word either. But she, like the others, wondered if the kid had anything to do with the disabled truck.

About two hours later the door to JT's office slammed shut. Rachel heard the bang all the way from her office and then saw JT rush by and out the back door. She went up to Amalia who was still cringing at the front desk. "What happened? Did JT just get a call from Ortiz Auto Repair?"

"Yes," Amalia said, still wincing. "I guess the news wasn't good. I couldn't hear a whole lot until he shouted, 'A new engine!' The next thing I heard is the door slamming and him saying he was quitting for the day."

Chapter 8

"Sugar in the gas tank?" Rachel's eyes showed lack of surprise. She was sitting with Buddy in the Plantation Room having pie and coffee. "We should have guessed it after what happened to the brake line. And I think we can guess how the sugar got in there, too," she added, remembering Toro's story of the boy with the paper bag in his hands. "Well, I can understand why JT wouldn't tell me."

"Now why would that be?" Buddy's voice was serious but his twinkling blue eyes gave him away.

"I'm sure it couldn't be that he might suspect I'd want to go poking around in his business," she answered with light sarcasm as she scraped the last few crumbs of pie crust onto her fork and ate them.

"And would you?"

Rachel looked up with green innocent eyes and a mischievous smile. "Of course, I would."

Buddy laughed, signed the check, and tossed a couple bills on the table for the tip. "Come on, let's go over to my place and get a nightcap."

"Sounds good to me." She stood up and walked out the door with him. "Let's take the long way through the garden, though. You need to stretch your legs after that plane ride and I need to walk off that pie."

"I do need to stretch my legs. That Beech Baron pulled in ahead of me again and I had to wait my turn and circle around a couple times."

"The Baron with the body-builder pilot and the odd-looking guy?"

"He's not odd-looking, Rachel. He just looks odd *here,* out-of-place. I recognize a hand-tailored Italian suit when I see one and nobody around here wears one. I'm sure the gold he wore was the real thing, too. At least it looked that way the one time I saw him close up."

"And of course, you'd notice the shoes."

"Of course. You could tell he was loaded, but he looked—you know—slimy. Even with the gray hair. He was just too slick."

"Interesting. Only two people in a six-seater."

"Well, I'm only one person and my plane has four seats."

"True. But you don't look odd."

"I guess I can take that as a compliment."

"You don't *look* odd, but that doesn't mean you *aren't* odd," Rachel teased. After they stepped outside, she took Buddy's hand. "By the way, did JT get any more poetry from his admirer this afternoon?"

"Why do you ask?"

She stopped. "Buddy, I saw the letter. You ought to know by now I find out everything. You might as well tell me what the crazy poet said and save me some time."

"Why? I thought maybe you'd want to try to pry it out of me later, at my place," he said with a sly smile.

"So that *was* another poem for him that I saw lying on the front desk." She continued walking.

He pulled her back. "That was a bit sneaky, you know."

She smiled from under her lashes. "I know. But so was the little trick you just tried to pull. Now tell me what the poem said."

"Okay." He pulled out a little piece of paper and handed it to her. "You win. I made a copy for you."

"Hmm. So you were just playing hard to get," Rachel teased, held the little square of paper up to the light above the walkway, and read it aloud.

> "'Daisies are white
> Violets are blue.
> You just got a taste
> Of what I can do.'

"Scary, but at least he admits to doing the deed," Rachel said.

"Yes, but with an implied warning there's more to come."

"That is the scary part. He could strike anywhere, anytime. But why, JT? He'd never hurt a soul. He's honest, fair in his dealings—generous. Who would want to hurt him? That terrorist can't possibly be a disgruntled employee. We don't have any. And there's not a soul that doesn't respect JT."

"Did Deputy Tucker ever check the letter for fingerprints?"

"Yes, he did. In fact, he called Heather this morning. There was nothing but her and JT's fingerprints on it. And the envelope was a peel and stick, so if you were going to suggest checking for DNA from saliva, that's out. There was just no way the note could be traced. So the person who's doing this is not stupid, either."

"No, he's not. But he's dangerous. JT could have been killed going down that hill."

"Yes, he could have, and Tucker needs to do something about it. He needs to get his act together and catch that lunatic." Rachel's voice had gone up an octave and rang with anger.

Buddy pulled back, studied her, and swung into his imitation of a southern belle: "Why, Miss Rachel, ah do believe that is a look of genuine concern on yo' face for yo' brother-in-law."

"Why shouldn't it be?" she asked, defensively. "He is my sister's husband. I do care about him. I don't want him hurt."

"So you *do* love him, after all. Now there's a tasty bit of information I can pass on to JT," Buddy teased, touching Rachel's nose affectionately with his finger.

"Don't you dare."

Buddy leaned into her and lowered his voice. "Well,

I could *possibly* be persuaded not to reveal a word to anyone." He flashed his brilliant, charming smile. "What's it worth to you?"

ぐっぴっつ

Early the next morning Heather drove down the mountain to Golden Vista. A murky haze fanned out over the western sky and she rolled up the car windows tightly against the smog. It looked like Venkman Farms was burning off one of their wheat fields and the wind had changed, holding a thick layer of smoke close to the earth.

Miss Emma Hornsby was already waiting on the veranda, holding a lace hankie over her mouth and nose. Heather quickly loaded her into the car and brought her back to the hotel for Emma's favorite breakfast special. Rachel arrived late and dragged herself into the corner booth.

Dolly followed right behind her in her squeaky white waitress shoes, her bleached-blonde hair tied back with a ribbon and a silk hibiscus blossom tucked in it, island style.

"You want the special, honey?"

"Oh, no thanks, Dolly. Just bring another carafe of coffee and a short stack. Extra butter." Rachel looked around, greeted Heather and Emma, and then asked. "Where are the guys?"

"They went into town to a businessmen's breakfast at the country club," Heather said. "I thought it would be fun to have a little get-together with us girls at the same time."

"I sure appreciate that," Miss Emma piped up. "I get tired of the same old choices for breakfast. And we never get steak. Can't blame 'em really. I mean, there's not many of us old folks left with our own teeth."

Heather looked down at her mug and tried to keep from laughing, but her auburn hair bounced and gave her away. "I thought Rachel could give you a ride back to Golden Vista later. She's going to Long John's memorial service, and it's close by."

"I'll say. It's across the street. Perfect location, isn't it? A funeral parlor right across the street from the old folk's home," Emma quipped. "But I decided not to go to funerals anymore. Don't even plan to attend mine."

"Great idea, Miss Emma. I'll hold you to that," Heather said. "But actually, I suspect Rachel is going primarily to do a little spying." She gave her sister a sidelong glance. "Right, Rachel?"

Rachel put her mug down. "Guilty as charged, I'm afraid. I've read murderers often go the funerals of the people they kill and I'm curious to see if certain people show up."

"You mean Brick Krutzer, right?" Emma asked.

"I can see you both are too sharp for me first thing in the morning." Rachel laughed then lowered her voice. "I just *know* Brick had something to do with Zoe's disappearance, and if he did that, he had to be involved with Long John's murder, too."

Dolly arrived at their booth with a large tray filled

with platters. She set them down carefully with a warning of "Be careful, ladies, hot plates," and after checking the water and coffee levels, quickly disappeared, leaving a waft of Evening in Paris in the air.

After everyone ate a little, Rachel turned to Emma. "What do you know about Brick and his early life? You kind of alluded to the fact that he had often been in trouble."

"I know plenty, but I'm not sure you ladies are up to hearing about it. It ain't pretty, I'll tell you that."

"We're not naïve," Heather said. "I doubt anything you say could shock us."

"Okay, I'll tell you what happened, but you were forewarned," Emma began and let out a deep breath. "Brick was a little hellion all through grade school. He was a big kid and kind of a bully. No, he wasn't kind of a bully. He *was* a bully. When he got to high school, he became a big football hero and hung around with Ron Emmett and Adam Tackett. There was also one other kid, David Cutter. They used to drink and cruise around and hangout at Rattlesnake Pass, driving dune buggies and things like that. They got in trouble—you know, typical teen-age stuff—but nothing ever came of it because Brick's dad was a U. S. Marshall, one of those types that believe their kid can do no wrong."

She paused to take another bite of pancake. Her eyes shifted from Rachel to Heather and back as if she was checking their reaction.

"Go ahead. Continue," Heather urged.

"Okay. One night they all got loaded, picked up this

girl, Brandi Weaver, and took her out to Rattlesnake Pass. There was a bunch of kids out there, all drinking, smoking pot, less than a dozen all together. Brandi was raped and beaten. Then somebody dumped her off at home."

Emma quickly looked down at her plate, embarrassed, and took her time cutting a small piece of steak and eating it. She then pushed some scrambled eggs around. She didn't look up at either woman.

"It's okay," Rachel said, reaching out and gently squeezing her hand. "It's really important that we know." She tried to sound calm, but she was seething inside. "Can you tell us what happened after that?"

Emma nodded, took a sip of coffee, and then continued chewing and looking down at her mug as if mentally debating what she was going to say. "Brandi's mother got home around two in the morning and found her daughter beaten up and crying. She dragged Brandi over to the sheriff's office and made Brandi tell deputy Stanky—he was the deputy at the time—what happened. She named Brick and his three pals as the guys who raped her.

"Well, Stanky first wanted to arrest Mary Weaver for drunken driving, but decided to go ahead and investigate after Mary brought Brandi to the hospital and threatened to call the newspaper. Stanky rounded up all the kids that were out at Rattlesnake Pass that night but they all denied seeing anything, every one of them. He talked to Brick and his gang, but they claimed she was just fine when they dropped her off in front of her house that night. Brick said they dropped her off early and then went out in the desert and spent the whole night behind Blood Mountain. Truth is, they did go out there afterward and had a camp fire and spent the rest of the night in their trucks so they'd have an alibi. Had a bunch of soda cans out there, left plenty of tire tracks, and made it look like they had been there a long time. That's where Stanky found them. To make a long story short, it never went to trial."

"What? You mean none of the other kids at Rattlesnake Pass agreed to be a witness?"

"Oh, there was one *witness*." Emma spit the answer out. "But in the end he didn't have the courage to speak up. See, this kid, he had a dog. It was going around town that he was going to testify about what happened, but then his dog was killed. Brutally killed. The kid ended up saying it was dark and he was drunk and he really couldn't tell if Brick and his friends were there or not."

Rachel silently nodded in understanding.

"And the prosecutor?" Emma's voice was tinged with disgust. "He was a lulu. He dropped the case, said there wasn't enough evidence for a trial. Brandi had taken a bath and they didn't have DNA testing then, at least not here. Heck, they didn't even have rape kits or women officers. Just a couple of men who figured if a girl got raped it was because she asked for it. Later, at the end of his term, the prosecutor found the money to run for a judge position somewhere else in the state and won. Some people in town were pretty upset about the whole thing, but nobody dared speak up. Brandi's mom was a single mom, just a nobody. They lived in a trailer down in one of those places on the edge of town, and she didn't have the world's best reputation."

"That's really horrible," Heather said, her voice cracking. "What happened to Brandi after that?"

"Everybody kind of distanced themselves from her, like she had some kind of disease or something. She got into drugs, went a little crazy. It was quite a while back, and in those days they didn't have much in town to offer a woman who was abused—especially a woman who was half Indian."

"That's really horrible—that poor girl." Heather had already pushed the remains of her breakfast away and she sat staring into her coffee mug, blinking her blue eyes, trying to keep the tears back.

"Yeah, I agree. I always felt sorry for her. She didn't have much of a chance from that day on." Emma looked at her two friends. "I told you it was an ugly story."

"It was, but we needed to hear it," Rachel said. "I've had the feeling Brick was a secret woman hater. Now I *know* he is—and a low-life rapist to boot."

"That he is, and you need to stay far away from him, Rachel. I saw you talking with him the other day at Golden Vista. It looked like Brick gave you the tour of the place."

"Yes, he did. And that's when I got the bad feeling about him."

"Good. Then I'm glad I told you that story. It helps to reinforce your intuition. I didn't want you to go around thinking he was some kind of golden boy."

"No need to worry about that."

Emma looked down at her plate, sighed with relief, and then lifted her head. Her perm had loosened up and a halo of soft gray curls surrounded her face. The corners of her lips turned up. "Then how about another round of pancakes?"

Chapter 9

Rachel delivered Emma Hornsby back to Golden Vista shortly after ten-thirty. When she helped the old lady into her transport chair, she couldn't help notice the recently-remodeled mortuary across the street where Long John's memorial service was being held.

A large tree in front of it looked as if it had been completely covered with huge orange-red blossoms overnight. "Look at that, Miss Emma," she said, pointing to the brilliant display.

"Amazing, isn't it? A Royal Poinciana. It will stay that way for a few weeks and I can see it every day from my apartment. One of the few good things about living here." She looked up at Rachel with a gloating smile. "Plus the fact that I can see who comes and goes."

As Rachel rolled Miss Emma toward her apartment, Emma handed her a piece of paper. "You will remember what I told you about being careful, won't you?" Emma asked.

Rachel glanced at the note. *Be careful of what you say in this place. I think they have it bugged.* She dropped the note into her purse and hugged Miss Emma goodbye with a clear promise to drive carefully. After moving the Hummer over to the parking lot on the side of the mortuary, she unfolded the note and read its message again. *Someone bugged Miss Emma's apartment? Or was this simply the manifestation of an old lady's paranoia?* She stared at the attractive assisted-living facility across the street, trying to discern its secrets. *But then again, the sleeping pills were real, so maybe Miss Emma is right. Just in case, I'll be careful what I say at Golden Vista from now on.*

⁕⁕⁕

The mortuary felt cool and smelled like a flower shop when Rachel entered. She noticed Danny Long up front with an older man and woman—his aunt and uncle—she guessed, who were surrounded by a bevy of people including several attractive young women. Deciding to pay her respects after the service, Rachel slipped into the next-to-last row, where she hoped she would be unobserved.

Brick was seated three rows ahead with his two cohorts, Adam Tackett and Ron Emmett, both of whom were cleaned up for the event. Rachel watched them frequently, noticing that they often exchanged glances during the service. *Interesting.* She took note of the other people sitting nearby as well and saw several people she recognized.

The service itself was short, much to her relief, and included an invitation to lunch at the home of Danny's aunt and uncle. As Rachel walked in the procession to greet the family, she gazed down at the table laden with photos and mementos of Long John's brief life. More than a dozen, colorful floral arrangements sat on stands around it.

When she approached the family, the brutality of Long John's death finally broke through to her as she felt her protective shell crack.

She found herself in front of Danny, frozen and speechless, only to be hugged tightly in return. After she finally managed to whisper a few words of sympathy, Danny thanked her and in a whisper he added, "Jesse Albarran needs to talk to you before you leave." He then reached out to the person behind her.

Rachel stumbled along until she stepped outside, the hole in her heart from her parents' deaths now torn open and bleeding once more. *It was a mistake to come here, you idiot! When will you ever learn?*

The sunlight fell harshly on her face when she stepped away from the covered walkway. It was already getting hot. She reached for her sunglasses when, all at once, Jesse Albarran was at her side.

"Danny told me what you've been doing. I have some information for you, if you want it," he whispered.

Then he looked around as if he were checking to make sure no one could have heard him.

"Sure," she responded in a dull voice, pulling herself out of the past. "Do you want to walk me to my Hummer?"

He took another quick look around. "No. I don't want anyone hearing me talk about this. Can you meet me at River Park? Do you know how to get there?"

She nodded, now able to sense his anxiety. "Let me leave first. You talk to a couple people, make yourself visible, and then take off."

River Park consisted of acres of green grass and trees that lined the edge of the river. Rachel drove down to the lower parking lot so her Hummer wouldn't be seen from the street and strolled along the curving path to a pavilion. The air felt heavy with humidity and smelled faintly of swamp grasses and river water. She sat down at one of the picnic tables and watched a lone older couple fishing near the water's edge. She mentally distanced herself from Long John's death and buried all thoughts of her parents. A few minutes later she heard footsteps behind her.

"Hey, thanks for meeting me, Rachel."

Rachel turned and looked up at Jesse. "No problem. I wanted to talk to you, too. Do you want to move farther away? There's another table ahead."

"No, this is fine. No one can see us from the road." He glanced around the area. "You never know who's watching these days." He sat down on the bench beside her. "Danny told me you were investigating Zoe's disappearance."

"Investigating? I guess I was just trying to help out my friend Hank Levinson. He lives at Golden Vista and had a really big crush on her. He was very distressed when she turned up missing and I kind of volunteered to help find her."

"He had a really big crush on Zoe?" Jesse looked skeptical. "I bet that was a one-way deal."

"Yes, I imagine it was, but it ended when Hank began to see what she was really like."

Jesse grunted in a show of disgust. "Man, I'm sure he didn't know the half of it."

"I'm sure *I* don't know half of it either, but I've kind of gotten sucked into the story anyway. There've been a lot of odd things going on at Golden Vista and I think Brick Krutzer knows a lot more about Zoe's disappearance than he's letting on. I've talked to him a couple of times and I have a bad feeling about him." Her eyes strayed back to the old couple at the water's edge. They were pulling in a small fish.

"Rachel?"

She looked back at Jesse. His dark eyes looked large and intense behind his black glasses. "You'd best be staying away from him. I'm telling you the truth for your own good. He's a dangerous man."

"Yeah, I just heard the story about his youthful activities with a poor girl named Brandi."

"Then you know about the rape."

"Yes, and the fact that he got away scot-free."

They were both quiet for a while and Rachel's eyes were drawn to a small group of people who had arrived in the parking lot and were making noise unloading coolers and balloons.

"I've been trying to figure that guy out. It sounds to me like Brick may have a problem with women in general. I mean, like one of those guys that secretly hates women and needs to dominate them or something."

"You mean the kind of guy who has a controlling mother that messes up his brains?"

"Yeah, that, too."

"Well, Brick sure fits the profile on that one. Hester is a mother straight from Hell. A genuine spawn of Satan."

Rachel blinked at his directness and looked off toward the river, recalling her meeting with Hester and the stories Hank and Miss Emma had passed on to her. She thought about the effect a woman like her would have on her offspring.

"Is it possible that Brick could be involved in all of this..." She paused and looked up at Jesse, meeting his eyes. "...you know—Zoe's disappearance and Long John's murder?"

Jesse gave her a skeptical look. "*Could* be involved? Man, the whole thing is probably—"

The group of partiers headed their way was now within earshot. "Hey, guys," one of the men said. "We have this pavilion rented for the afternoon. We need to set up."

"No problem," Jesse said. "We were just leaving."

He turned to Rachel. "Come on. Let's walk back to the parking lot."

After they were out of hearing range of the group, Rachel stopped and said, "I have been racking my brain to try to figure out what has been going on but I start thinking about Brick and his sidekicks and my brain just goes in circles."

"I can tell you what I know, but let's go back to my truck, first." His gaze shifted over her pale arms and face. "You don't need to be standing out here in the sun."

When they climbed inside the late-model Dodge, Jesse flipped open the cooler between them. "Want some water?"

"Sure." Rachel picked up a bottle and cracked open the cap. "I know Long John was a long-time friend of yours. A good friend."

"Yes, he was. He came over the night after Zoe turned up missing. He didn't want to tell me what was going on, but I got pretty upset and told him I wouldn't help him unless he did."

"So what did he tell you?"

"He said he made a key for Zoe that fit a lock that was inside Golden Vista. It was to a door that nobody was supposed to open. Apparently, Zoe had told him the boss only showed up at night once a month, so she would sneak John in sometimes when Brick wasn't due to come in. It was one of those times that Long John made a model for the key."

Rachel nodded. "I'm guessing that key he made was to the back annex of the home, the part that the Krutzer's never remodeled. Right after Zoe disappeared, Adam Tackett installed a heavy-duty padlock on the door by the nurses' station that led to it. The thing is, the door already had a dead bolt on it. So I'm wondering why they would need an ugly padlock on it, too—unless they were hiding something and figured out that somebody had a key to the deadbolt."

"That makes sense. John told me Zoe was suspicious there was some kind of illegal activity going on and she wanted to check it out. That's why she manipulated John into making the key—against his better judgment, I might add."

"Do you think she was planning on blackmailing Brick after she found out?"

"I'd bet on it, man. John said Zoe kept saying if her hunch was right, they'd both make a pile of money and she'd marry him." A wave of sadness appeared to wash over him and his whole body seemed to sag. "I honestly don't know what he saw in her, but she seemed to have some kind of power over him. She could get him to do whatever she wanted."

"Well, if part of what she wanted was to blackmail Brick, it looks like it backfired."

"That's one thing about Zoe Liddy: her brains aren't exactly her strong suit."

Rachel took a long sip of water and leaned back against the seat. "Did Long John say anything else of importance?"

"The main reason he came to see me was to ask me if he could come back that night and sit up on the hotel roof with binoculars. He wanted to spy on the backyard of Golden Vista, hoping to catch sight of Zoe, or hoping to see some kind of activity that would indicate that something illegal was going on."

"You mean something like drug smuggling?"

"Man, who knows? It could be anything. But whatever it was, I bet it's very lucrative."

"Yes, I understand Brick owns a huge mansion on the golf course."

"No he doesn't. Hester owns it. Brick lives there with her."

"Really? He lives with his mother? That's kind of odd for a guy his age."

"You're not the only one who thinks that. He has the whole north wing to himself, but it's still freaky-weird for a man that age and that rich to live with his mother."

Jesse finished his water and put the empty back in the cooler. "Anyway, that was the last I ever saw of John." He continued to stare at the cooler and his goatee began to quiver.

Rachel reached out, squeezed his hand, and allowed him to gather himself together before she spoke.

"Danny told me Long John came by his house later, about three in the morning, and got him out of bed. He said his brother told him he had to leave town right away and that he was in big trouble. I think that was the last time anyone ever saw him alive."

Jesse nodded, but never looked up. "That makes me wonder if he saw something he shouldn't have seen up on that roof top."

"Something scary enough to make him want to leave town in a hurry?"

"Yeah, only he didn't get very far."

Chapter 10

Rachel felt the sun hot on her face as she drove back to the hotel. She guessed there was still time to meet the others for lunch and pulled up in front of the café. She spotted the group in their booth, but decided to pick up her messages first. Just as she did, she noticed Deputy Tucker and Jared Johnson coming in the back door. Neither one of them looked happy.

"Have you guys eaten?" she asked.

"No," Tucker said. "We thought we'd talk to JT. He around?"

"He's in the corner booth with Heather and Buddy. I'm heading over that way myself. Why don't you join us?"

"Twist my arm," Tucker said, without a smile.

On the way through the lobby, Rachel sided up to Johnson. "May I have a private moment with you before we go in?"

He gave her a puzzled look but nodded and then told Tucker to go on ahead.

Tucker shot Rachel a what-are-you-up-to-now look, but kept on moving.

Rachel and Johnson moved to a sofa at the end of the lobby and she started right in. "Did Tucker tell you about my parents?"

Johnson nodded. "He said you and Heather thought they were both murdered, but the police told you it was a murder-suicide."

"That's right. I was the one who found them. I was thirteen at the time it happened and I was very, very traumatized. But I can tell you this, Jared, there's no way my father would have shot my mother, *ever*. Not in a million years. He absolutely adored her.

Johnson nodded his head again. "And you want me to help you with this, somehow, right?"

"Right." Rachel looked straight at him. "I'm hoping you'll have some kind of connections, maybe know somebody who knows somebody, who still works in Grand Rapids."

"And if I did?"

"I was wondering if it were possible for you to get copies of the records of the case, and maybe the photographs of the scene." She twisted her hands in front of her and looked away. "You see, when it all happened, when I came home from school and walked into the living room, I just kind of went into shock. I flipped out, went crazy, whatever you want to call it. I ran out of the house incoherent and a neighbor came in and called the police."

Johnson stared at the young woman and fought back the emotions he felt. He had remembered hearing about the story years before and his heart had gone out to the two daughters even then. He reached out, clasped both of Rachel's hands inside his massive ones, and held them. "I promise you," he whispered solemnly, "when I get back home, I will help you any way I can."

They walked in silence to the café, aware of the commitment between them. When Rachel slid into the booth next to Heather, her sister gave her a puzzled look. Rachel returned it with a smile and a wink to let her know she was okay. Tucker looked over at Johnson, but Johnson just gave him a quick glance before ordering the daily special.

As they were all finishing their lunch, Deputy Tucker pulled a couple flyers out of the file at his side. "I hate to show you this, but the sooner I get these out there, the better. This girl was abducted last night."

"She looks thirteen!" Heather exclaimed, horrified.

"She *is* thirteen," Tucker said.

"Where's she from?" JT asked.

"Yuma. She was taken about nine o'clock, walkin' back home from the Dairy Queen on Fourth Avenue. She was within a block of her house."

"She looks Hispanic," Rachel said. "Do you think it's the same guy? I thought he liked blondes."

Tucker shrugged. "We don't know anything for sure. The only witness we've got said they saw a white panel truck cruising by the area, but we got a lead on someone here in Mesquite."

Heather and Rachel looked at each other, and then Rachel asked, "Does he work for Brick Krutzer?"

If looks could have killed, Tucker would have sent Rachel to her grave right then. "The guy we're goin' to get don't work for nobody. He's a two-time, level-three sex offender and he just got out of prison." The deputy glanced at his watch. "Ya'll please excuse me, but I got to be gettin' back to my office. I'd appreciate it if you'd put these posters up right away." He slid out of the booth and picked up his Stetson. "I'll talk to you later."

Rachel looked across the table at Jared Johnson. "You're not going with him?"

"No, ma'am, not me." He shook his head. "I'm not part of that little party. Besides, Lilly and my grandsons are on their way back and should be arriving any time. We'll be leaving here tomorrow morning."

"Oh, no. We hate to see you go," Heather protested.

"You know, I kinda hate to leave, too. Tucker thinks we've just started to make some progress on this case. This guy they want to pick up—Tucker thinks he could have knocked on the door at Golden Vista, and when Zoe came to the door, convinced her to open it."

"So he does think it's possible Zoe was abducted," Rachel said.

"Oh yeah, but don't tell him I told you."

"Never," Heather said. "But you can't stay a couple more days?"

Johnson shook his head. "I'm afraid not. We've got to get the boys back home. Their momma is missing them way too much. And she wasn't too crazy about what happened in the desert."

"I can understand that, having raised twin boys myself," Heather said. "So do you have anything special planned for this evening?"

"Well, I was hoping you folks might be able to suggest something."

"I have the perfect place to the take the boys, and I'd like to volunteer for that," she offered.

"Do you mean Cooper's?" Rachel asked.

"Yes, I think it would be fun for them. They have the best hamburgers and all those arcade machines." Heather looked around at everyone. "All of us could go."

"Mmm. I was kind of hoping I could take Lilly out to some fancy place—"

"Yes, Heather," JT added, "Jared might like to go out with his wife *alone* after not seeing her for a while."

Heather blushed and looked down at her plate. "Okay, I get it." She lifted her head. "Then how about if we take the boys to Cooper's and Jared and Lilly go out to eat, say at Domino's?"

JT gave her an incredulous look. "Domino's?"

Johnson blinked at her. "A pizza joint?"

"Oh, no. Not pizza. It's a very fancy French place. They named it after a large mannequin dressed in a harlequin court-jester's outfit. And Lilly would love it. The food's great, it's very luxurious, and it's located in a historic building in Old Town, right near Cooper's, so you would be close to the boys."

She shot a quick look to JT. "Just because Anna

Venkman is a competitor doesn't mean she doesn't have a great place to eat."

"I think it's a great idea," Rachel chimed in. "What do you think, Jared?"

Johnson smiled broadly. "It sounds like a great plan to me—especially the babysitting part."

※※※

The group didn't set off for Old Town until nearly 7 p.m. Lilly was tired after driving all the way from Yuma and needed a nap, so the boys were happy to be able to go swimming for a couple of hours. Rachel worked late, to make up for the missed morning of work, and followed the group out to Cooper's in the Hummer.

Jared and Lilly enjoyed looking at Cooper's décor while Thomas and Willie commandeered the arcade area. When it was almost time for their dinner reservations, Lilly gave her grandsons final instructions on behaving properly. She sat them at a high table with the Carpenters and Rachel to await their hamburgers and fries.

Thomas and Willie made quick work of their meals and rushed back to the arcade with more quarters. Rachel and the Carpenters lingered over their burgers while they enjoyed watching the boys and the rest of the crowd.

"I hope they'll like Domino's," JT said, a frown creasing its way across his forehead.

"Don't be silly," Heather said. "Of course, they will. Lilly is a classy woman. She'll appreciate all the fancy little details and the gourmet menu."

About five minutes later Rachel looked up and spotted Jared and Lilly Johnson coming toward them. "Uh-oh."

JT jumped off his chair to meet them. "What happened?"

Jared and Lilly looked at each other and started to laugh. "The gal that runs that place hates all of you."

It was Heather and JT's turn to look at each other.

"Oh no! I didn't even think of that," Heather cried. "What happened?"

"Well nothing happened at first," Lilly said. "The place was gorgeous. Everything was fine until she was showing us to our table and I mentioned how you referred us there."

"And that's when she just went crazy," Jared said. "I mean, right there in the middle of the restaurant, she started screaming at us. Screaming stuff about you and Tucker and spies and some guy named Domino."

"Yeah, right up until the time we literally ran out of the place," Lilly said. "I have to tell you, folks. There is something seriously wrong with that woman. Uh-huh, definitely up here," she said, nodding and pointing to her temple.

"I am so, so sorry," JT said, looking aghast. "We did have a problem with them when they first opened. Deputy Tucker took a date over there to spy on them, but it's a long and funny story. We'll tell you all about it on the way back to the hotel. When we get there, we'll take you to the Plantation Room and treat you to the best meal you'll ever have in Yuma County."

"Now that's a deal I'm not going to turn down," Jared said. "The people running *that* restaurant know how to make a guest feel like royalty. And that prime rib is the best—"

"What?" Lilly said, glaring at her husband. "Prime Rib? Since when do you eat prime rib, Mr. Johnson? The doctor said you're supposed to be eating broiled chicken and fish."

"I, ah, well..." Jared said, as he looked around helplessly. "JT? Help me out here."

Just then Rachel's phone broke into song, and she reached for it with an apology. "Excuse me," she said, reading the name of the caller and walking a few steps away.

The excited voice of Hank answered her greeting: "Come quick, Rachel! I saw Brick drive two men around to the back and fat Emmett follow behind them in the panel truck. They were there just a couple minutes and then they came around front to his office. I bet any money he's buying drugs off them right now! They might have even stuffed Zoe in the panel truck."

Rachel, momentarily stunned, suddenly remembered what Miss Emma had said about the rooms being bugged. *If she's right and the phones are bugged, too...*

"Stop that right now, Hank!" she scolded. "I've heard enough of that stupid talk about Zoe. You're making yourself crazy over this."

A dead silence filled the air, then, "But—but Rachel—how can you—"

"You've got to stop all this foolishness and find

something else to do with your time, Hank, other than imagining all these weird plots you're dreaming up. I'm coming over right now, so be at the front door to let me in." That said, she hung up quickly and turned back to the group.

Heather looked at her, puzzled. "Who was that?"

"Trouble. And I've got to go. I'll catch up with you all later," Rachel said as she dashed off.

"Rachel, wait!" her sister called out, but Rachel never looked back.

Within three minutes Rachel pulled up beside Brick's Cadillac at the entrance to Golden Vista. Hank was already waiting outside the entrance for her with part of his wheelchair wedged in the doorway to keep it open. A frantic look was frozen on his face.

Rachel bent down to give him a hug. Whispering in his ear, she told Hank she suspected his phone and apartment were bugged. She explained that in case someone was taping their conversation, she wanted Brick to think she was no threat to him.

A look of relief washed over Hank and he sagged in his chair. "I didn't know what to think," he said, shaking his head. "I was afraid you really thought I was crazy."

"Well, now you know what's going on, but you still have to back off from this, Hank, or you'll get the both of us in trouble."

He looked down at his hands in his lap. "You're right. And the last thing I'd want to do is see you get hurt."

"Very well, then. No more phone calls." She pulled a

small, flip phone out of her purse and handed to him. "Unless you use *this*. And then only if you call me from the bathroom with the shower on."

Hank looked at the phone then up at her and his eyes shined with admiration. "Oh, Rachel, you're my girl. Now, how about if we go back to my apartment and put on a little show for our audience?"

∽∾∽

Earlier that same evening, Zoe Liddy sat listlessly gazing at the bed in the red room, her dirty, chestnut-colored hair hanging limply, obscuring her vision. She heard the door pop open and her stomach heaved. She didn't know who to expect this time, but it was always the same horror regardless of who showed up to administer her nightly punishment. As the men entered, she began to rock back and forth in her chair, and her mind slipped back to the night when she first opened the door to the room that had been her prison ever since.

A deeply-tanned man dressed in a hand-tailored Italian suit entered first. He was followed by a tall, muscular black man whose jacket opened and exposed the butt end of a .41 Magnum. Brick followed and closed the door behind him.

Zoe watched the men walk toward her in a gray fog and her mind slipped farther away. She saw the red room again just as it was when it flashed in front of her eyes that first night. The image was burned into her brain: she saw herself creeping down the hallway, opening the door, and being shocked by the image of the blonde with her waist-length hair. Her head was swollen and tilted off the side as she hung from the ceiling with the belt tightly looped around her neck.

Time had stopped for Zoe right then. She had stood mesmerized at the sight and the flashlight slipped from her hand. Then she heard Brick's taunting voice. It was the last thing she remembered before everything went black.

She had awakened to a nightmare, a brutal assault from Brick. The next night it was Ron Emmett who pressed her against the bed. Then Tackett…

The men inside the room were speaking to each other with angry voices, but Zoe heard it only as the buzzing of bees. She continued to sit on the metal chair and rock back and forth until she felt someone yank her head back by her hair.

With a faraway look, she gazed into the face of a man she didn't recognize. She saw herself reflected in the blackness of his pupils, but she dreamily did not recoil from his anger or react to the sneer on his lips. She heard him curse somewhere in the fog of her drug-induced world and then felt him let go of her hair. Her face fell forward and she rocked back and forth on the chair again. The men stepped away and she heard the click of the door resonate in the red silence of the room.

After the three men got back in the car, Brick drove around to the front of the building. The trio strode through the lobby, now unoccupied except for an old lady appearing to sleep in a chair with a magazine on her lap, and took the corridor that led to the sound-proof offices of the owners.

Once inside, the deeply tanned man raised his voice to an angry pitch. "What do you mean, one of the blonde ones died?" he screamed and followed his accusations with a stream of insults and profanity. "I told you last time, it better not happen again."

Brick Krutzer answered with icy coldness. "Don't blame me for that one. She hung herself."

"So she was the one in the paper? The one that was strangled that some gold digger found out in the desert?"

Brick looked down at the floor, thinking he'd like to strangle that stupid Tackett.

"Are you totally brain dead? Did you think I wouldn't find out?" The man waved his arms and paced. "You better not have buried her close to the first one. You know the FBI will be out there with a body finder."

"Don't worry about that. They've come and gone. Emmett put her on the other side of the mountains, way to the south. No one will ever find her there."

"Doesn't matter. The police are probably all over the place anyway."

Brick finally raised his head in an effort to assert himself. "What do you care? I'm the one taking all the risk here. I could get the death penalty for this."

"And that's supposed to be my problem? It's your man who killed that girl, not mine. The paper said she was brutally raped. You need to have better control over your employees and understand that these girls are commodities, not whipping posts."

"Maybe so. But things happen. Besides, I got you a replacement."

The man made a noise to indicate disgust. "An old, fat, redhead is my replacement?"

Krutzer wanted to say thirty-three was not old and double D-cup breasts were appreciated by most men, but he knew the man's client wanted high-school age girls or younger. "Look, if you don't want her, get rid of her. You don't have to pay me. I just can't afford to bury another one around here. I've got enough people snooping around as it is."

"You created *that* problem yourself. It's not my look-out. We agreed to buy two blondes and two darks. All under fourteen. Now you tell me you've only got one blonde, and you're trying to dump a used-up, fat broad on me—one who's clearly in la-la land. Do you think I'm stupid?"

"Look, I already said I'd get you another one, even if I have to risk finding one here in town myself. Just give me another couple days. In the meantime, take the broad, no charge. Right now she's in shock and we had to dope her up a bit, but she'll snap out of it. She's a registered nurse and could be very useful to you. Think about it. Who's better with a needle than a nurse?"

The mention of a needle and a nurse caught the attention of the deeply-tanned man. He touched his chin and stared down at the floor in thought. The old broad could have possibilities.

Brick used the moment to his advantage and his eyes took on a penetrating gaze. "You think about this, too,

Mr. Shandellan. You either take all four women or you take none. I can find another buyer."

Shandellan stared back in a contest for domination before he spoke. "I'll pay you for three, and deduct two thousand to get rid of the old broad. I also expect to have the blonde—and she better well be a young one—in one week. My client does not like to be disappointed."

He set the briefcase on the desk, took several piles of cash out, and placed them neatly on the desk. He closed the briefcase. "Okay, load them up. We're ready to go."

Shortly after the trio of men drove around to the rear yard, the back door of the old annex opened and Ron Emmett and Adam Tackett emerged. Each man led a young Hispanic girl out. The girls, both blindfolded and gagged, appeared to be dazed and hesitant as they descended the ramp that led from the back door. They were quickly put into the panel truck where the men bound their hands and legs.

That done, Emmett and Tackett returned to the building and quickly returned with two other women. One was a blonde, thirteen years old, the other was Zoe Liddy. The blonde went obediently into the van, but when Zoe felt the cool, fresh air on her face, something snapped in her mind. She realized she had been released from her dungeon of horrors and was being transported to…where? Her death? In that one lucid moment she tried to twist herself out of Emmett's grip and fell on the ramp. Her ring slipped off as the fat man lost his grasp on her hand and it bounced onto the gravel and under the edge of the ramp. Emmett yanked her up roughly before she could turn away and shoved her into the Ford, knocking her to the floor.

Shandellan drove the panel truck a little under the speed limit all the way to the airfield with his pilot in the passenger seat. He drove onto the tarmac, and when he pulled up next to the Beech Baron, Emmett and Tackett emerged from the rear of the truck. Under the cover of darkness, the pilot and Shandellan readied the plane for flight while Emmett and Tackett silently moved the truck's cargo into the plane. In less than ten minutes the plane took off for Los Angeles with two men and four women hostages on board. As soon as it was airborne, Tackett drove the truck back to Golden Vista. Emmett sat in the passenger seat contemplating how he would spend the bonus he would be getting that night.

Chapter 11

The same moment Rachel had seen the Cadillac pass by the window, she grabbed her purse, prepared to leave Hank's apartment. When she heard the soft knock on the door she left without a word and stepped into the lobby. Miss Emma Hornsby, who had been sitting in the lobby pretending to sleep, stood there and motioned her out.

"The visitors left in the panel truck," Emma whispered. "Dapper Dan was driving and the body-builder guy was sitting in the passenger seat."

Rachel shut the door behind her. "What about Emmett and Tackett? And Brick?"

"I couldn't see Emmett and Tackett, so I'm guessing they were in the back of the truck. At least one of them would have to be to drive it back from the airport. And they're both too stupid to tackle a job like that alone.

Brick came inside by himself and went back to the office."

"You're sure about that."

"Of course I'm sure, girl. They've done this before. Besides, after Brick and his visitors tromped through the lobby, I went right to my apartment and waited for them to leave. My window overlooks the driveway, remember?" A sly smile lit up her face. "I don't have lace curtains for nothing."

Rachel was off in her Hummer in less than a minute and soon found herself tailing the white panel truck. She hoped she stayed far enough back to keep from being spotted, and once the Ford passed the city limits, she backed off even more. Lazy eucalyptus trees lined the edge of the road, their branches swaying in the breeze, their leaves nearly gray in the twilight. Rachel kept the Hummer's headlights off and followed in the near darkness.

When the panel truck took the turn to the airport, Rachel slowed down even more, knowing it would take the men time to transfer whatever it was they were hauling to the plane. After she made the turn, rather than follow the road, she navigated the Hummer through a stand of stunted tamarisk trees that bordered the south side of the airport parallel to the runway. She shut off the engine, climbed out of the Hummer and went around back to get her binoculars.

Rachel fished through a box of gear: a gallon of water, jumper cables, neck pillow in a bag, can of compressed air, tool box. *Where the heck are my binoculars?*

Panic crept through her as she moved more junk aside, finally dumping everything out of the box. *They're not here*! Then she remembered the last time she used them was when she took them gold prospecting. *They must be in JT's truck.* Muttering an obscenity, she slammed the back of the Hummer shut and then froze at the noise. *Could they hear that?*

She crept alongside the vehicle and parted the long-hanging branches of the tamarisk tree in front of her. The sticky needless clung to her top. *My white sweater! Why did I have to wear that tonight?* She peered through the needles only to see the tall pilot facing her direction. Panic flooded over her again. *Is he watching me? Can he see me in here?* She brought the branches slowly toward her, trying to cover her ivory face and white top as her eyes searched out the activity taking place by the plane. She picked out Tackett and fat Emmett moving about. *What's that they're moving?* Emmet threw something over his shoulder, something big. *What in the world is it? It looks like...like...a body? People? Is that people? Are they smuggling people out?*

She could do nothing but stare and then gasped when she thought she saw a glint of chestnut-colored hair in the moonlight. *Zoe? Is that Zoe? Oh no!* She reached for her phone and punched in Deputy Tucker's number.

It rang several times before Tucker answered, his voice nearly breathless.

"This better be good, Rachel."

"Get down here to the airport now, Dewey!" she whispered urgently into the phone. "I think they've got

Zoe Liddy! They're loading her into a plane. I'm sure of it. They've got her, they've got her!"

"What? Hold on there. What are you talking about?"

"It's Brick Krutzer! His men, that Emmett and Tackett, are loading people, I think women, into a plane. The women look unconscious. There are two other men getting the plane ready to take off and they all just left Golden Vista. He's the one, Tucker, it's Brick! It was him all along! Hurry!"

"Where are you, Rachel?"

"I'm in the stand of tamarisk trees by the east-west runway. They can't see me. Just hurry!"

"All right, all right, I'm on my way. I'll be right there. And for heaven's sake, don't move. Don't do nothin' stupid!"

Rachel's heart beat furiously and then sank as the plane started up the runway. She looked at her watch as the white panel truck sped off the tarmac and held her phone through the branches hoping to get a couple of pictures of the panel truck and the plane taking off before they both disappeared from the airfield.

When they were out of sight, Rachel pulled out of the grove of tamarisk trees and raced to the turn off. There she met Deputy Tucker coming toward her.

She jumped down out of the Hummer as he rolled down the window of his truck. "They've gone," she said, her energy sapped. "What took you so long to get here?"

"I was in the middle of somethin.' I do take a little time off now and then, ya know. Now show me this place where this thing happened."

Rachel and Tucker pulled onto the tarmac and got out of their vehicles to look around. They both inspected the ground thoroughly with flashlights.

"Are you sure this is where they were?" Dewey Tucker asked.

"Of course I'm sure. I was right over there," she said, pointing into the grove of trees.

"Humph. There's nothing here."

"Of course there's nothing here *now*. They all left! What took you so long to get here, anyway? You only live a couple blocks away." Rachel caught a whiff of something, something that smelled familiar, and looked at him, her eyes narrowed. "You weren't home, were you?" she added, remembering where she had smelled that old-fashioned perfume before.

"Where I was, young lady, is none of your cotton-pickin' business. Now, are you gonna tell me what happened or you just gonna stand there all night?"

೧೨೧

Heather rushed to answer the pounding on their casita door and yanked her sister inside. "What happened? Where were you? I was afraid something happened to you."

"It's okay, it's okay" Rachel said, trying to calm her. "I'm fine. But let me settle down and tell you what happened."

JT walked into the living room. "I want to hear this, too," he said, trying to suppress the anger in his voice.

"And it better be good because Heather was worried sick about you."

"We better all sit down because this is quite a story," Rachel said, heading toward the sofa. She related the events of the evening starting with Hank's phone call. When she finished, Heather looked horror-struck and JT just sat shaking his head in disbelief.

"Are you positive you saw the men carry those girls into the plane?" JT asked. "It was pretty dark."

"Well, maybe not a hundred percent sure, but I'm pretty sure. What else could it have been?"

"I have no idea. So what did Dewey Tucker say? Did he believe you?"

"He was a little reluctant at first. He went out to the place in the grove of trees I was in with the Hummer and looked out. He kept asking me if I was sure about what I saw."

JT nervously rubbed his hand along his hairline. "*Are* you sure about what you saw? That's a pretty big accusation you're making here."

"I know. But what else could it have been? A department store dummy? A Saint Bernard?"

JT got up from the sofa and began to pace, the carpet muffling the sound of his footsteps. "Maybe a big sack of something?"

"But, JT, sweetie, remember all those missing girls?" Heather asked. "You have to admit what Rachel says makes sense."

"Yes, it makes sense, honey, but you've got to remember the distance from where Rachel stood and where the plane was. And it was dark out."

"Are you saying you don't believe me? I did take pictures. I can't help it if they didn't come out very well."

"Of course we believe you, sweetie," Heather answered.

JT stopped pacing. "It's just that people can't be a hundred percent sure they are seeing what they *think* they are seeing."

Rachel wanted to snap back but managed to hold her tongue in check.

JT turned to her. "Is Tucker going to act on this?"

"After I hammered on him awhile, he finally told me he would try to go to Golden Vista tomorrow with a search warrant and check out the old annex."

"That's something he should have done right away," Heather insisted.

"There's a lot of things our illustrious Deputy Tucker should have done right away," Rachel said. "But no. He decided one of the local sex offenders had to be the one responsible. He never stopped to consider that Bricknell Krutzer is the worst sex offender of them all," Rachel said, her voice rising.

"Now Rachel, let's keep it calm here," JT said. "Tucker is doing the best he can. He is waiting for the DNA results from what they found on the dead girl's body. It's easy to second guess the man and say he should have done this or that, but he makes the best judgment he can at the time."

"He may make his best judgment, but his judgment is pretty poor. And I don't know why you're always sticking up for him. He's never helped *you* out any. He can't even figure out who's terrorizing you."

"Okay, okay enough!" Heather demanded. "You two need to stop this right now. You're like two little kids and I already have a headache from all your arguing."

"I'm sorry, honey," JT said and then turned to his sister-in-law. "You're right about one thing, Rachel. We are no closer to finding out who our anonymous terrorist is now than we were from the very beginning."

"Have you received any more notes?"

Heather and JT exchanged glances. "Yes," he replied, appearing to be resigned to the fact that Rachel would find out anyway. "I'll go get it for you."

When JT returned from the bedroom, he handed Rachel the folded piece of white copy paper. Again, the paper was generic and the poem was printed in Times New Roman type. Rachel read the few lines out loud.

> "If you weren't such an evil pig
> I wouldn't go after you.
> But you are, and I will.
> And you'll see what I can do! "

"An evil pig? Would a man say that?" she asked.

"I think it sounds more like something a woman might say, unless it's some kind of clue," JT replied.

"A clue? An evil pig? I can't connect a pig with anything I know. Did you show it to Tucker?"

"Ah, I figured the deputy had his hands full with other problems right now."

"So you didn't tell him?" Heather burst in with a look of disbelief on her face. "You didn't even *call* him? Why, this letter is even more threatening than the last one. And you could have been killed when your brake line was cut. Didn't it occur to you that would have been murder?"

"Okay, okay," JT said, throwing up a hand. "You're right. I should have called Tucker. I promise I'll call him first thing in the morning. Maybe he'll come over for breakfast."

"Maybe by then we'll have confirmation about what was going on at Golden Vista, too," Rachel added. "All Tucker has to do is find some kind of evidence to indicate that women have been stashed in that old annex."

He looked at Rachel steadily. "Why do I think that would make things just a little too easy?"

❧❧❧

The following morning speckles of clouds dotted the sky like flakes of white pepper and the air smelled of petunia blossoms. Heather and Rachel met on the sidewalk and decided to walk through the courtyard to check out the new annuals that maintenance had planted the day before.

When they approached the pool area, they noticed the large mass of petunias in various shades of purple. A gray-haired guest also appeared to admire them as she passed by the garden and stepped into the pool.

"That Mrs. Thornton sure has courage," Heather declared. "It's still too cold in the morning for me to get in the water, even if it *is* heated."

"I agree. You'd have to pay me a million bucks to jump in there right now."

As they watched the woman swim toward the Jacuzzi, Rachel recalled how JT had re-built the whole pool himself with the rocks from the mountain and a bucket loader. He also added some boulders he made himself from chicken wire and cement, turning the whole end of the pool into a grotto complete with a cave with a waterfall entrance.

Mrs. Thornton swam to the waterfall and disappeared underneath. A horrific scream burst over the water and a series of shrieks followed it. Without thinking, Rachel kicked off her shoes and jumped into the pool.

She swam to the Jacuzzi as a cloud of red water tumbled through the pool. Seeing the billow of red, Heather screamed, and then Toro bounded out of nowhere and jumped into the pool splashing a huge wave of red water over the flagstone decking. Two more people who were within hearing distance raced to the pool's edge.

Toro and Rachel appeared from within the cave half-carrying Mrs. Thornton, who was now sobbing hysterically, out of the area. Upon opening her eyes, Mrs. Thornton saw the red water and sagged into the pool in a faint. In one swift motion, Toro lifted her up and waded to the edge of the pool with the older woman in his arms.

Heather ran to the rack of towels and rushed an armfull of them over to the two soaked women as Toro laid Mrs. Thornton on a lounge. At that moment JT burst out of the back door of the hotel and came charging toward Heather.

She and JT wrapped Mrs. Thornton in towels as she shivered and sobbed.

"Th—th—the body!" the woman gasped. "It was a b-body!"

"What!" JT exclaimed. He looked at Rachel who was still dripping wet. She put a finger to her lips then pulled a couple of towels around herself.

Heather hugged the gray-haired guest and soothed her with soft, reassuring words, but JT turned to stare at the pool which was now half filled with blood-red water. "Toro, what are you doing?" he called to his maintenance manager who was now back in the pool headed toward the cave.

Toro looked back, held up a hand, but continued on.

"Don't touch anything!" JT called out again and ran along the edge of the pool to the cave.

Toro stepped back out of the Jacuzzi. "It's a pig," he said, with water dripping down from the top of his head.

"What?"

"It's a pig," Toro repeated. "Someone put a dead pig in the pool."

"A pig," JT repeated, and immediately recalled the "evil pig" line in the last threat he had received. "Don't touch anything. Just come out of the pool, and dry off. You have some extra clothes?"

"Yes, sir, Mr. JT. I'll—or maybe I better wait."

JT turned his head in the direction Toro was looking and noticed Deputy Tucker coming toward them. Tucker stopped and looked at Toro chest high in the pool of pale red water, looked the shaking, gray-haired guest wrapped in towels like a mummy, looked at Rachel who looked like a drowned cat, and finally looked at JT.

"What in thundering tarnation is goin' on?"

Rachel gave him a quick explanation and the Deputy walked over to the edge of the pool and stared down. "I don't think that's blood," he said. He looked back at Toro who was now out of the pool and had a towel wrapped around his shoulders, barely reaching his chest. "You say it's a pig? You're sure?"

"Deputy, sir, I know what a pig looks like. My step-dad used to raise them."

"Do you think you could get back in and get the pig out?"

"Yes, sir." Toro threw off the towel and jumped back in the water. In a minute he waded out pushing the bloated pig in front of him.

When he got to the edge of the pool he lifted the pig out over the rim and it rolled over on its side, its mouth open, its dead eyes staring at the group of people huddled around the pool.

"Well, I'll be hog-tied. It *is* a pig." Tucker bent over and stared at the pig wondering how it happened to find its way into the Jacuzzi, and then finally turned his attention back to Toro. "Anything else back there, Toro?" he asked, hoping he wouldn't have to jump into the pool himself to find out.

"Some kind of wire, sir."

"A wire?"

"Yes, sir. I think it was some kind of trip wire that had been stretched across the entrance to the Jacuzzi. It looks like when that lady went inside the hot pool she tripped the wire and the pig popped up."

"And that's maybe when the red stuff emptied out, too," the deputy mumbled, more to himself than the others. "I'll need some kind of clean container if you can get one from the kitchen. I'll drive over to Yuma and have that coloring analyzed right now."

He looked over at Mrs. Thornton, who was still covered in towels and sitting in a lounge chair, whimpering and shaking. "You okay, ma'am?"

"Now that I know it's just a p—p—pig, I'm okay," she replied, still shivering, "but I about had a h—h—heart attack when that thing p—popped up out of the water. Who would ever d—do such a terrible thing?"

"Who indeed?" JT asked, his eyes scanning the area.

"Can we take her to her room, now, Deputy?" Heather asked. "She's had a terrible fright."

"Yeah, go ahead. I don't think we can do anymore here." Tucker said, just as his phone buzzed and he reached for it. "Yeah, Pete. What'd ya find out?"

A few seconds later Tucker snapped his phone shut. "I gotta go. Somebody get me that container real quick so I can get a sample of his stuff."

While everyone had been talking, Rachel wandered off to the edge of the flagstone decking and studied the contents of a trash can. "I think you might want to look at this, Deputy."

Tucker plodded over, looked inside the container,

and pulled out a pair of plastic gloves from his pocket. After donning the gloves, he reached down into the bottom of the trash can and pulled out a small box. "Dye." he announced, holding the box up for everyone's inspection.

"Dye?" JT asked.

"Yep. Permanent red fabric dye. I'll still have the tests run, but I'd be willing to bet this is what's in the pool."

"Oh, no," Heather moaned, looking down into the pool. "Our beautiful pebbled surface is now pink."

JT also looked down. But instead of a pink, pebbled surface, he saw hundred-dollar bills flying out of the water.

༄༅༄

Pete Diaz and Deputy Tucker pulled up in front of a dark stucco house with a Mexican tile roof. This time they merely glanced at the yard that had been attractively designed and meticulously cared for. They navigated the curved brick pathway to the front door and rang the bell. Luce Escamilla came out with a surprised look on her face.

Deputy Tucker and Officer Diaz introduced themselves and a look of apprehension replaced her surprise.

"What happened?" She asked before either man could speak again.

"Everything's fine, Mrs. Escamilla," Pete said. "We have been waiting for you to come back from your cruise so we could ask you a couple of questions."

After she invited the officers inside, Tucker pulled up a file. "We'd like to show you some photos of several men to see if you might recognize any of them. Do you mind if I spread these out on your table? We are looking for someone who might have come to your yard sale—the one you had just before you left for the Panama Canal.

She pulled back a bit and turned to Officer Diaz. "You knew Tomas and I went to the Panama Canal?"

"Yes, ma'am. We needed to find you as quickly as possible so we contacted friends and family to try to locate you."

"Then this must be important."

"Yes, ma'am, it is. I wish we were at liberty to tell you more."

"Okay," she said, looking at Diaz steadily. "What is it you want me to look at?"

As Tucker spread the photos out he suggested she take her time to see if she remembered any of the men attending her sale.

"This man here, he came." she said, pointing to a photo in the top row. "I think he bought an old wallet we had. And this guy here, he walked around and didn't buy anything. He looked a little creepy to me so I watched him because I was afraid he might want to steal something. We had a lot of nice, quality stuff to sell."

"I understand you had a pile of...er...men's magazines, like *Penthouse* and *Hustler* for sale."

Luce's face flushed. "They were my step-son's. I

found them in his room after he went back to college. I don't think it's illegal to resell those magazines."

"No, ma'am, it's not. We're just trying to find out who bought them."

She looked back at the photos on the table. "Well, it wasn't any of those guys."

Tucker was clearly surprised. "Are you sure? None of them?"

"That's what I said. *Somebody* did buy them, though. Didn't even quibble about the price. I got top dollar."

"Can you describe the person who bought them?" Diaz asked.

"I can do better than that. I recognized the man, although he didn't remember me."

"Who was he?"

"Well, I don't know his name, but he's one of the new tellers at Sand Savings and Loan, the one with the blond hair that looks real young, like he's seventeen. He acted real nervous, too, didn't even want to look me in the eye."

"Huh." Tucker grunted and turned his face to the photos on the table. "And you're sure it wasn't one of those guys?"

"I remember who bought the magazines, Deputy," Mrs. Escamilla said, asserting herself. "I've got a good memory for faces and I even remember wondering why a young-looking, clean-cut kid like him would be buying stuff like that."

"But you sold them to him anyway."

"Listen, I was just happy to get rid of those magazines so my good-for-nothing step-son wouldn't have them when he got back from school."

Tucker led the way back to the truck, looking crushed. "I was *sure* we'd nab Shorty on a parole violation, at least."

"I was hoping we had our man, too," Diaz said, "but I guess it would have been too easy." He opened the door to the truck on the driver's side. "Where are you gonna go from here?"

Tucker slid into the passenger seat, his shoulders sagging. "You remember Rachel Ryan, the woman who found that girl buried in the desert?"

"Do you think I'm blind? Of course I remember her."

Tucker gave Diaz a sideways glance. "I don't know what you guys see in that white-washed sack of bones."

Diaz just laughed. "Tucker, you are way too old to start judging women, you know that?"

"I'm not too old to appreciate a good-looking woman, but I just happen to like a little meat on the bone, you know?"

Diaz just shook his head and smiled. "So what about Rachel?"

"She called me last night and claimed she saw Ron Emmett and Adam Tackett loadin' some women into a plane at the airport and that the women looked unconscious. She said she was sure one of them was Zoe Liddy. She's got this idea Brick is kidnappin' women and temporarily holdin' them in the old annex at Golden Vista."

"I wouldn't put it past him. And there have been a lot

of missing persons in the last year or so, so it could be possible, I guess. What did you end up doing?"

"I did what I had to do. I went out to the airport but when I got there, there was nothin' going on. Rachel said the plane had taken off just a couple minutes earlier. But I went ahead and got a search warrant early this morning. I know old Hester will raise hell when I go there, but it's somethin' I should have done right away. When they first reported Zoe missin' and I went to check it out, I noticed the door to the old part of the building was locked. I just took Brick's word for it that it was just storage and that he had the only key."

"Don't second guess yourself," Diaz said, pulling the truck into the street. "At the time, everyone just assumed Zoe took off somewhere."

"Yeah, that's the trouble. I just assumed." Tucker turned his head and looked away. "And then her boyfriend was murdered. Whole different ballgame then."

"So when are you going to check the place out?"

"Now. And I ain't lookin' forward to it."

Chapter 12

The temperature had reached eighty-four degrees by the time Deputy Tucker arrived at Golden Vista, not very hot for a local, but Tucker found himself sweating before he reached the front door.

He felt even worse than that when he went inside.

"You've got *what*? How could you!" Hester Krutzer screeched, jumping up from behind her desk. "You know all you had to do was ask. You don't have to come storming in here like some kind of gestapo with a search warrant."

"Now, Hester, you recall I did ask, but Brick said he didn't know where the key was and that there was only storage back there." Tucker kept his demeanor calm and his voice low, determined to hold his ground in spite of the fact that Hester came charging around the side of the desk toward him and sweat was pooling up on the back of his neck.

Totally ignoring his comment, Hester went to the phone and called Brick. "Deputy Tucker is here with a search warrant to see the old annex. What do you want me to do?"

After a pause she slammed the phone on the cradle. "He says to come to the office and he'll take you over. He insists on going with you because the men have done some work over there and he wants to make sure it's safe."

"Fine with me." He turned on the heel of his red lizard boots and left the office. Brick's office was down the hall and although Tucker took just a few seconds to get there, he felt a sense of urgency to get to the back rooms of the property.

Brick was cordial—unlike his mother—and took precious seconds to apologize for his mother's behavior and to assure the deputy that he was happy to comply with the warrant. He began looking through the desk for the keys, heaping supplies of paper clips, pens, erasers, and thumb tacks on top of his desk.

Tucker shifted his weight from one foot to the other, feeling the seconds slip away. *What if someone was removing crucial evidence from that area right now? I'm in my rights to take a crow bar to the entrance. But if don't find anything, I'll have to buy them a new door, and with my budget—*

"Wait, I know where it is," Brick declared cheerfully. "I remember putting it on the little key ring I rarely use." He walked to the opposite side of the room and fished through a credenza before finally holding up a small ring of keys. "Okay, shall we go?"

A relieved Tucker followed Brick as the younger man meandered through the lobby, greeting all the residents they met on the way. Once at the entrance to the annex, Brick unlocked the padlock and then searched through his ring of keys trying one, then another, before he finally unlocked the door.

The deputy noticed the hasp and padlock was a recent addition but kept that thought to himself. He glanced around impatiently and noticed Hank Levinson standing in the doorway of his apartment, watching them.

Tucker glared at Hank, but Hank was undeterred and remained standing in the doorway until both men disappeared down the hallway headed toward the unrestored part of the old hospital. Then he went into the bathroom, turned on the shower, and called Rachel.

Brick shined his flashlight straight down the corridor, walking a step ahead of the deputy into the cone of light. "Sorry about the electricity," Brick said, "The overhead fixtures haven't worked in years."

Frustrated at the limited visibility, Tucker removed his own flashlight from his belt and splashed a small beam of light around the hallway and floor. He ducked under the black widow hanging from her web, walked a few steps, and stopped. He pulled out a small camera from his pocket and flash-photographed the floor.

"What?" Brick asked and turned back to look at him.

"Footprints. And they look pretty new." Tucker laid a pen beside the smaller pair and snapped a photo of the clearest looking print, then shot another one a little farther down. He did the same with a couple of the larger prints. "Hmm," he mumbled, looking over at the prints Brick had just left on the floor. "Them larger prints look to be about the same size as yours." He looked up at Brick and noticed the stocky man's smile had disappeared.

They both stayed silent until they passed through a set of fire doors. "What's that?" Tucker asked, splaying the light over a door on the left.

"It's nothing," Brick said, "Just a small supply room," and continued on.

"I'd like to see it."

Brick let out a huff of air in a pretense of irritation and trudged back to the door. He opened it to a small room filled with shelves and dust. "Satisfied?"

"Yep, just go ahead on," the old deputy said, not in the least intimidated by the younger man's sarcasm or annoyance.

Brick took his time closing the door and turned back to the hallway. A short distance later he came to a "T" in the corridor and faced another door.

"Tucker flashed his light at it. "Looks like you done some work around here. This is new."

"Yeah, it's fairly recent," Brick said. "We had some water damage. Thought maybe we'd make over some of the rooms back here, but we never got around to it. I'm pretty sure this is more storage."

"Open it."

Brick didn't answer but tried the knob. It didn't open

to a twist in either direction so he sifted through the ring of keys in his hand, trying each one until he finally found the one that worked. "Go ahead in," he said.

"No, you go first," the deputy said, and waited until Brick entered the room, splaying his light around the interior. Four old beds, now folded up, stood in the middle of the room surrounded by a pile of corrugated boxes and some old equipment and a couple metal folding chairs. The two windows had been boarded up.

Brick scanned the room. "I think this was once a ward room when the hospital was operational."

Tucker continued to move his light around the interior and floor of the room. "That sound proofing on the walls?"

Brick flashed his light on one of the walls and shrugged. "Looks like it. We didn't put it up. Maybe it was the looney ward."

Tucker studied the room another minute longer before he turned to exit the room.

"We have a similar set of rooms on the other end, if you're interested in seeing them," Brick offered.

"Durn right I'm interested," the deputy said, all the while feeling like he was being led on a wild goose chase.

They walked down the hallway until Brick reached the door to the first room. As he opened the door, Tucker spoke.

"I noticed none of the doors are locked except the one to that room with the new door."

"That's right." Brick turned to face him with a frown, decidedly annoyed. "We decided to put locks on the doors, but so far, that's the only door we've needed to replace. When, and if, we go ahead and remodel the rest of the building, we'll put locks on all the doors."

The deputy grunted his acceptance of Brick's explanation but still had an uneasy feeling. He pointed his flashlight into the room. Pushed to the middle of the floor were four more folded hospital beds. An old, saggy loveseat and upholstered arm chair sat next to them.

The last room they entered was similar—old dusty furniture and two beds. "Are you finding what you're looking for, Deputy?" Brick smirked. "By the way, what *are* you looking for? A drug smuggling operation, perhaps?"

Tucker decided not to dignify his question with a response. "Where were Emmett and Tackett last night?"

"They both were on the job. They had some clean up and repairs to do."

"I suppose if I ask them, they'd be able to tell me what they did."

"Of course." A wide, fake smile spread across his face."

Tucker looked at him steadily. "Okay, I think we're done. Let's get out of here."

"Whatever you say, Deputy."

൙൙൙

Rachel jumped up from behind her desk when she noticed Dewey Tucker enter the lobby, heading her way. "What happened?" she asked, rushing up to him.

"JT in? Let's go to his office." He had a stern, almost angry look on his face, and the vibes Rachel was getting off him sent a sick feeling to the pit of her stomach.

JT stood up and greeted them both when they came in. He turned to the deputy and said, "By the look on your face, I get the feeling things didn't go that well this morning."

"They sure as hell didn't. In fact, I got so much egg on my face I could eat another breakfast. It may be a while before I can convince Judge Brenson to give me another search warrant. Especially for one for people as prominent as the Krutzers."

"It went that badly, huh?" JT commiserated.

"Depends on whose side you're on, I guess. Everythin' was on the up 'n up. I went in all the rooms. Everything was either empty or filled with junk from the old hospital. Layers of dust everywhere."

Rachel sank back into the sofa. "I can't believe this. There *had* to be something there. Long John purposely went up on the roof of the Hotel Rios just to spy on the back yard. He must have seen *something* scary enough to make him want to leave town in a big hurry. Maybe he saw the same thing I did." She turned to Dewey Tucker with pleading eyes. "You *do* believe me, don't you?"

The deputy dropped his shoulders in weariness. "Rachel, you don't even *know* what you saw for sure. You'd be crazy to think a prosecutor would press charges on somethin' that you think you saw from that far away at that time of night.

"What?" Rachel reeled back, ready to jump up.

"What else could it possibly be? A short mannequin with big boobs and long red hair? And what about Long John? He mysteriously gets murdered the same night he tries to flee town after watching the action at Golden Vista? Do you think that's just a coincidence that he gets shot in the back of the head?"

Tucker looked down at his hands.

"Well? Don't you have an answer for me"?

Rachel opened her mouth to attack again when JT leaned into her. "Back off a bit," he said softly. "We all need to put our heads together to figure this thing out."

He turned to the deputy. "So Dewey, did you come to any kind of conclusion about Brick and Golden Vista?

Tucker looked up at JT and scratched his head. "Conclusions? Heck no. All I got is a bunch of questions."

"Questions? What kind of questions?"

The deputy nervously twirled his Stetson in his hands. "Well, for starters, if there's nothin' but worthless junk in the annex, why did Brick have to add a big padlock to the door that already had a deadbolt on it?"

"I noticed that, too!" Rachel said, jumping in excitedly. "That padlock didn't go on until *after* Zoe disappeared. That's why I think that door was the one Zoe had Long John make a key to. And I'm willing to bet any money she went in that door the night she disappeared."

"Okay, Rachel, how about letting Tucker finish?" JT asked. "We can discuss your questions later."

Rachel clamped her hand over her mouth and tried to look repentant.

"The whole place was filled with dust," the Deputy continued, "and I noticed in the hallway there were two sets of footprints, one that could have been a woman's, one from a man. I snapped photos of them, but if Zoe made a set of those prints the night she'd gone missin', she'd still be wearin' those shoes, so it wouldn't be of any help to us." A gloom covered his face. "Unless we found her body somewhere with the shoes still on her."

"But you could at least check for the size," Rachel blurted.

"Rachel!" JT roared.

Rachel clamped her hands over her ears. "Okay, okay, I'll shut up. I promise."

Deputy Tucker let out a tired breath. "Then there was that one room that didn't make sense to me. It had a brand-new door, still hadn't been painted, and it had a lock on it. Ain't none of the other doors had one. The only stuff in the room was four folded up beds and a bunch of junk—nothing valuable in it that needed a lock on the door. Brick said they had some water damage so he put in the new door, but I didn't see any stains on the ceiling or any other stuff like that. The paint job in the room and the hallway was old—what you could see of it—and you couldn't see much of it because somebody put up soundproofing panels all over the room, including the back door.

"Everything I seen so far was dusty and dirty, but that dang floor was *clean.* I mean, newly washed clean, all over, not just in front of the door. It looked like it had been cleaned in the last day or so. Not only that, it was cleaned with some kind of disinfectant. I could smell it.

"So I'm thinkin', why would Brick have someone do that? Was he tryin' to cover something up? Did he really hide Zoe—and whatever—in there and needed to clean up a mess? He would have had plenty of time to clean the room and put things together before I got there with the search warrant, but why would he bother unless he got tipped off that I might be coming by?"

Rachel's mind raced. *What could have tipped Brick off? Did someone spot me following the panel truck? Did someone say the wrong thing and a bug in one of the rooms pick it up? Or maybe this has been going on for a long time and they always cleaned up the room after they delivered the plane load of hostages.* She looked over at Tucker who looked as drained as she'd ever seen him. *On the other hand, at least Tucker is seriously considering my theory this time.*

JT's voice jogged her back to the present. "So, Deputy, do you think it's possible Brick could have used that back room to stow Zoe in after he caught her poking around?"

"Well, accordin' to that Albarran kid, Long John said Zoe suspected Brick of doing somethin' illegal back there and she was gonna blackmail him when she found out what it was."

JT shook his head. "Stupid girl."

"Yeah, he's way out of her league," Tucker said and paused. "If she's still alive, that is."

"These young women that are missing," Rachel said softly, "do you think it's possible Brick is selling them to that man with the plane? Could he be using them somewhere as prostitutes?"

Tucker's face turned grave. "Maybe. Or the guy who bought them is sellin' them to someone else. I read a report there's at least 18,000 women being trafficked in America a year. Maybe twice that many we don't even know about. A lot of the young girls who are reported missing in this area turn up in the trade somewhere like LA or Houston."

"Like maybe that thirteen year old girl?" JT asked.

"I'm afraid so."

Rachel stared at Tucker wide-eyed and speechless.

"All those posters of missing children you've been bringing in since we've opened," JT began. "Do you think all those young girls and boys..."

"I didn't at first. But then I read that report. You don't want to know about some of the stuff I read."

"Then you need to go after that guy!" Rachel exclaimed. "That slimy one that flies that plane. Surely the airport has a record of the planes that go in and out of here."

"Ah, I don't think so," JT said. "First of all, it's not an airport, it's a landing strip. Second, there's no tower and no personnel."

"Oh," Rachel said, sinking back, remembering her own flights with Buddy. No one else was ever there, not even another plane. "Then what can we do? We can't just sit here."

The deputy sat with his arms folded across his chest for a long time before he spoke. "I got some ideas, but bein' way out at the end of the county like this, the county ain't gonna send me any more help." He turned to look at Rachel. "They don't even see the connection between the body you found diggin' for gold that day and Long John's murder. A missin' person like Zoe Liddy ain't high on their priority list, either."

Rachel squinted at him. The deputy's eyes were turned down in an effort to avoid hers. "So what are you trying to tell us, Deputy?"

Dewey Tucker nervously pulled at end of his walrus mustache, looked at JT, then back at Rachel. "I'm gonna need some help," he finally admitted.

Chapter 13

Rachel thought about their plan of attack while she stood in the shower washing her hair. She felt almost overwhelmed that Deputy Tucker hadn't ridiculed her ideas and actually listened to what she had to say. *We really have everything we need to make the plan work, and I'll bet I can have my crew ready for tomorrow tonight.* By the time she had towel dried her hair and dressed in jeans and a sweater, she was already feeling restless.

She checked her watch for the third time. *What time did Buddy say he was coming back? I have so much to tell him, I don't know where to start.* She pictured his face with his movie star smile, crooked nose, and tousled sandy hair. The hair was always a mess, she thought, but on him it looked great. It was easy to understand why women fell in love with him—too many women. And the fact that he had been married and divorced three times before he was forty wasn't that great of a record. Yet—

She stopped in the middle of combing out her hair and stared at her likeness in the mirror. "Rachel Ryan, you are missing that man!" she admonished herself out loud. "You better watch it or you'll soon find yourself—"

The sharp knock on the door snapped her out of her reverie and she checked her watch again. *Can he be here already? I was supposed to pick him up at the airstrip.*

She yanked open the door ready to hug him and stopped short, her mouth open in astonishment. Instead of Buddy, a tall, broad-shouldered man with dark, wavy hair and deep brown eyes stood smiling at her. "Alex Tucker! What are you doing here?"

"Now, is that how you greet an old friend?" Alex cocked his head flirtatiously and looked at her from underneath thick lashes.

"I—I wasn't expecting you," Rachel stammered. Her mind flooded with images of the times they'd been together, the feelings she had felt for him. "I didn't know if I'd ever hear from you again. I didn't think you'd just pop up out of nowhere—"

"Pop up out of nowhere?" Alex's expression changed to one of disbelief. "Did you think I would just go home and forget about you? Is that what you thought?"

"I—I didn't know what to think. I never heard from you after the last time you came by."

"I never heard from you, either." His voice and his eyes turned cold.

"I don't chase after men."

"You don't chase after men? What do you think this is, 1950?" he scoffed.

Rachel turned away. *This certainly isn't starting off very well.* She extended her hand toward the sofa and asked softly, "Why don't you come in?"

She seated herself, leaving plenty of room for Alex.

He sat close to her, took her hand, and pressed it to his lips. "Can we start over again?"

A shock went up her arm and through her body at his touch and Rachel remembered the first time he had said those words to her. She had been swimming and he brought over margaritas as a peace offering after a rough initial meeting. When he grabbed her wrist to keep her from leaving, the same spark shot through her. And then there was the time on the north side of Blood Mountain when the electricity between them was more than they could stand. He kissed her and she thought she would melt right into the rocks.

"Rachel?" Alex asked softly, the gaze from his dark, brooding eyes catching hers. He looked at her with hunger. It was a deep hunger he felt when he wanted a woman.

Rachel felt like she was drowning. He wasn't handsome in the in classic sense, but she felt a primal attraction to him, his deep-set eyes, his chiseled jaw. She had a vision of the two of them the afternoon he suddenly showed up and they were alone in the Plantation Room. She could barely restrain herself from throwing herself at him right there in the booth. What was happening to her?

She abruptly broke away from his spell. "Yes, let's

start over," she began in a tone that sounded businesslike. "First tell me, have you seen your uncle Dewey? And what you've been doing lately?"

Alex took a deep breath and let it out, obviously disappointed. "I did meet with Dewey and he briefed me on all that's been going on around here. But the big news is that I've been working with the FBI on a big case in my jurisdiction."

"Really? That is big news. Isn't it a bit unusual for the FBI to work with anyone?"

"Yes. I wish I could tell you more about it, but I can't right now. But if things turn out right, I could be headed off to Quantico in a couple of months and may be working for them in another year."

Rachel drew back. "Is that what you want?"

"I'm seriously thinking about it. And they are seriously thinking about me. We'll just have to wait and see what happens."

"That's pretty exciting."

"Yes, but not as exciting as you." Alex looked deeply into her eyes.

Rachel could not pull her gaze away from his face and she felt like she was in a free fall. Drawn to him like a magnet, she caught the scent of the aftershave he wore and pictured herself pressing her face into the crook of his neck, his chest—

And then he kissed her. It was a long, passionate kiss that made her feel as if she were melting into him like a snowflake on your tongue. When he released her, they were both breathless.

He cupped her chin in his hand and leaned into her. "I've missed you terribly, Rachel."

Heat radiated through every pore in her body. To make love to him would be thrilling...like cascading down a waterfall, and she felt herself yielding to his touch.

Then an orchestra broke into song. Literally.

They both turned to look at Rachel's cell phone on the table by the door.

"Leave it," Alex said.

"I can't. I'm expecting a call."

"Let them leave a message and call back."

"No. I can't." Rachel pulled away and went to the phone. "Are you here?" she said after clicking on, and then paused. "Okay, I'll be right there." She turned to Alex. "I'm sorry, but I have to leave to pick up someone."

He turned cold again. "Can't someone else do it?"

"No, it's personal."

"Buddy?"

"Yes. I have to pick him up at the airport so we can get his car at the garage."

"And nobody else is capable of doing that?"

"I promised him I'd be there, Alex. We're going to have dinner together."

"I see." His voice was tinged with what? Annoyance? Regret?

"I'm sorry to disappoint you, but you should have called me ahead. I wouldn't have made other plans. We could have spent the night together, Alex."

"The whole night?"

She looked away from his eyes. "I'm really sorry, but you need to go. I need to leave." She grabbed her purse, went to the door, and opened it. She stepped aside waiting for...what? A hug? A kiss good-bye?

But Alex rushed by her without a look and kept on walking. Rachel rushed out to her car and one-handedly drove through town, while combing her hair. She managed to apply a little blush and lipstick while waiting at the stop lights. When she arrived at the airport, Buddy had already tied down the Bonanza and stood on the tarmac waiting for her. She jumped out of the Hummer and rushed over to him. In the emotion of the moment, she threw her arms around him and gave him a passionate hug and kiss.

"Wow!" Buddy said, stepping back and surveying her. "You must have really missed me."

"I did. I truly did. You were gone a long time."

"I know. Right at the height of tax season, my best accountant decides to have her baby early. I didn't have a whole lot of choice in the matter."

"And you are such a sweet boss I'll bet you didn't even bring her work to the hospital," she teased. "Come on, get in the truck and we'll go get the BMW. Armand's staying open late just for you."

"You look excited. Something happen?"

"Yes, lots of things are happening. But let's get the duties out of the way and I'll tell you the whole story over dinner."

It was nearly eight when they found a private booth

at the far end of the Plantation Room. After ordering the lobster flown in that day from the west coast, they settled down with their margaritas and Rachel filled Buddy in on the latest happenings with the Golden Vista case.

By the time they finished their entrées, Rachel had explained her and Tucker's plan of attack.

"So all the helpers are meeting you for lunch tomorrow? Even the two oldsters from assisted living?"

"Yes, and they both are excited to help."

"And you're positive Dewey Tucker agreed to have you all help him this way?"

"Girl Scouts honor," she said, holding up a hand. "I'm a little in shock myself. But I think our deputy realizes he's stuck and there's just not enough man-power in the county available to him."

"So you probably need to get to bed early and get a good night's sleep?"

"Well, maybe not *too* early." She gave Buddy her warmest smile. "We definitely have time for a night cap, if you want."

"Mmm. Well, that will do for a start."

൞

Rachel was still rubbing the sleep out of her eyes when she answered the insistent knocking on her door. She wouldn't have opened it except for the fact that her sister was eyeing her through the peephole.

"What's going on?" Rachel asked when Heather pushed her way in with two cups of coffee.

"Miss Emma just got kicked out of Golden Vista!"

"What?" Rachel needed a moment to absorb the news.

"Miss Emma was just given notice that she had to be out of Golden Vista within a week. Period."

"But—but why? Oh, come in and sit down and let me have some of that coffee. Tell me from the beginning."

They both sat at the table on the edge of their seats and attacked their lattes.

"Miss Emma called me late last night," Heather said between sips. "Brick gave her written notice she was being evicted. The reason sited was that she was a disrupting force among the guests and staff."

"Oh no," Rachel cried. "This is my fault."

"It doesn't matter whose fault it is. The problem is, she is being kicked out."

Rachel's head was throbbing. It was too much for her brain to absorb so early in the morning. "So what can we do?"

"I came up with a temporary fix. It's not perfect, but for the time being—"

"She's going to stay here? At the hotel?"

Heather nodded and Rachel looked around her suite. Yes, it could work if she got the ground floor, except...

"I know. You're wondering how we can manage meals and meds."

"Exactly what I was thinking."

"You and I will have to do the meds. She's got one of those little pill boxes so we only have to fill it once a week. It's the meals that will present the problem."

Rachel sipped her latte and thought a bit. "I hope you aren't thinking of room service. She can't spend twenty-four hours a day in her room."

"I know. We'll just have to have bell staff take her back and forth to the café in the wheel chair, or even give the maids extra time. We can figure out a payment for her that will be about what she's paying at Golden Vista."

Rachel nodded. "That could work."

"It will have to, until we can figure out something else."

"Don't worry, Heather." Rachel clasped her sister's hand in friendship. "We can work it out. It's better than having her stay where she is and have sleeping pills forced on her. At least we know she'll be safe here at the inn."

"Very much so. I just had to run it by you to make sure I made the right decision."

"You did." Rachel glanced at her watch. "Is it eight o'clock already? I overslept!"

Heather had an impish smile cross her face. "I couldn't help but notice you got in awfully late last night. I got up to go to the bathroom and got a glass of water. I saw you coming up the steps at two this morning."

"Heather!"

Heather was smiling broadly now. "Hey, it's okay. I'm glad you had a good time with Buddy."

"It—it's not what you think," Rachel insisted, turning pink.

"Sis, I'm not thinking anything, okay? I'm just happy you and Buddy are getting along well. Especially after Alex dropped by."

"What? Heather, are you spying on me?"

"No, for heaven's sake. We just happened to walk home from dinner at the same time he climbed the stairs to your suite. Did he tell you the news?"

"The news? What news?"

"You know—about Benny Ammato?"

"Benny Ammato?" Rachel's brain spun. She had tried to forget that name and the man who caused so much trouble for them. "What about Benny?"

"He left, skipped out on probation for some dumb thing he did in LA before he came here. Alex thinks he might be hiding out in town."

"What? Benny Ammato was on probation in LA? What did he do?

"I didn't ask. I was just upset that he could be back here."

"This is lot to take in. Alex never said a word about it. Nothing."

"Maybe he had more important things to talk to you about."

Rachel swallowed a sip of coffee and stared off. "Yeah, like why I didn't jump with joy when he pops in unannounced after not talking to me for weeks?" Her eyes shifted back to her sister. "Did he actually think I was going to fall into bed with him just because he shows up and tells me he missed me?"

"Did you?"

"Fall into bed with him? No. Of course not." Rachel

locked onto Heather's penetrating gaze and shrugged. "Okay, I was tempted."

"But?"

"Heather, he doesn't *love* me. He just *wants* me. It's not good enough."

Heather squeezed her sister's hand. "I'm glad. He may be a handsome hunk, but you deserve someone who will love you until death-do-us-part."

"I'm not sure that's what I want, either," Rachel said, turning away. "But a one-night-stand once every couple of months is definitely not it. And it really makes me angry he never mentioned anything about Benny Ammato."

"I admit that wasn't too nice. Especially if he wanted you to think he came by just to see you."

"That's for sure. But why would Benny skip out on probation and come back here? And how would Alex find out about that?"

"I don't know, but Benny did have at least one friend here, remember? Not to mention he's got a big grudge against all of us."

Rachel clutched her forehead. "The poems! Could he could be the one who's stalking JT?"

"JT was talking about that this morning with Deputy Tucker. It's a possibility isn't it?"

"Did Alex spend the night with his uncle? He was pretty angry when he left here."

"No. Tucker said he saw Alex just briefly. He just pops in and out of *his* life, too, it seems."

"We'll talk more about this later. I've got to get dressed and get to work." Rachel's smart phone beeped.

"A text message this early in the morning? I better check." After reading her message, Rachel turned to her sister, white-faced. "It was from Hank Levinson. He was afraid to call me, afraid they planted more bugs in his room. He said Hester brought over an eviction notice early this morning for him. He has to be out within a week."

༺༻

The rest of the day was hectic. Rachel and Heather decided it would be best to move Hank and Miss Emma over immediately so Heather made the arrangements to have their personal items moved to the hotel and their furniture moved into a storage facility.

Toro had the maintenance crew do the work in short order, and Heather and Rachel helped Miss Emma pack up the myriad of personal items she kept in her studio.

By one o' clock they had enough of the moving project under control that Rachel was able to have both Hank and Miss Emma at the hotel in time for the meeting with Deputy Tucker. She also invited Jesse Albarran and Danny Long to be part of her plan.

Deputy Dewey Tucker sat at the round table, in the middle of the private room, looking his usual gruff self. Miss Emma sat on one side of him and Hank sat on the other, both of whom looked exhausted from their moves. Rachel sat directly opposite Tucker with Jesse and Danny on either side of her.

Deputy Tucker began by explaining their plan for solving the mystery of Zoe Liddy's disappearance and possibly the murder of John Long. "If we are correct in our beliefs, our very lives could be in jeopardy if any of this information about what we are doing leaks out." He looked at Miss Emma and Hank. "In fact, I understand Hank and Miss Emma here have already been asked to leave Golden Vista just for the little bit of snooping around they've done already."

"Which kind of proves they're guilty of something, doesn't it?" Emma remarked. "I mean, if they aren't doing anything illegal, they wouldn't have needed to boot our butts out, would they?"

"That's right, Miss Emma," Rachel said, trying to suppress a smile as she handed out a schedule to each person. The plan was simple, she explained. Each couple would sit in a darkened apartment on the top floor of the Hotel Rios Apartments. She paired up Jesse with Miss Emma and Danny with Hank as partners. There the couples would take turns sleeping and watching the back yard of Golden Vista for any type of activity. If anything unusual occurred, they would call Deputy Tucker immediately. Rachel would act as the floater, the extra person who would take care of anything else that came up.

Using the apartment had been the brainchild of Jesse Albarran. After studying the hotel at night, he suspected Long John had been observed on the roof of the hotel because his binoculars had reflected off the hotel lights. So the roof of the building was out. However, in a stroke of luck, one of the apartments facing Golden Vista had just been vacated and was scheduled for remodeling. The dark interior would be the perfect cover for them, and the bathroom and kitchen would be available for personal needs.

When the meeting was over, Rachel notified the kitchen it was time to serve lunch. Chef Henri, himself, wheeled out the first cart with scrumptious plates of a variety of Italian specialties along with side salads.

"Oh man, real food!" Hank exclaimed. "I think I died and went to Heaven."

"This is wonderful, Henri, thank you so much," Miss Emma added. "I don't think I'll miss Golden Vista one bit."

Rachel had to laugh, but then considered she had become spoiled by having mouth-watering meals available to her every day. After Henri and his assistant had left the room, Tucker answered a few questions from the crew and everyone was looking forward to the first night of surveillance.

After finishing their lunch, Jesse and Danny both hurried off to return to their businesses. Emma and Hank followed behind them to supervise the remains of their moving project.

Deputy Tucker and Rachel were the last to leave the room. "So what do you think, Dewey?"

Tucker contemplated the question and stroked his mustache. "I think it could definitely work," he said then paused. "As long as you don't go off and get a wild hair to do somethin' stupid."

"What? That's not fair. How can you even think that?"

He raised his eyebrows and looked at her steadily.

"You don't really want me to answer that, do you?"

She lowered her gaze to the floor. "No, I guess not," she replied and hurried toward the exit and her sister's casita.

After one knock on the living room door, Heather pulled Rachel inside. She had been waiting to hear if the plan was a go.

"Well?" she asked. "Tell me!"

"Yes, we're on, and believe it or not, I think with the crew we have, we could end up solving this whole case."

"Oh, wouldn't that be wonderful?" Heather clapped her hands in glee. "Especially if Zoe Liddy were found alive."

"I'm hoping that if the missing fourteen-year-old is one of their current hostages, we can save *her* life," Rachel said. "But I'm afraid I'm not holding onto too much hope for Zoe. She's been gone too long, and I swear I saw her being loaded into that plane."

"Well, there's always hope unless her body turns up somewhere."

Before Rachel could reply, her cell phone rang. "It's Jared Johnson!" she said breathlessly, checking the phone and clicked on to his voice. "Jared, how *are* you? How's the family? I'm so excited to hear your voice." She stepped over to the sliding glass door and opened it, hoping to improve the reception.

"Lily and kids are fine," Jared said. "They're getting used to being back in the colder weather, and are still talking about their trip to everyone. How is the Long John case going?"

Rachel brought him up to speed about the crew they had put together for the nightly surveillance of Golden Vista.

"That sounds like a great plan, Rachel. And I'm glad to hear you're working with Tucker so well."

"I can't exactly say we are getting along wonderfully, but we are making it work so far. Our crew is going to start tonight at nine, and we'll just have to wait and see what happens."

"Well, I'll be praying for you all," he said and then paused. "The main reason I called was because I have some information about your parents' case."

"You found something out about my parents?" Rachel repeated, and her heart pounded.

"Yes, but I'm afraid some of it is not too good."

"Oh, no" Rachel said, her face crestfallen.

"But by not being too good, it makes it actually better for you."

"What do you mean?"

"Well, here's what happened. I sent off for the case and got a complete copy, except all of the photos were missing."

"They were?"

"Yes, and when I called back, nobody knew what happened to them. I thought that was kind of strange, so I went over to Grand Rapids and looked though the file box myself, and the photos weren't anywhere in there. I mean, I looked through every single file in the box, thinking they might have been misfiled. Nothing. But I did find out the name of the photographer who shot photos of the crime scene."

"You did? Is he still alive?"

"Yes, he's still alive, and I was able to talk to him. But the best part is, he keeps a personal file of every photograph he takes. He's going to send me copies of all the photos he has of the case, even the ones that didn't come out so well."

"Oh Jared, that's wonderful!" She could see Heather anxiously watching her out of the corner of her eye.

"Yeah, I thought so, too."

"When do you think you'll have a chance to study them?"

"It depends on how long it takes to get the photos. It sounded like he'd had them stored in bins a room in the basement. He had them labeled by years so he should be able to find them pretty quickly. I'll call you in a few days, regardless of whether I have them or not. But until I have them in my hands and see what's there, I can't say for sure."

"I understand, and I thank you so much for all the trouble you are going to, Jared. I can't tell you how much better I feel just knowing you'll be able to review the case. There was always something that bothered me about that room, but I just can't remember what it was."

"Not to worry, little lady. If there's anything there that doesn't fit right, I won't let it go until I figure it out."

When Rachel clicked off, she turned to her sister and hugged her. "He's got the file, and he's going to the get the photos in a few days, and promised to study the case."

Heather turned, silently sauntered over to the sliding glass door, and pulled it closed. Her hair caught the light from the afternoon sun, causing it to glow like burnished copper. She turned back to her sister and gazed at her steadily, a deep frown line forming between her eyes. "Rachel? Try not to get your hopes up. I don't want you to get crushed if this doesn't turn out the way you expect."

"I know what you're saying, sis, but there's no way it could turn out to be worse than what it is now." Rachel's face took on a resolute look as she crossed her arms in front of chest. "You and I both know our father was innocent. And I've decided, no matter what it takes, or how long it takes, I am going to prove it."

Chapter 14

The next day seemed to last forever for Rachel. At last nine o' clock arrived and she drove over to the Hotel Rios Apartments with an excited Miss Emma in the passenger seat.

"I'll tell you, this is the wildest thing that happened to me since Gertie's tit got caught in the ringer. I sure don't miss having to move out of Golden Vista one bit."

"It sounds like you have a new lease on life, Miss Emma."

"You bet your boots I do! It's great to be out of that prison."

A few minutes later Jesse met them at the back door of the apartment building armed with a cooler filled with drinks and snacks. "You guys all set?"

"We dang tootin' are! Let's get going," Emma said, as Rachel pushed her wheelchair into the building. They took the back elevator up to top floor of the building where a darkened apartment awaited them.

"Give your eyes a couple minutes to adjust," Jesse said, opening the door for them, and they all entered the sparsely furnished room.

"This is where the real work begins," he continued. "If you look behind you, you can see the bathroom. There's a dim night light in there to help you navigate, and Emma, the door is wide enough to accommodate your wheelchair."

"Great. Thank you. Now let's see what you brought for snacks. Rachel brought a pie, but let's have our main meal first."

Rachel smiled at that comment. By now, she was used to the vast amount of food that tiny little woman could eat. All three of them sat, gazing out the windows with their binoculars as the town slowly fell asleep.

Time ticked away and Rachel's leg began to shake up and down like a jack hammer.

"You don't have to hang around," Jesse said, noticing her nervousness. "Miss Emma and I can handle this. Really. You might as well get a good night sleep so you'll be fresh for tomorrow."

Rachel had to admit to herself that after four hours of staring out the window at nothing, she was totally bored. "Okay. You're right. Just make sure that if anything happens, you call me and wake me up. I'll leave my phone right beside my head all night."

"We promise," Miss Emma said. "Now go home."

ೞಣಲ

The next night wasn't a whole lot better when Danny and Hank sat in the apartment with Rachel. The streets were deserted by ten and Rachel had already paced the floor several times.

Danny turned to Rachel and Hank about midnight. "This gives you an idea about what most police work is like—waiting."

"At least on a stake-out," Hank replied. "Then there's the driving around in the patrol car looking for doughnut shops."

After a long period of quiet, Danny asked, "Anybody know any good jokes?"

Rachel gritted her teeth in frustration. "I wish something would happen! It's horrible just sitting here and wondering what is going on inside that building. It looks quiet out there, but as far as Golden Vista is concerned, looks are deceiving."

"I know," Hank said. "There may be some young girl trapped inside, scared to death."

"I wonder if we could contact her, like maybe if we tapped on the wall or something," she said. "Even with the windows boarded up on the inside, maybe she could hear knocking. Or maybe there's some kind of clue in the yard."

Danny looked over at her. "What are you thinking?"

"Nothing, really." She glanced at her watch, the time barely visible in the dim light. "It's still early."

At one o' clock Rachel looked at her watch again. "I have an idea."

Hank looked at her. "No."

"Hey, you don't even know what it is."

"Don't matter. You're dangerous when you get ideas."

"Well, let's hear it, anyway," Danny said.

"I was just thinking that maybe Danny and I could walk over by the north wall," she said with an innocent look.

"And?" Danny asked.

"Well, then you could give me a boost over and I could climb into the yard over by that pile of stuff that's got the tarp over it."

"No! Too dangerous," Hank said, jumping in.

"Why? There's not a soul out there. And if someone shows up I could simply duck under the tarp. No problem. When they leave, I climb back over the stuff and Danny helps me down from the wall."

"No. Deputy Tucker will blow a gasket when he finds out."

"So who's gonna tell him?" She looked from one man to the other.

Danny thought a bit. "I kind of like the idea, but I think I should be the one to climb over the wall."

"No. Not good." Rachel shook her head. "If you get caught, Brick will have you arrested and that would ruin your reputation in town. But if *I* were to get caught, I'm already in trouble with him, so what would be just one more thing."

"It's a stupid idea," Hank insisted. "If Brick caught you, he could—"

"Not if you're here and call Deputy Tucker right

away. And I could call out to Danny if I got in any kind of trouble at all."

"No way," said Hank.

The three of them sat in silence for about minute. Then Rachel stood up. "I'm going, with or without you, Danny." She moved toward the door.

"Okay, okay. I'll come." Danny sighed. "At least I'll be right outside the wall if they happen to come back. I can call out and let you know they're coming so you can hide."

"That'll work. Let's make sure our cell phones are on vibrate so we can contact each other." She turned to Hank who was glaring at her. "I'll be okay," she assured him. "As soon as I get inside the wall, I'll call you."

"I still don't like it," Hank replied. "I think it's a mistake.

But Rachel had already turned and headed toward the door. When she and Danny reached the wall, they double checked with Hank by phone to make sure the yard was still clear. Danny gave Rachel a boost to help her clear the wall.

She threw a small duffle bag over first and then landed easily on the covered pile of junk in the corner and climbed down. She ran to the building, climbed the few stairs and tried the door, just in case in opened. It didn't.

She went back down the stairs and got down on her hands and knees. She popped a small flashlight in her mouth and thoroughly searched the area around the steps.

Her phone buzzed. It was Hank. "You forgot to call

me. I've been watching you, but I still need to know you are okay."

"Sorry. I did forget. I'm done working around the steps so I'm going to check the building in hopes that I can find a window they covered over with the stucco. If I do find one and someone is inside, they possibly might hear me tap and tap back."

"Okay, but don't stay too long."

Rachel started on the north side of the building and had gone about twenty feet when Danny's voice boomed out from behind the wall. "Rachel! Hank just called. The panel truck is heading this way. Hide quick!"

Rachel grabbed the black bag with the tools and ran to the pile of junk against the wall. She lifted the tarp and crawled underneath just as the truck pulled up in front of the gate.

She settled in as the truck pulled into the yard and the doors opened. The men were joking and laughing about something and Rachel began to relax knowing she was out of sight.

Then she felt something on her neck and froze. A spider! In a panic, she swiped at it, but whatever was there had moved to her cheek and she swatted at her head and neck, forgetting Brick and his men were close by.

"Did you hear that?" Brick's voice boomed out into the night.

Rachel froze, terrified, not daring to breathe. Her cheek no longer tickled, but images of black widows flooded her mind and her body broke out in a cold sweat.

She heard the footsteps coming closer. She even

closed her eyes—as if that would help—and tried desperately to remain still.

She heard other steps and then quiet.

"What's under there?" Brick asked.

"Nothin', just junk," one of the men said.

More quiet. Rachel held her breath.

Then someone lifted the tarp. Rachel opened her eyes to take in Brick glaring at her while his two buddies stood there smirking.

She smiled. "Hi Brick."

In answer, he pulled her up to her feet. "You better explain what you're doing here."

"Okay, okay. I know it looks bad, but my new cat got away and jumped into your yard so I climbed in after her. Then when you came, I felt foolish so I thought I'd better hide so you wouldn't think that I had trespassed on your property."

"You *did* trespass on my property!" Brick's face flamed with rage.

This isn't going well, Rachel thought. "Well, yes, I suppose you're right," she said, hoping to defuse his anger, "and I apologize, so I guess I'll just be on my way." She turned to leave but Brick grabbed her arm.

"Oh, no you don't!"

"Ow! Your hurting me!"

He yanked her toward him. "That's nothing like you're gonna hurt."

"Help! Help! Call the sheriff!" she yelled.

"We already did. He's on his way," Danny shouted.

"What the—" Brick said, turning to the voice.

"That's Danny from next door. He's the one that gave me the cat."

"I don't believe you had a stupid cat."

"Well, I *did*, and you better not touch me again or I'll have you arrested."

"You'll have *me* arrested?"

The siren on Deputy Tucker's truck screamed within hearing range and the spinning lights soon reflected off the building. Brick smiled at her in a contemptuous way. "I'm going to have *you* arrested for trespassing. I've had enough of your snooping. In fact, I'm even going to file a restraining order against you."

Before Rachel could reply, Tucker squealed to a stop. He popped the door open and pounded at the gate and yelled for them to open up. The angry deputy was followed in by a sheepish-looking Danny Long.

"What's going on here?" the deputy demanded.

Rachel quickly related her story about the cat before Brick could say anything.

"You don't honestly believe that story, do you, deputy?" Brick asked.

"I think it's too late to sort this out right now and I'll take it up again in the morning."

"What? I want her arrested! She trespassed on my yard."

Tucker looked at Brick as if he were looking at an idiot. "Forget it Brick. The district attorney would laugh you out of the courtroom. Now, do you really want to open this whole thing up to an investigation?"

Brick stared at him and considered the implications.

"Then I want to sign a restraining order against her. I don't want her stalking me or being anywhere near this building."

"Fair enough. Come down to my office tomorrow and sign the papers." He walked them out to the gate and locked the door behind them.

After they all left the yard, Deputy Tucker ordered Danny to go home. Rachel stepped up her pace behind him in a hurry to get away. She barely made it to the sidewalk when the deputy called out to her to stop. She waited for him and her heart sank as she watched the expression on his face.

In a frighteningly calm voice he finally spoke. "Rachel. It's all over. "

"What do you mean?" she asked meekly, not daring to look him in the eyes.

"You broke our agreement."

She hung her head. "I know. I—I just wanted to look around."

His voice was low and sounded tired. "I know you wanted to look around, but the deal was you watched from inside the building. Now he knows we're on to him. You just blew it. It's over."

He shook his head and walked away.

"But wait," she said. She ran up to him and pulled something out of her pocket. "Look," she said, holding out her hand.

Tucker reached out and took the ring she gave him. "What's this?"

"It's the ring Hank gave Zoe the night she disappeared. See? It's fake but it's got those little blue stones surrounding that large one? I know Hank would be able to identify it."

The large deputy sighed deeply and just looked at her. "It doesn't prove anything, Rachel. Sure, it's possible Zoe dropped the ring in the yard, but it doesn't prove she was abducted. It only proves she was here some time that evening—here outside the building where she works. She could have come out for a smoke."

Rachel felt as if someone had punched her in the gut. Tears began to well up in her eyes and she wanted to defend herself. *Zoe doesn't smoke.* Her mouth opened and closed but nothing came out. Her gaze followed Tucker as he walked away. Tears leaked down her cheeks. She hung her head and noticed her designer shoes were covered with a layer of dirt. They seemed to mock her. *Rachel Ryan, you really messed up big this time.*

༺༻

Rachel rolled over in bed the next morning and groaned. "I don't want to get up," she moaned. She pulled the covers over her head. *I feel so humiliated. Everyone will know. Even JT.* Rachel pounded her fist into her pillow. *Well, so what? He already thinks you're an idiot. Who cares about him? Buddy will understand and so will Heather. So get your butt out of bed.*

She sat up and looked around. Another thought jolted her and she threw the covers off. "I've got to call Jared Johnson." The phone beside her bed rang as if on cue.

"Jared! I was just thinking of you!"

"You must have known I'd have some news by now."

"I was hoping. What is it?"

"I received the photos and studied them. Then I read through all the notes again and tried to fit them together."

Rachel's stomach lurched. "Did you come to any conclusions?"

"I don't want to send them—especially the photos—to you." He paused. "I think it would be too traumatic for you to see them. But I think I can tell you how it all came down."

"You're probably right about the trauma," Rachel conceded and lay back down on the pillow. "I think I can handle it if you just describe the scene to me, though. I know it's difficult, but it's something I have to do. I'm determined to get this handled once and for all."

"And if you don't come to the conclusion you want? What then?"

"I'll just have to deal with it, that's all."

"Okay then. If you're ready, this is what I got…"

Rachel lay back on the pillow and closed her eyes.

"Your mother was shot first, in the forehead. She fell to the living room floor."

Rachel took a deep breath and let it out. "That's what the police said."

"Well, it looks like they were right."

"What about my father?"

"This is the part that I have a problem with."

"What do you mean?"

"He's half-lying on the sofa, as if he recoiled from the gun blast. It's a large caliber gun, the kind you'd get a kick back from, but you'd use two hands to hold it steady."

Rachel had stopped breathing, waiting for Jared to continue. "And?"

"Here's the part that I don't get. There's residue only on his right hand, none on the left, so that means he only used one hand, and the gun was lying on his hand backward. It's kind of hard to explain. But his fingers would have been twisted if he had held the gun the way it was lying in his hand."

"Wait! Wait!" Rachel sprang up in bed. "You said the gun was in his *right* hand?"

"Yes, it was kind of—"

"Jared! That's not right! My father was definitely *left* handed! He couldn't do *anything* with his right hand."

There was a long pause. "Are you sure?"

"Of course I'm sure! My mother was left-handed too, and Heather and I are both left-handed. It runs in our family."

There was silence on the other end of the phone. Jared's deep voice finally punctuated the quiet. "This presents a whole different picture."

"You mean someone would have had to put the gun in my father's hand, and they put it in the wrong hand."

"That's one explanation I can think of."

Rachel was excited. "What's the other explanation?"

"I can't think of any off hand."

"This is amazing, Jared. I am so excited!" Rachel

was up out of bed now, standing by the phone, wanting to jump up and down. "Can I talk to the investigating officer?"

There was a pause. "I'm afraid not, Rachel."

"No? Why not?"

"The investigating officer, Captain Blackmer, is dead.

"What? He died?"

"He died, but now I'm not sure how."

"What do you mean?"

"When I called to talk to him, I found out he had gone over a cliff with his brand new truck about two weeks later after the incident."

"Was it an accident?"

"The official report said yes, but now I'm not so sure."

"You mean someone might have pushed him off the road?"

"Possibly. The accident report sounds a little hazy to me. But what's even more important is that Blackmer had deposited seventy-five thousand dollars, in cash, in his bank account the week before—which is unusual to begin with—and then took fifty thousand out to buy the truck."

"Oh, boy. That is kind of odd. I wonder what it means?"

"Rachel, it could mean several things. But if you're right about your parents being murdered, then it's possible Blackmer was paid to cover that up. And then who ever paid him the money decided they wanted to make sure there were no lose ends."

Rachel sagged to the edge of the bed. Her mind was racing again. "But who? Who could have done all this? And why? My parents didn't have any enemies." She nervously gripped a clump of hair with her hand. "Is someone going to re-open the investigation?"

"I'm going to take it over today to the Chief of Police and see what I can get started. Of course, I'm officially retired so I can't really be involved."

"I understand that. But will you call me and keep me posted?"

"Yes, of course I will."

"I just thought of something, Jared. I need to call my crazy aunt Lydia."

"Your crazy aunt Lydia?"

"Yeah. Everyone has a crazy aunt, don't they?"

"If you say so," he laughed.

"She was close to my father and she needs to know. And she may have a guess as to who might be responsible."

"Call me if she thinks of anyone, will you?"

"You bet I will. And, Jared? Thanks for everything. This is the best thing that happened to me in a long, long time. You have vindicated my father!"

Chapter 15

When Rachel hung up, she wasted no time in calling her sister. "Heather, I'm coming over as soon as I get my clothes on. I have great news!"

It took Heather a few moments for the truth about their parents to sink in. "This is amazing news," she finally said, stunned. "After all these years—and the police never figured that out? They never even asked if he were left-handed. They just assumed he killed our mother and then…" Her voice dropped off as she dabbed her eyes with a tissue.

"But we knew the truth, didn't we, Heather, even if the police didn't. I never for second doubted Dad was innocent. There's just no way he would have killed Mom."

"I never doubted him either." Heather looked down at crumbled tissue in her hands. "But I just can't imagine anyone wanting to kill our parents. Everyone loved them! They were wonderful people."

Rachel reached over to hold her sister's hands. "Yes, they were. But somebody did kill them. We just don't know why."

"Well, we *do* know it wasn't a robbery gone wrong. Nothing was taken."

"We don't know that. Just because we couldn't find anything missing doesn't mean something wasn't taken. Somebody tore apart Dad's desk and files. They were definitely looking for something. Whether they found it or not, we don't know."

Heather thought about that and slowly nodded. "You might be right. They were looking for something, something important, and Dad wouldn't tell him where it was. Either that, or he didn't know."

"Exactly. So if we could find out what the killer was looking for, we might know who the killer was."

"That makes sense."

"Yeah, the problem is, I have no idea what he was looking for."

They sat quietly for a couple of minutes before Heather finally spoke: "So what's next?"

"I'm going to fly up to see aunt Lydia."

"What? Are you sure that's what you want to do? She may not be able to help at all. You know she's got some problems."

"I know. I remember the day she had the breakdown." Rachel silently shook her head as she recalled the scene from their past. "I'm not sure she can help, either, but she has the right to know what really happened to Mom and Dad. She's also the only one who could have known if there was anything unusual going on with Dad. She was close to him. He might have confided in her."

"But Lydia's a hermit, she's mentally ill. We haven't seen her in so many years—why she could even be institutionalized or even dead by now."

"No, we'd know if something happened to her. She sent you a Christmas card a couple of years ago, remember? Besides, what else do we have to go on? You got any other ideas?"

Heather shook her head. "No. No, I don't."

"Then I'm going. I've got to do something, and it's the only thing I can think of."

"But Aunt Lydia…she's…she's…crazy."

"So what? I'm a little nuts myself," Rachel said and pulled out her phone. "I wonder if I can get a non-stop flight from Phoenix to Grand Rapids."

☙❧

The next day Rachel hoisted her suitcase off the turn style, nearly falling over in the attempt. *I've got to stop with all these clothes. But then again, it still gets cold in Michigan in April. I really need those long pants and sweaters. And I need to—*

"Rachel!" A feminine voice cried out. "Rachel, it's me!"

Rachel turned to the voice and stared, momentarily puzzled. "Aunt Lydia?"

"Yes, yes, of course, dear!" a large, chestnut-haired woman answered and then enveloped Rachel in her fleshy arms. "I just got your message, and oh, I'm so happy to see you, my precious, precious niece!"

Rachel blinked in surprise. "I didn't expect you. But I'm so happy to see you, too, Aunt Lydia," she said, trying to recover. "You look so…so *well*. You look *good!*"

"Yes, my dear, I *am* well. I am *very* well." She laughed heartily and added, "I am no longer the crazy aunt everyone warned you about."

"Oh, Aunt Lydia! You are still the funny woman you used to be."

"Yes, that part I haven't lost. But we can talk later. Right now I need to get you home."

She grabbed the huge piece of luggage as if it were a box of popcorn and toted it behind her. "My car is parked close by on level 2."

"But I need to rent a car."

"No, you don't. Save your money. I have one you can use."

Rachel gazed at her aunt in amazement. *She never used to have a driver's license. Did an alien inhabit her body?*

When they arrived at Lydia's house, Rachel stared at it. "Your house looks brand new."

"Oh, yes. I've been doing lots of work. Repainted the whole thing. And wait 'til you see the inside."

They wheeled the large suitcase into the living room, and Rachel paused a few seconds to take it all in. Gone were the waist-high stacks of magazines and newspapers, the tubs of knickknacks and dishes, the piles of clothes that didn't fit in the closets. She remembered how she used to navigate a path through the living room overcrowded with junk. "What happened? Where's all your stuff?"

"Gone, gone, and more gone!" Lydia cried, raising her arms. "Isn't it wonderful? I am no longer *trapped* by things."

Rachel walked ahead though the dining room and entered the kitchen. Everything was clean and spotless. "I need to sit down," she said, bewildered.

"Great. Let's have some tea. I just baked some cookies."

Still stunned, Rachel stood up and walked back to the dining room, looked around the whole area, turned a complete circle, and came back.

"Pretty exciting, isn't it?" Lydia said, taking a couple of mugs from the cupboard. "I understand now that I had a brain problem. My chemicals were all messed up. I had OCD. That's the term used for my hoarding problem. I saved everything—and that was in addition to a few other things I had wrong with me. But I finally went to a shrink and he prescribed some medication for me. Three years later, this is the result."

"Of course," Rachel thought. *The Ryan curse. My father, his sister, and me. I'm glad I've never had kids to pass those genes on to.*

"Sugar?" Lydia stood with the mug in her hands.

"Yes, please." Rachel spooned some in her tea and took a small sip. Still in awe, she turned her gaze to the stylishly decorated dining and living rooms and extended an arm toward them. "Medication did all this for you? Your house looks like something from a magazine."

"Well, I also had the help of a couple of friends." Lydia's eyes twinkled and then her expression became serious. "The only regret is that I waited too long to finally get it together. You need to forgive me for that."

"Forgive you? What in the world for?"

"This." Lydia sighed, got up from the table, and walked to the pantry. In a few seconds she came out with a large manila envelope. "I have to ask your forgiveness for this."

Rachel sank back against the chair. She looked intently at the blank envelope Lydia handed her. "What is it?"

"I don't know."

"You don't know?"

"That's right. I haven't opened it." Lydia's tone became solemn. "Your father gave this to me a couple of days before he was killed. He told me it was important and said for me to hide it somewhere." She snorted a laugh. "That's rich. I guess he figured if someone tried to rob me of it, they wouldn't be able to find it in my house in a million years."

"Yes, I remember. Heather and I used to play hide and seek in your basement."

Lydia nodded. "My house was so filled with junk that I put the envelope somewhere and couldn't even remember where it put it." She shook her head in disgust and took a long sip of tea. "I found the envelope last week when the organizing team and I were tackling the junk in the basement."

"Oh my—"

"Yeah." Lydia's voice sounded tired now. "It was only a couple days after that, after I hid the envelope, they were both killed. Then I completely lost it. Remember? They took me away and put me in the hospital. They wouldn't even let me out for the funeral."

"Aunt Lydia—"

"No. Let me finish," Lydia said, holding up a hand. "Thank God, Heather and JT took over. I don't know what would have happened to you."

"I'm afraid I didn't fare a whole lot better than you, Auntie. It was a terrible time. And I gave Heather and JT a terrible time, too."

"It was a bad time for everyone, Rachel. When I finally got out of the hospital, I had totally forgotten about the envelope. Heather and JT had already gone back west and took you with them. I just went on with my life."

"Until last week."

"No. That's not quite true. About three years ago, I renewed a relationship with a friend I had from where I used to work. He was another biologist and his wife had died. He knew I had problems. He'd seen the house. He was the one who encouraged me to get an appointment with a psychiatrist. That's when my life changed."

"Wow. That's quite a story."

"Yes. Yes, it is. After I started to get better, I realized I had to get help to clean out the house. I didn't need to live that way anymore. Besides, by then Samuel and I were getting serious. Last year he asked me to marry him. We want to get a smaller condo so we can close it up for the winter and head south. So you could say I'm getting rid of a lot of extra baggage."

Rachel clutched her forehead. "You're getting married, too? So much has happened, my brain feels like it's going to burst."

"I know what you mean. I can hardly believe it myself—and that I actually hoarded all that stuff."

"But you found the envelope."

"Yes, the minute I saw it wrapped up in that old quilt, I remembered what it was. Then I was afraid to open it. In view of what your father had said, I realized I made a significant mistake." Lydia dropped her head in embarrassment. "But when they finally let me out of the hospital, I had totally forgotten that whole month prior to the incident. Except that I knew my brother and his wife had been killed."

"So you *never* opened the envelope?"

"No. Before I could decide what to do, you called and left the message. So I thought: you're the heir—you and Heather. It's yours to open. So I saved it for you."

Rachel stared at the envelope and envisioned the scene of her father handing the parcel to Lydia. *He was obviously worried. He could have been scared.* "I think we need to open it now. But first I need to tell you what I found out about what really happened."

"What really happened—you mean about the murder?"

"Yes. You got any real food in that refrigerator? I'm

starved and a sandwich would be great right now."

"I can make you an egg salad sandwich," Lydia said, getting up from her chair.

"Cut in little triangles?"

"You bet. Chips and root beer, too."

By the time they finished their sandwiches, Rachel had finished her story about meeting Jared Johnson and how he helped her find out the truth about the murder of Joseph Ryan and his beloved wife.

"I never believed he killed her. I think that's what made me snap," Lydia said. "They closed the case without really investigating anything."

"Me, too. But that's in the past. We know the truth now. We just have to find a way to prove it."

"So do you think what's in the envelope will help?"

"There's only one way to find out, right?"

Lydia pushed a knife over to her and Rachel carefully cut through the seal. She pulled out some papers and an eight-track tape. She held up the tape. "We'll have a do a little bit of leg work to hear what's on this."

Lydia laughed. "No we won't. You haven't seen the basement yet. I bet there's four tape players down there waiting to go to auction."

"Wonderful! That saves us a bunch of trouble."

Rachel held up the first piece of paper, a letter from her father in his own unique hand. She began to read out loud.

> "'I, Joseph Ryan, have been employed by Varner-Walther Pharmaceuticals since August, 1982, as a research biologist. The enclosed tapes

will explain how, on January 10, 1996, I was approached by Martin E. Varner, CEO of Varner-Walther, and asked to find an antidote for the contents of a sealed test tube. Upon investigation, I found the contents to contain the amoeba Naegleria fowlerie, a rare but deadly type, not commonly found in the USA.

"'I wondered why I had been asked, in particular, by the CEO, to work on something that people would rarely encounter unless they traveled frequently to tropical countries. It didn't make sense financially, since it would take a while to complete this work. I was aware some layoffs were taking place within the corporation and it might present a financial drain to spend money on something that didn't seem like it would pay off. However, it was not my place to question the CEO.

"'I was only three days into my work when I accidentally overheard part of a conversation between Varner and Benson Hildebrandt, the corporate treasurer, which answered some of the questions in my mind about the work I had been ordered to do. This is explained in detail in the tapes enclosed with this letter and papers. The bottom line is that after a little more investigating, I slowly came to the realization Varner and Hildebrandt plotted to infect a portion of the population with Naegleria fowlerie by poisoning water supplies in the United States—swimming pools, lakes, water systems—any place people's noses could come in contact with the amoeba. Then Varner-Walther Pharmaceuticals would "rescue" the country with the antidote medication I was working on.

"'It was almost beyond belief when I finally came to this conclusion. I know this is a horrible accusation, a frightening, almost unbelievable one. I have to confess at this point, that during this period, I illegally broke into the company computers to look for information. I am in the process of gathering evidence of what I believe is happening, (see enclosed papers) and the motive (see accompanying financial records) but at the same time I am trying to appear "normal" and am working in the lab, as usual, on the antidote. I realize what I've done is illegal. However, if anyone is reading this now, then it won't matter. I will have been eliminated.

"'Also, if my assumption is correct, I realize that once I've finished the assigned work and the antidote is at hand, there is a good chance my life will be eliminated anyway. I am going to pretend to do the work required until I gather enough facts to be able to hand everything over to the Federal Bureau of Investigation.

"'Even now I am starting to wonder if Varner suspects that I know what's going on. He has been acting strangely around me and stops by almost daily to see how the project is coming along. This is something he never has done in the past.

"'Because of this, I am getting this material out of our house to a safe place. Hopefully, within a couple of days, I should have all the information I need. In the meantime, if anything should happen to me, please call the FBI immediately and give them the contents of this envelope.

"'Written in my own hand,
"'Joseph D. Ryan'"

When Rachel put the letter down, all she could do was to stare at her aunt. Neither of them could speak. When she recovered enough, she simply said "I need to make a phone call."

She pulled out her smart phone and tapped in the number for Jared Johnson.

Chapter 16

Three days later, Rachel sat holding hands with Buddy in the Carpenter's living room, telling all of them about her experience in Grand Rapids.

JT nervously rubbed his hairline as he read the letter aloud from Joseph Ryan. When he finished reading he looked up at everyone.

"This is makes perfect sense—now that we know what really happened. Once they suspected Joe Ryan had caught on to the underlying reason he was assigned to that project, Walther had to eliminate him. But the Naegleria fowlerie virus? How in the world was he planning to get it into the water? I had never even heard of it before."

"I don't even understand what it is," Heather said, dabbing at the tears that flowed from her eyes.

"It's a microscopic amoeba that's found mainly in the tropics," Rachel answered. "It's rare but deadly. It lives in water and if you get some water with it up your nose, the amoeba goes to the brain, grows rapidly, and kills you. They actually named it the brain-eating amoebia."

"It sounds horrible."

Rachel stood up. "It is." She wandered nonchalantly around the room. "Jared called me this morning and told me the local police have been working on that aspect of the case. They found out Varner-Walther went bankrupt in 1998 after the board of directors sold all their stocks. A lot of people lost a lot of money in that deal. The FBI is now trying to track down any former employees who were there at that time. It appears both Varner and Hildebrandt made some trips to water plants in the south to see their operations. But that had been the previous year. It appears they were still in the planning stage then."

She stopped in front of the entertainment center. "The police are thinking that they somehow had planned to penetrate the water supply in several southern states along with the lakes and ponds where people swim," she added, poking around the open shelving.

"But why southern?" Heather asked.

"Because the water's not warm enough in the north for the amoeba to survive."

JT watched Rachel. "Yes, but in the audio transcript, Joe Ryan said that was one of the things he was instructed to do—modify the amoeba to survive in colder temps—and he told them that would take years of research. He thinks that they had been aiming to drop their little bombs all over the country. He also told them finding a cure for it would be a lengthy process, too." He frowned at Rachel. "And what in the world are you doing over there, anyway?"

"I don't know. Just thinking."

"Well, you're making me nervous flitting around. Can't you think and sit down at the same time?"

Heather laughed. "That's not possible when she's following her nose. Right Rachel?"

"Right. And I found the orange blossom beads." Rachel sniffed at the jar. "It smells like March in Yuma."

"Great," JT said with sarcasm. "But can we please get your attention back to the letter?"

"Yeah, I'd like to know what we're going to do now." Buddy said, reaching for his coffee.

"I'm sorry," Rachel said. "I think this whole thing is so stressful to me, my brain checks out. I'm truly sorry."

Before anyone could reply, Rachel's phone stole everyone's attention.

She took the call, answered in monosyllables, and hung up. "We need to go over to Miss Emma's place," she said, turning to Buddy. "I'm not sure it's anything, but we need to check it out."

"I'm staying put," JT said, "but let me know if it's anything important." He reached out for Heather's hand and gave it a quick squeeze, indicating that she should also stay.

Rachel and Buddy left immediately, and when they reached Miss Emma's suite, the door was open.

"Come in and shut the door," Miss Emma called out, waving them in. She sat at the table with her laptop in front of her. Hank sat alongside. She smiled up at him. "I called Hank when I needed some technical help."

"Yeah, you guys need to take a look at this," the old man said and pointed at the computer.

"Where did you get that?" Buddy asked, staring at the group of photos on the screen.

Miss Emma gleamed with self-satisfaction. "When I was still living at Golden Vista, my daughter gave me a new camera phone to have fun with so I started practicing. I had no idea how to put the pictures on my computer, but just kept taking photos of everything interesting I saw, trying to figure out how to work the darn thing."

Rachel bent over Miss Emma and gazed at the photo of a dark, elegantly dressed man walking next to a tall black man with a body-building physique. "You got their photo! This is priceless, Miss Emma. You are quite the woman."

"I thought you might appreciate these. And there's more."

She clicked through several photos, some with Brick Krutzer in them. "That's all I got."

"That's more than enough." Rachel turned to Buddy. "This is wonderful."

"So what do we do with them? Buddy asked.

"Let's make copies for Deputy Tucker. And let's make another copy for Alex Tucker."

"We could fly them out to Alex ourselves. Maybe he has some way to identify these guys if they really are from LA."

Rachel hesitated. "That might be a good idea." She

turned to Emma. "Are there any other photos—like maybe of Zoe Liddy?"

Emma flicked through several more photos taken at Golden Vista until she found one of Zoe standing face front. "Ask and you shall receive."

"Oh, Emma, this is wonderful." Rachel cocked her head and gave Buddy a grin. "We could ask Alex to give copies of Zoe's photo to the vice squad so they could be on the lookout for her."

"You couldn't just fax them?" Hank asked.

Buddy shook his head. "No. I have his home address and I'd prefer if we just dropped in so we aren't left out of the loop. I want to be sure he's willing to help us. He's not that far from my office so I could check in with my staff while we're there."

"So, okay," Rachel said, looking around at everyone. "Let's print these babies out."

∽∽∽

When they arrived in LA, Buddy decided to stop by Byron Edward McCain & Associates first. Rachel had been in the dramatically designed building before—which had been decorated by Heather—but it never ceased to impress her every time she saw it.

Buddy jovially greeted his employees as he and Rachel walked past several offices.

A client, who was conferring with one of the accountants, turned in her seat and spotted them. The statuesque redhead cried "Buddy!" and jumped up out of her seat. She ran to him, wrapped her arms around him, and gave him a wet kiss on the mouth. Rachel took a step back.

When Buddy disentangled himself from the young woman's grip, he mumbled an introduction to Rachel. The woman barely touched Rachel's outstretched hand.

"You look familiar," Rachel said.

"You may have seen me in the magazines," she replied with a raised eyebrow. "I model for Samantha's Closet."

Rachel felt a prick in her heart. She was familiar with the catalog and the sexy lingerie it promoted—along with the leggy, large-breasted models. "Yes, I recognize you now." She forced a smile and didn't care if it looked genuine.

Buddy awkwardly led Rachel out of the area. "She kisses everyone like that. Don't worry about it."

"Did you think I was worried?"

"Not really. But I didn't want you to get the wrong idea."

Later, in the car, Rachel asked, "Do you date her?"

Buddy turned his head. "Who?"

"You know—Miss Boobs."

Buddy laughed. "Heck no. I have taken her to lunch, though. I often take clients to lunch, especially the ones who will steer more business our way."

"And she has?"

"Oh, yes. Most of Samatha's models are our clients."

Her curiosity satisfied, not to mention her jealously quelled, Rachel turned her attention to the road. "We must be pretty close to Alex's house by now. It looks pretty residential here. Somehow he didn't seem like the homeowner type."

"You never know. According to the GPS, the house should be on the next block. If he's not home, we'll call."

The house was a typical California tract house built during the 80s, with a grass front yard. Alex's truck sat in the driveway in front of a two-car garage. It was four o'clock when they pulled in behind the truck and got out of Buddy's car.

Rachel started to feel anxious as they approached the door. *Maybe we should have called ahead. He was pretty upset when he left last time. What if he's rude or angry? What if—*

Buddy interrupted her thoughts with a hug and reassuring smile and pressed the doorbell.

Alex opened the door and stared speechlessly at the faces of Rachel and Buddy. His face registered something between shock and horror.

Rachel's face flooded with embarrassment. *Oh boy, this was a big mistake.*

Buddy spoke first. "Hi, Alex. May we come in? Or is this a bad time?"

Alex opened his mouth to speak but before he got a word out a feminine voice called out from the kitchen. "Who is it, honey?"

Rachel froze at the sound of the female voice and a wave of nausea washed over her. *What? He has a wife?*

"Friends from Arizona," Alex answered, and his voice cracked.

Rachel's mind raced. *He's married*? She stared at him wide-eyed as the shock passed and anger surged through her blood. *Of course! The liar! How could I have not seen it?* Before she could speak, an attractive young woman appeared, wiping her hands on her apron. Her eyes were sparkling, and inky black curls fell past her shoulders.

"Hi, I'm Marcie," she said, extending her hand. She had a glowing smile with white, even teeth. "Welcome. Come on in. What can I get you to drink?"

Chapter 17

Although a thousand thoughts swirled around in her head, Rachel shook the hand held out to her. "Thank you, Mrs. Tucker," she said, recovering, "but we're fine. We aren't going to stay long."

"Oh, please call me Marcie," she graciously replied. "We're pretty informal here. Come in and sit down."

Marcie turned to lead their guests into the living room and Rachel took the moment to give Alex a look of fury and disgust.

"Have a seat," he said quickly, his voice breaking with nervousness. "It's great to see you guys."

"It's nice to see you again, too, Alex." Rachel glared at him, her face hard and unforgiving.

Marcia caught the look between them and an awkward silence swallowed up the room.

Buddy cleared his throat and snapped open his briefcase. "I know you're busy, Alex, so we'll make this quick. We had some business in LA so we thought we'd stop by to show you some photographs. We're hoping you'll be able to help us identify the people in them."

"Photos?" he asked with relief. Sweat shined on his forehead and he held out his hand. "Sure, I'd be glad to take a look."

Buddy handed over three of the photographs Hank had printed out of Miss Emma's computer. "First, I'd like you to look these over. They're shots of Zoe Liddy and we were wondering if she might be in your area. Your uncle told us a lot of women who are kidnapped in the southwest are either taken to Houston or LA to be used as prostitutes. You might remember hearing about her—the woman who went missing from Golden Vista?"

"Yes, yes. I know all about what happened." Alex became deeply engrossed in the prints, trying to avoid Rachel's eyes. "So you're thinking she might be working in LA?" His eyes were fixated on the photos. "It's very possible she could be here, considering the amount of women moving into the area. I could give these to vice and they could try to find her."

"That's what we're hoping for. I have some other photos I'd like you to look at, too." Buddy handed another stack of prints to Alex. "These are two men whom we believe are buying young girls from Brick Krutzer."

"Yeah, Uncle Tucker mentioned that, too, the last time I saw him. But he thought maybe some local sex offender was involved."

"Some sex offender *was* involved," Rachel said, "but he just hasn't done any time. Not yet, anyway. Brick

Krutzer is probably the worst sex offender of them all, but nobody has been able to pin anything on him." Her gaze settled on Alex and she could feel him squirm in his chair.

He studied the photographs again and finally turned to his visitors. "I know these guys."

Rachel's eyes widened. "You do?"

"Yeah, their names are Jim Shandellan and Robert Hampton." His voice was tinged with scorn.

Buddy leaned forward anxiously in his seat. "Do you think they could be buying girls from Brick and flying them back to LA? If they are, they probably transported Zoe in the last group of girls."

"Yeah, they definitely could be up to something like that." Alex tapped one of the prints. "This shot here is very important—this one with Brick. It ties them together at his rest home." He looked up at Buddy. "This could help both of us. I'll personally see to it that these photos get in the right hands."

Buddy closed his briefcase and stood up. "We'd appreciate anything you can do, Alex."

Rachel stood up and turned to Marcie. "Thank you for letting us take up your husband's time, Marcie."

"I wish you could stay longer," she offered. This time her voice sounded tentative.

Rachel reached out to shake her hand. "Thank you so much. That's very kind of you, but we need to get back to Arizona tonight."

Alex followed them out, shutting the door behind him.

Rachel suddenly turned to him and extended her hand. "Good-bye Alex," she said, looking directly into his eyes. "And don't worry. I won't say anything to your *wife.*"

"Rachel, let me—"

"Good-bye Alex," she said again, refusing to listen to any explanation. Then she quickly turned away.

Buddy held the car door open for her. She slid into the passenger seat without a glance in Alex's direction.

Buddy turned on the ignition. Rachel turned to him and watched him until they pulled out into the street. She turned her head and stared out the windshield. "Did you know?"

"No." He hesitated and softened his voice. "I kind of wondered if he had a girlfriend, but I didn't want to say anything in case I was wrong." He paused. "I didn't expect we'd find out like that."

"Me neither."

"You okay?"

Rachel thought a bit while pieces of the puzzle of Alex Tucker fell into place. She turned to Buddy and her eyes lit up with a smile. "Better than I have been in a long time."

They drove on, comfortable with each other, and when they were about an hour from home, Rachel called Heather. "Hey, sis, you still up?"

"Yes, and we want to see you. We'll wait up. Just come by."

"Is everything okay? You sound a little—"

"We'll explain when you get here. There's no need

to worry." Heather hung up the phone and sat on the sofa next to JT.

He raised his eyebrows. "You just told your sister a big, fat lie."

"No I didn't. We'll figure something out. We have to."

Silence filled the living room like a heavy weight. JT looked down at the stack of books on the end table, the single rose in the crystal vase, the scented candle flickering under the slowly rotating ceiling fan. *What can I do? How can I protect my wife?* He unfolded the paper in his hand.

Heather leaned into him for comfort. "Read it out loud again."

"You have it memorized."

"I know. But I can think better if you read it."

JT's deep voice filled the room.

> "'Your time is now up—
> It's the end of your story.
> You're all going out
> In a big blaze of glory.'"

જ�જ�

It started spitting rain at eight o' clock the following morning. Heather and Rachel shared an umbrella on the way to the café when a faint rainbow arched itself over the western sky. "Look! A rainbow," Heather cried, pointing to it. "That means there's hope. Everything will work out."

Rachel watched the rainbow quickly fade from sight. "Even if it didn't last long?"

"Oh, ye of little faith," Heather responded and then heard Buddy call to them.

"Hey wait up! Is Tucker coming for breakfast?

"Yes," Heather answered, stopping to wait for him. "JT called him early this morning and they're already inside."

The three of them slid inside the large booth in the corner and exchanged greetings with the Deputy Sheriff and JT.

Buddy asked if they came to any conclusions about the poems.

The deputy nervously pulled at his long walrus mustache. "The only thing we can figure out is that whoever the guy is, it sounds like he's gonna either torch the inn or plant a bomb somewhere."

"I have to agree with that and it sounds horrible," Rachel said, stirring her coffee, "but I still don't understand the motive behind it. If we could figure that out, we might know who the poet is."

Buddy nodded in agreement. "Right. But who'd want to hurt JT? And who's strong enough to wire up a pig in our pool?"

"The trouble is you folks think too kindly of others," the deputy said. "You don't realize there are some people out there crazier than bestsy-bugs. They don't gotta have a motive."

Rachel smacked her forehead. "That's it! Crazy is the operative word here. It has to be the Venkmans. Remember how they went bonkers after Otto's death and blamed *us*?" She turned to Heather. "And what about the time when the Johnsons went to eat at Domino's? Lily said Anna went psycho when she found out you guys recommended the place. She said there was definitely something wrong with her, remember?"

"That's right," Heather recalled. "But do you really think Anna could do something like that? I mean try to murder people? She'd have to have help. And even as big as she is, there's no way she could have done that pig-in-the-pool trick alone."

JT finally spoke. "Anna would have had to hire some help, that's true, but then she's got the money to do that. She may even be angry that her restaurant isn't doing all that well and blames us for that, too."

Tucker cleared his throat. "I'm bettin' you folks ain't heard the latest on that deal."

All eyes turned toward him.

"I heard Anna Venkman is bein' sued for using the Domino's name."

"What?" JT asked. "You've got to be kidding."

"I ain't kidding. A famous pizza place ain't gonna take kindly to other people usin' their name. I don't blame 'em, either."

JT's eyes filled with dread. "Oh, boy. If only we knew for sure that the Venkman's were at the bottom of all this—"

"Then what?" Heather asked.

The table turned quiet as everyone digested what was said and contemplated the big question.

Rachel held up a finger. "I have an idea."

❦

By the middle of the afternoon, speckles of clouds were floating west, forming a blanket on the horizon. Heather drove Rachel to Old Town Mesquite and parallel parked in a spot not far from Domino's.

She frowned and studied Rachel carefully. "Are you sure you want to go through with this?"

"Yes. We've got to do something to force her to show her hand."

Heather nodded in understanding. Rachel opened the passenger door of the Hyundai and slid out. "I just hope I can get her mad enough to do something stupid."

"Please be careful, sweetie. I'll be right here by my phone if you need to call for help." She gave Rachel a half-smile. "At least I know you can run faster than she can."

Rachel walked away, turned, and gave her sister a quick reassuring wave.

It was less than a minute later when she arrived at the restaurant with the large black and white sign announcing Domino's. *I wonder how long that sign will stay up there—if Anna is really being sued, that is. It could be just another one of Tucker's juicy rumors.*

A couple of people were sitting in the sidewalk café drinking tea and eating French pastry. It was the hottest time of the day, a hundred and three, and it was three o' clock, the slowest time of day in the restaurant business.

Rachel stepped inside the entrance, glanced around, and was immediately impressed with the massive crystal chandeliers and gilt-framed mirrors that beckoned people in. She had seen the restaurant only once before when she was able to gain entry while it was still under renovation. She was concerned, even at that time, that Domino's would be a formidable rival. It certainly was a beautiful place, but thankfully, at that hour, the restaurant was void of customers.

A new Domino manikin was stationed near the hostess station and Rachel approached it, her heels tapping on the marble floor.

She smiled as the harlequin-patterned figure turned its head and waved its arm to welcome her.

"Hello," it said in a mechanical voice. "Welcome to Domino's."

Rachel noticed the manikin was attached to the wall with a length of wire. Anna Venkman apparently wasn't taking any chances on her precious Domino falling to the floor again and meeting an untimely demise. Too bad.

Before she had the chance to check out the place further, Anna tramped toward her. She was nearly six feet tall and outweighed Rachel by seventy pounds.

"What do *you* want?"

"I want to talk to you for a minute."

Anna stared at her with narrow eyes filled with hatred. "Just get out."

"I will, but not before I tell you that we know all

about your little plan," Rachel chirped, blinking with innocence.

Anna's blonde hair was pulled back severely in a bun and her steely blue eyes glared at Rachel. "I have no idea what you're talking about," she said, turning her face away. She spoke in a cold monotone as if talking to the interloper were a total waste of her time.

"The cutesy little poems?" Rachel continued, ignoring the order to leave. "Very amateurish, by the way. I did better in the second grade. Your meter was off and they weren't very original, you know."

Anna's turned back at the insults, her face flushed with anger. "I told you I have no idea what you're talking about. Now get out!"

Rachel remained calm and kept her voice conversational. "I can't help wondering, though, how you managed to pull off that pig thing. I can't picture you climbing into the pool all by yourself, lugging a pig. But then again, you're muscular and big enough to lift one." Her eyes went up and down along the woman's frame. "Fat enough, too."

Anna's jaw clenched and a vein popped out on her forehead. Her hands tightened into knots and she slowly advanced toward Rachel.

Rachel took a step back and noticed a movement at the edge of the main room. "What? Is that Benny Ammato?"

Anna quickly turned her head to see if Benny was standing there. He wasn't.

Rachel continued on in a voice loud enough to be

heard all over the room. "My, my, Anna. Now you're keeping company with known felons? You can come out now, Benny. I've already seen you. In fact, you might want to pack up and head out of town if you don't want to end up in the slammer again."

Anna raised her hands, fingers like claws ready to pounce, and her face twisted into a grimace.

Rachel wisely took another step back, her hands raised slightly in surrender. "I'm leaving, don't worry, but I'm looking forward to seeing you at the inn. We're watching your every move, Anna. Your *every* move. We'll be expecting you soon." She beamed her insincere, condescending smile. "Just wanted to let you know." She turned and rushed out the door.

When she jumped into the car, Heather asked her how it went.

"Better than I had hoped."

"She got mad?"

"I ran out just before she lunged for me."

"Great!"

"Yeah. She was mad enough to do me some major damage."

"Then it was good that you got away before she could get to you."

"Even better, I figured out who she had helping her," Rachel said and punched in Deputy Tucker's number.

༺༻

The women went home to tell JT and Buddy what

had transpired at Domino's. They were at the Hibiscus Café having coffee and pie. The room was quiet except for an older couple who were just leaving.

When Rachel finished her story, JT voiced his concern. "Are you sure it was Benny Ammato?"

"Are you kidding? I'd know that little weasel anywhere. He tried to duck when he spotted me, but I saw him."

"That whole pool debacle makes sense now," Heather said. "Benny was very muscular. He could have easily lifted that pig. He was familiar with the swimming pool, too, and I bet he rigged up that mechanism to make it pop up when Mrs. Thornton touched the wire."

JT rubbed his head. "I never would have imagined he had a connection with Anna Venkman."

"Yeah, we might have figured this whole thing out a lot sooner if we had known," Rachel said.

Heather clasped her sister's hand. "That's okay. But we know now, so that's all the really matters, right?"

Buddy finished his pie and pushed his plate away. "So now we go to step two, right?"

"Right," Rachel answered. "One of the maintenance guys is already stationed at the bottom of the hill behind a curve and some boulders," Rachel answered. "There's only one way up and one way down, so Anna, Benny, or whomever she sends, has to go right by him."

"What if the person climbs up the mountain instead?" Heather asked.

"Climbs up the mountain with a gallon of gasoline or a bomb? It's at least a half-mile."

Heather lowered her eyes. "Not too possible, I guess."

"No. In fact, I think she'll wait and make her move at night like before, with or without Benny."

⁙

Earlier that afternoon, as soon as Rachel had left Domino's, Anna Venkman spun around and stormed back to the alcove. She accosted Benny Ammato. "You idiot! Why did you let her see you?"

"Obviously, I didn't think she would," he snapped back. "It doesn't matter now, anyway. I'm done. You need to pay me what you owe me and I'll be on my way."

"Absolutely not! You'll stay and finish the job you agreed to."

He raised an eyebrow at her. "Oh really? Well, here's a news flash, Anna: I'm history. And I want the cash right now for the pig thing, cutting the brake line, and getting the kid to do the truck."

"No. Not a cent until you complete the work."

Benny stared at her. "Don't be stupid, Anna. All I have to do is make one phone call and it's all over for you." Benny's lip curled into a sneer. "But knowing you, you might enjoy prison."

Anna's eyes opened in anger. She crossed her arms over her chest and her voice turned low and taunting. "Go ahead and call. You'll be the one that gets arrested. You're the one who found the guy with the bomb. I don't even know who he is. You're the one who hired the kid and wired up the pig. I knew absolutely nothing about it. It will be your word against mine, and you're a felon who's running from the law."

Benny and Anna glowered at each other for several seconds.

Anna never noticed Benny slip his hand under his jacket. But she definitely noticed the pistol when he pointed it at her.

"Give me my two thousand," Benny said in a quiet voice. "I know you've got it in the safe. And you owe me the money. So let's calmly walk over to the office right now."

Anna stared down at the gun in silence.

"Don't even think about it, sweetheart. I got nothing to lose. The LA cops are looking for me to do some serious time, so we can part friends or you can be looking at the pearly gates. It's up to you."

They glared at each other for several seconds, and Anna blinked first. Her face sagged in defeat. "Okay. We'll part friends, but I still need the bomb. I don't even know who's got it."

Benny looked off, contemplating what he should do. "Okay. It should be ready by now and I can get it for you. I'll even show you how to set it, but you'll have to give me another grand when I do. I'm taking a risk by doing that. If I were ever to get caught with it, it's all over for me."

She clenched her teeth and thought a minute. This was her one chance to even the score with JT Carpenter. "All right. Let's get it done."

Chapter 18

Rachel opened the door to the maintenance shop. Toro was standing behind the workbench repairing a dresser drawer.

"Hey, Miss Rachel. What's going on?"

"I just wanted to double check with you about tonight." She walked up to the table and stood beside the huge Indian. "Did you grow an extra four inches?"

Toro chuckled. "No. You just changed your shoes."

Rachel looked down at the turquoise-beaded sandals that matched her slacks and laughed. "Yeah, I forgot about those."

Toro finished tightening the vise he was working with. "So you think Anna's gonna show up tonight?"

"I'm betting on it. We need to be ready, regardless."

"I'm with you there. I'm gonna relieve Javier at ten-thirty. As soon as someone comes up the hill that I don't know and passes the curve, I'm pulling out and following them like cat hair on black pants."

"And you'll call me, right?"

"You bet."

Rachel's gaze swept around the little room and she sat on the metal stool next to the bench. "I wanted to ask you about something. It's a little personal, but you don't have to answer if you don't want to."

Toro looked down at her. "What do you want to know?"

Rachel shifted around on the stool trying to get comfortable. "Remember you told me about the scar on your face, and how you went to prison for killing a guy in a bar fight?"

Toro's eyes narrowed a bit and he answered with hesitation. "Yeah…"

"You never said who the guy was."

"I know."

Rachel softened her voice. "I heard it was David Cutter, one of the guys that hung out with Brick Krutzer."

Toro looked at her steadily, but said nothing.

"You were protecting Brandi that night, weren't you."

He turned his face away.

Rachel waited, letting the statement hang in the air.

He let out a breath. "She told me what they did to her that night, the night they picked her up and brought—"

"I know what happened, Toro. It was horrible."

"A few weeks later, I was drinking at the Snake Pit. Brick and his crew show up, drunk or high on something.

I leave the bar, and that's when I see them outside. I had a few beers, a couple of shots, but I was sober enough to see who was there. Then Brandi comes up looking for her mother. She used to hang out at the bar a lot. They see Brandi and try to stop her from going in and start messing with her and taunting her. I tell them to shut up and leave her alone. Cutter gets in my face and I'm pretty sure I push him away. He falls. Then we really get into it."

Rachel saw the pain in his eyes. "I can understand that. You were her friend."

"I hated Cutter," Toro said with emotion. His eyes narrowed and his gaze drifted away. "I hated all of them for what they did. And I was drunk. I lost control, totally lost it." He slowly shook his head. "I beat him to death. I didn't even know he died until they came after me the next day."

Toro hung his head and was still.

"Oh, Toro, I am so sorry that you had to spend time in prison for that." Rachel looked at him with an aching heart. "But I'm not sorry you killed him," she added bitterly. "I wish I could kill the rest of them myself."

"Oh, don't say that, Miss Rachel. It's a terrible thing to have to live with all your life."

"Maybe so. But it's a travesty they got away with such a heinous crime."

"Yeah, it was. But that's the way life is sometimes."

She looked up at Toro with deep sadness in her eyes. "I tried my best to find out what there were up to at Golden Vista, but I screwed it all up. I even got served with a restraining order. I am so sorry, Toro."

"I heard about what happened. But that's okay. It ain't over yet."

"What do you mean?"

"Just that it ain't over yet. They'll keep on doing what they're doing, and they can't keep it up forever. It'll catch up with them sooner or later."

"Maybe so. I just hope I live to see it, Toro."

"Yeah, I hope I do, too."

༺༻

At ten-thirty that night, Rachel received a phone call from Toro.

"I just took over the shift from Javier. He said nobody came up the road that didn't belong here. I'll be here until four, and then Jason will come in to relieve me."

"That's a long shift, Toro. Are you going to be okay?"

"Yeah. I went home and took a long nap after my regular hours. I'm feeling great and ready for whatever happens."

"Thank you, Toro. I'm just grateful we have you on the job."

Rachel set her phone down on the café table and looked at her companions. She and Buddy were sitting opposite the Carpenters at one of the booths in front of the windows. The restaurant was officially closed and they sat in the semi-darkness. From their position they could see the lights of the town of Mesquite and the edge of the road that that led to the valley.

"This is great," Buddy remarked. "From our vantage point, we can see everyone who comes up the hill."

Rachel pushed aside the placemat aside she had been folding. "Now all we have to do is wait."

"Couldn't we just take turns?" Heather asked. "This is kind of nerve-wracking."

Rachel's phone rang again before she could speak.

It was Toro. "Anna Venkman just passed by, going up the hill, and I'm following her now. I called Deputy Tucker and he said he was on his way."

Everyone was suddenly alert. They sat quietly and watched the edge of the road from the window.

In a short time, a new red Lexus came up the hill followed by a cloud of dust. It pulled into the middle of the parking lot, circled around and faced the road. Anna seemed to take a while to pull herself together and get out of the car. Toro pulled up next to her.

The group in the café could see them talking, both appearing to be calm. They watched Anna turn and lumber her way toward the café. Toro faced them and shrugged.

JT spoke: "Well, this was unexpected. Let's get ready." He exited the booth and stood; the others followed. He reached around behind him and felt for the gun he had placed there earlier.

Heather grimaced. "I hope you don't have to use that."

"I hope so, too."

Anna Venkman sauntered into the lobby, then into

the dim light of the café as if she were in no hurry. She had a bland expression on her face, almost one of peace. JT felt the hair on his neck stand up.

"What are you doing here, Anna?" he asked.

She continued strolling up to them and set her designer tote on one of the chairs nearby. She held up her hands and spoke calmly. "I'm not packing, so you can relax."

"So what do you want?"

She shot a look at Rachel. "I want you to keep that skinny bag of bones away from my restaurant." Her voice was firm and oddly calm. "I don't want her, or any one of you, accusing me of whatever you're dreaming up these days. If you do, or if I ever hear that you have maligned me or my family in any way, I will take you to court so fast you won't even be able to blink."

"So you deny sending me notes?"

"You've got to be joking," she said haughtily. "I'm far too busy with my restaurant to be sending anybody anything." She swung her arm out and pointed her finger at Rachel. Her venomous anger spewed out of her mouth. "And, *you*! Don't ever show your ugly face near me ever again!"

Everyone jumped back, and they all stood there momentarily speechless as she turned and tromped out of the café. They watched her reach the parking lot and looked at each other.

"Well, that was interesting," Rachel said.

Before she could say another word, Heather sprang forward. "Look! She left her purse!" Heather made a dash for it, and before anyone could speak, she picked it up and ran after Anna, calling out to her.

JT and Rachel looked at each other and had the same thought. "A bomb!"

Rachel took off like a shot and the others ran after her.

"Stay back!" she screamed at them and called out to Heather to stop.

Anna had stopped near her car, and saw Heather running toward her with the purse. "No!" she said, holding out her hands. Heather continued running to her and Anna backed away until she brushed against the car. "No!" she shouted, "Go back!"

At the same time, Heather heard Rachel screaming at her to stop. She did, only to see her sister madly tearing after her. She turned back to Anna and was puzzled to see the super-sized woman run toward the road.

Rachel screamed at her. "It's a bomb!"

Heather looked down at the tote and finally realized, with horror, what she was holding. "Oh God, help me!" she cried, as she gently set the purse down next to the car. She quickly turned and ran toward the café with her hands over her ears. Rachel spun around and joined her.

When they arrived at the hotel entrance, Buddy grabbed them and pulled them far into the lobby. JT ran to the lounge. It had no windows, but he had no idea what kind of damage the building could sustain from a bomb blast.

He screamed into the room, "Everyone get down on the floor and cover your heads, NOW!" Everyone stared at him. "*Now*! *Do it*! There's a *bomb*!"

When JT's deep voice shouted out the word "bomb," the patrons in the lounge all scrambled at once to get to the floor and crawl under the tables. JT ran back out to the lobby and huddled with everyone against the wall.

ත්‍රේ

When Deputy Tucker responded to Toro's call and drove up the hill to the Inn, he caught Anna in his headlights running down the road like a mad woman. He squealed to a stop beside her, kicking up a cloud of dirt. Anna continued running down the hill past him, and he called out to her to stop. At that moment a bright light flashed in the night, and a loud explosion shook the ground.

Two of the café windows blew in. Pieces of a new red Lexus flew through the air. Some hit the outside of the bar and landed on the roof. The rest burst into flames.

Rachel was crowded together with the others when the shock hit. They stared at each other, realizing how they all narrowly escaped death, and Heather shook from the aftershock.

Rachel was the first to speak. "No more designer purse," she said, solemnly.

Heather burst into laughter at the incongruity of the statement and then sobbed from the tension of narrowly escaping being blown apart. JT wrapped his muscular arms around her and held her tightly.

Back outside, Tucker was thrown against his truck

from the blast and a piece of the Lexus flew against the door and bounced at his feet.

Anna was also hit with a shock wave and fell into a ditch by the edge of the road. As she did, she felt her ankle crack.

Tucker walked down the road and found her crying in the ditch. He looked at the pieces of Lexus scattered on the road then back at the whimpering woman. He had to repress a smile. "Too bad about your car, ma'am."

⁂

JT headed back to the lounge and made sure no one was injured. He was thankful it wasn't a weekend when the place would have been packed with dancers. There was no damage to the inside because the slump block wall provided protection for everyone. The patrons were subdued and JT informed them they could have a free pie and coffee while an emergency crew cleaned up the roadway of debris.

It was almost midnight when the ambulance took Anna away with its lights flashing. Evan, one of the EMTs, turned to Rachel before they left. "You know, we've got to stop meeting like this."

Rachel smiled. "This is the last time, Evan, I promise."

"You mean that?" Buddy asked, as he sided up to her.

"I do. I'm done with the detective business. I've decided I'd like to live a quiet life for a change."

"Ha!" JT said. "I'll believe that one when I see it."

"I gotta get going," Deputy Tucker said. "Duty calls. I'll be at the clinic with my prisoner if you need me."

"Thanks for coming when you did," Rachel said, placing her hand on his shoulder. "I'm so thankful you didn't get hurt from the blast."

"Nah. I'm too ornery for that." He looked at her with respect. "Well, your plan worked, little lady. I'm just grateful it ended the way it did."

"You and me both," JT said, holding his hand out to the deputy. "And I just want you to know I appreciate everything you've done to end this nightmare."

The deputy shook his hand and tipped his Stetson. "Just part of the job, my friend."

∽∽∽

Buddy and Rachel took the path through the courtyard back to their casitas.

"Did you really mean that about wanting to live a simple life?" he asked.

Rachel gave him a sideways glance. "Well, not simple if you mean a log cabin in the woods."

"You mean you're ready to settle down?" Buddy pulled her down on a bench.

"Well, maybe not exactly. The mystery of my parents is solved. That was the big thing, the thing that kept driving me. It kept me from any peace I might have. But now I know my father was a hero."

Buddy nodded. "He certainly was, and I can understand how you feel." He held her hand. "It must be a tremendous relief to know the truth."

"Yes it is, more than you'll ever know."

He squeezed her hand gently. "Have you heard any more from Jared?"

"Yes, but I wanted to tell you when we had some quiet time like this, so we could talk it over." She took a breath. "Remember the treasurer, Benson Hildebrand, who plotted with the CEO? They found his family. It turned out he hung himself not long after they had my father killed. They couldn't find any of the paperwork that my dad left, but they found out he hacked into their system and knew he would have left some kind of evidence against them. So rather than sweating out every day waiting for the FBI to come after them, they decided to drop the whole plan. They sold the company stock, closed the doors of Varner-Walther, and disappeared."

"How did Jared come to that conclusion?"

"He had to sort out bits of information and put it all together." Rachel dropped her gaze. "He—uh—also has an old FBI friend at Langley.

"Ah—and what else did the friend say?"

"They found Varner in Italy. He's now old and riddled with a horrible kind of blood cancer that eats your bones. They are going to extradite him to Michigan, but they're not sure when. He's got 'round-the-clock nurses and the morphine he takes has lost its potency. His wife died last year, he has no kids, and he's in agony all the time. He actually was relieved to be found and wants to come back to the U.S. to die."

"So he confessed?"

"Pretty much. He wanted to clear his conscience—or so he said—and confessed to the amoeba plot. But he blamed Hildebrand for planning and executing the murder. He said he had nothing to do with it."

"Do you believe that?"

"No. But it doesn't matter at this point. No matter what the state could do to him, it could never be worse that what he's going through now. He's suffering terribly and he knows he's going to die alone, a bitter and helpless old man. Jared thinks they might prosecute anyway because his crime is so heinous—if they can get him here before he dies." She turned away from his eyes and focused off in the distance. "I've thought about going out there, just to see the man. Maybe spit in his face."

"Really?"

"Well, maybe not the part about spitting in his face. But I have thought about going out there—just for the closure. It really messed my life up, you know."

"Yes, I do know. And if you really want to go, I'll go with you."

She quickly turned to him. "You would?"

"Of course, I would."

She pulled back a bit to look at him. "You're a jewel among men, you know that?"

"I'm glad you're finally getting around to noticing that," he teased. He pulled her up from the bench close to him. "So now we can celebrate two solved mysteries—your dad and mom's death, and the crazy, murderous poet. You *are* free to settle down."

"Yeah, except for the problem with Golden Vista," she said and began to stroll through the courtyard. "I feel really bad about how I let everyone down, Buddy."

"I don't quite understand that, but I'm sure you can explain it better to me back at my place."

She laughed a rich, full laugh. "Okay. We could use a nightcap to take the edge off, anyway."

They continued walking. "But I just got another idea!" she said.

Buddy stopped cold and turned to her. "You're kidding right?"

Her eyes twinkled. "Maybe. Or maybe not."

Chapter 19

It was about a week later when Rachel was in her office, gazing through the French doors into the lobby. The weight of depression felt heavy on her shoulders. She still struggled with the memory of the night she climbed over the wall onto Golden Vista's property—and got caught, ruining everything. Now she was totally out of the loop. Brick knew she was spying on him, and she felt helpless about being able to find Zoe or rescue any young girls Brick's crew might kidnap. She wished she had more faith in Deputy Tucker and the whole justice system, but she'd seen firsthand how the scales of justice were often tipped.

Restless, she stood up and began to pace. There had to be a way to help. "Just use your brain, Rachel," she muttered while she walked back and forth across her office. Her sassy red shoes seemed to mock her. *It's your own fault, stupid. If you'd just learn to follow orders, you could have helped to catch that scumbag by now. But, no, you had to take it upon yourself to go over the wall.*

"What are you doin' there, girl? Tryin' to wear out the carpet?"

Rachel jumped at the voice. Deputy Tucker leaned up against the office door frame with his Stetson in his hand.

"I was just thinking. If that's okay with you, that is. And don't startle me like that."

"Well, I had to say somethin' to get your attention. I didn't know you were wound up like a banjo string."

A flush of embarrassment rose up her neck. "So what did you need?"

"It's lunch time. You gonna eat? I got some news and thought you might want to hear it, too."

"Is it that time already?" She looked up at the antique clock. "Okay, let me get my purse." She locked the office door behind them and they headed across the lobby.

"Is it good news?" she asked. "I could use some right now."

"Can't say it's all good. You can make up your own mind about that."

When they arrived at the Hibiscus Café, JT and Heather were already seated.

"Where's your partner?" the deputy asked JT as he took a seat in the corner booth.

"He had to go back to LA. It's still tax time for him, you know."

"Yeah, I do know. I just sent mine in—late, like I

always end up doin'." He looked up at Rachel. "You can sit next to me. I ain't gonna bite."

Dolly came right over to take their orders. "Cuban food today, folks. Paella. And it's delicious." She winked at Tucker and gave him a special smile.

Everyone ordered the special with peach iced tea.

"Okay, Dewey, tell us the news," Rachel said. "Did they find Zoe?"

"They sure did. She started talkin,' too, once they got her sober."

"Wonderful!" Heather cried. "Did they arrest the guys that kidnapped her?"

"They're still lookin' for Shandellan and Hampton. But they arrested Brick Krutzer real early this morning."

"They did? Wow!" Rachel exclaimed. "I am so excited!"

"Yep. And they got the other two, Emmett and Tackett. Charged 'em all with enough felonies to wallpaper a bathroom."

The four cheered, happy to hear justice was served, but Deputy Tucker seemed subdued.

"Something wrong?" JT asked.

"Momma put up bail for Brick, so he's out runnin' around loose."

"No!" Heather moaned. "What a disappointment."

"Yep. But everybody's got a right to bail. Even folks who are the scum of the earth."

Rachel pretended to be occupied with folding her napkin into a fan. "So I wonder what he's doing now."

Tucker narrowed his eyes at her. "I think he's back at

Golden Vista. And I think you'd best stay away from him—as far away as you can."

"He's right, Rachel," JT said. "I'd say the man's pretty unhappy with you right now and his back is up against the wall. He's even more dangerous at this point in time, if such a thing is possible."

"Oh, don't worry about me. I've given up on all that. It's in the hands of the law now."

JT looked at her. "You promise?"

Rachel rolled her eyes and huffed.

"Well?"

"Okay, okay. I promise."

"Good. So what are you ladies up to this afternoon?"

"Whatever it is, you need to stick close to town," Tucker warned. "Wind blew all night from the west and the humidity's already dropped. Probably hit a hundred and ten today."

"Not to worry," Rachel said. "We're going to take Miss Emma to the Indian Museum craft show. I believe it's indoors."

"Huh." JT thought a bit. "Well, at least you gals won't get into trouble doing that."

The deputy raised his eyebrows and gave JT a look as if to say, "You wanna bet?"

JT turned to Heather. "You *will* stay out of trouble, right?"

"Of course, sweetie. Don't be silly," she said, squeezing her husband's hand with affection.

At the same time, however, Rachel's mind was spinning.

※※※

The wind had stopped by ten that morning and the radiation from the sun was at level 9. Heather unlocked the car door for Miss Emma. "I brought some sunscreen in case the craft show is outside." She looked up at the wide expanse of sky. "It looks like we're going to need it, too."

"I always pack mine," Rachel said, patting her tote bag. "So we're in good shape."

She helped Miss Emma get settled and then sat in the back, happy to be by herself. She thought about Deputy Tucker's news as they drove into town, and she felt herself bristle like a steel brush. Brick Krutzer was walking around free.

The alligator surface of First Street jarred her out of her angry thoughts when the tires kicked up a stone that hit the underside of the car. "They sure need to resurface this road," she grumbled.

Heather laughed. "Oh, Rachel, that's just part of the charm down here."

"Charm, shmarm!" Miss Emma said. "I think you could find something positive about the city dump, Heather."

"You're probably right," Heather said and laughed again as she turned onto River Street. "Everything always has an upside."

Rachel's phone broke into song. She looked at the caller ID and saw it was Jesse Albarran.

"Hey, Jesse."

"Rachel, I need to talk to you." His voice sounded urgent.

"Right now? What's wrong?"

"Man, I don't want to say over the phone, but trust me—it's important. Are you at home?"

"No. Actually we're in town right now, a block away from the Hotel Rios. I could stop by for a minute." She tapped off the phone and leaned over the seat. "Heather, can you make a quick stop at the Hotel Rios apartments? I need to talk to Jesse. He's got a problem."

Heather made a quick turn and pulled up in front of the apartment building.

"I'll be right back," Rachel said, jumping out of the Hyundai. She ran to the entrance where Jesse was already waiting.

"Thank you!" he said, "I can't believe you were so nearby."

"What happened, Jesse? I can tell you're upset."

"Please stay? It's important," he said, ignoring her question. "I'll get you to wherever you're going."

Rachel stared at the intense look on his face. "Can't you tell me?"

"Not unless you want to lie to your sister."

Rachel understood. "Just a minute." She ran out the door to the car and Heather rolled down the window.

"I need to stay a few minutes. Jesse has a problem. Please go on without me. Jessie said he'd drive me over to the casino afterward."

Heather frowned. "Are you sure? We could wait."

"No, no. I'll be there shortly and I'll call you so we can re-connect."

Heather hesitated.

"Go ahead. I'll be there soon," Rachel urged, then turned, and ran back into the building.

"Did you lie?"

"No. Now tell me."

He looked over her shoulder and watched Heather pull away. "Change of plans," Jesse said. "I think we can do this." He grabbed Rachel's hand and pulled her to the back door.

"Do *what,* Jesse?" she asked, as he tugged her along.

"I'll tell you on the way," he said, pulling her to a car.

"This is your ride? What happened to your truck?" she asked.

"I still have it, but I got a good deal on this baby. I just couldn't pass it up."

Rachel stared at the red Porsche as Jessie opened the door for her. "Wow!" she said, as she slid into the passenger seat.

Jessie's grin was wide. "I knew you'd like her." He closed the door, ran around to the driver's side, and started up the engine to a low purr.

"She sounds wonderful! Let her rip!"

Jesse squealed out of the parking place and spun a U-turn to get to River Street. "I know a short cut," he said.

"A short cut to where, Jesse?"

"I don't know yet."

"What? You're taking me somewhere and you don't know where we're going?"

"Sort of."

She squinted at him. "Does this have anything to do with Brick Krutzer getting out of jail today?"

"Smart girl."

"I heard Brick's mother bailed sonny-boy out."

"It wasn't his mother."

"What?" Rachel looked at him critically. "Deputy Tucker said she did."

"Tucker said she did because that's what he *assumed*. She *was* going to bail him out, but at the last minute she ended up in Yuma Regional because she had a stroke over this whole thing. Somebody else bailed him out." He grinned that wide grin of his again. "And I know who the person was because my friend Gordo Sanchez was the guy that handled the paperwork."

"Really?" Her mind began to click through the various possibilities. "So who paid the bail?"

"A great big bear of a guy, must have weighed three-fifty, with hands that looked like they could squeeze a pig in them. Gordo said he wore a black suit and tie. The guy's name was Bogavich or something like that. He could have been a Russian."

Rachel frowned. "I would have expected Shandellan to be the one who'd bail out Brick. Or Hampton." She stared out the windshield, thinking, never noticing the rows of Eucalyptus trees that lined the edge of the road near the airport. "But then again, the police are looking for him, and he probably knows it. So he wouldn't be stupid and show up at a police station. He'd send someone else."

"Well, there's more." Jessie stomped on the gas at that point and pulled onto a two-lane road. "I think we've gained on them by at least ten minutes."

"Gained on *who*, Jessie? You need to tell me what's going on!

"Okay, okay. Let me get on dead cow road and get away from traffic first."

She held her breath while Jessie passed several vehicles. In a minute he made the turn. The road dipped and turned, but it was free of traffic.

He leaned on the accelerator. "When Gordo called me early this morning, I sat in the office with my binoculars and watched everyone who went in and out of Golden Vista."

"What? You *spied* on everyone?"

"You bet I did, man." His face turned grim. "Rachel, I know darned well Brick killed my best friend. I intend to watch him day and night until I see him arrested for murder one."

Rachel glanced down at the speedometer. The Porsche hit 90. "So obviously you saw something."

"I saw the big Russian drive up to the entrance of Golden Vista in a black SUV with limousine-dark windows in the back. Brick was in the front passenger seat. The back door opened and out pops a guy who looked dark, foreign maybe. Very well dressed. He had a goatee and wore big black rimmed glasses. Another guy got out who was tall, very well built, a black guy. But he had on dreadlocks so I didn't figure it out at first."

"That they were Shandellan and Hampton?"

"Yeah. It took me a few seconds to realize that they were in disguise. But they weren't in the Navigator when the grizzly paid the bail and picked up Brick. So I figured there were holed up in a motel somewhere."

"Ah." Rachel nodded and her eyes shifted to the speedometer again. "You're going ninety-five, Jesse."

"Man, this baby will go 120 easy."

"On this road?"

"Haven't you noticed it on the turns?"

Rachel didn't speak.

"Okay. I'll slow down. We should be catching up to them pretty quick anyway."

"*Who*, Jessie? Are you talking about Shandellan and Hampton?"

"Yes. Shandellan, Hampton, Brick, *and* the grizzly."

"Brick, too?" She stopped to think. "I wonder if they're planning on smuggling him out of the state."

"Well, I saw them all go inside Golden Vista first. After about fifteen minutes, just Shandellan and Hampton came out. They drove around back before I realized what they were doing. I ran up the stairs with the binoculars. By the time I got to the roof, they were locking up the back of the SUV and the four of them climbed into it. The Russian drove and Hampton sat up front.

"Wow." Rachel pictured the scenario in her mind. "So you think they took him with them?

"Yeah, and if they picked up the girl, they had her in

there, too. So being that I was already up there on the roof, I watched them drive away, all four of them, plus maybe even the girl—if that's what they were doing back there."

He turned to her, with a big smile plastered on his face, then looked back at the road as he passed a pick-up. "When I couldn't follow them with the binoculars anymore, I used the telescope."

"You bought a telescope? To watch Golden Vista?"

"Actually, I'm taking an internet astronomy class from AWC." He looked guilty and hunched his shoulders. "But—"

"So you *do* watch them."

"Hey man, Deputy Tucker never told *me* I couldn't watch them."

Rachel's eyes lit up with excitement. "Great, Jesse! So what did they do?"

"I saw them turn, head out past the airport onto Dead Cow Road and that's when I called you."

"So they're going out to the desert?" Rachel asked.

"Possibly. Or they're going to take the turn that leads to I-10 and head back to LA. "That's my guess. After that, they would be in the middle of the desert, and there are no turns for about twenty miles. And I doubt they'd be going out there to watch the cactus bloom."

"So do you think we can catch up?"

"I thought you wanted me to slow down." He cast a glance at the speedometer. "We've gained about seven minutes on them already.

"Wait, look!" Rachel pointed out to a plume of dust

headed north east through the desert. "That's the road that goes to Shark Tooth Mountain. Do you think that's them?"

"Well, it's still fifteen minutes to the road that goes to LA. And that's about the length of time we've been behind them."

"Can you follow them in this car?"

Jesse braked. "The car can do anything, man. But are you sure you want to?"

Rachel wasn't sure *what* she wanted, but before she could make up her mind, Jesse backed up and turned onto the dirt road. "I'll stay far enough behind them so they won't even notice us."

"In a red Porsche? You've got to be kidding."

"It doesn't matter. They're in a Lincoln SUV. Even if they turned on us, they could never catch a Porsche."

Rachel glanced at the speedometer again. "At least not this one."

"Whoa!" Jesse cried, "There they are." He slow down and handed the binoculars to Rachel. "Read me the license number."

She started reading off the numbers on the California plate.

"That's them," he interrupted. "I'm heading back."

Chapter 20

Back at the inn, JT picked up the phone. The call was from Heather.

"Hi, sweetie. How are you doing?" her cheery voice said.

JT's eyebrows furrowed. "I'm fine. But why do I have a feeling you're not?"

"Oh, Emma and I are doing great. We saw the craft show and bought a couple of things, some really nice beadwork the Indians did. Then we had some Indian fry bread."

JT's anxiety antenna shot up and its signal was circling around the area. "And Rachel? Did she eat, too?"

"Well, I guess that's why I called. She's not with us."

"Oh? What did she do this time?"

"She needed to see Jesse Albarran about something and said he would bring her over to the casino in just a few minutes. But so far, she hasn't called or answered my texts. Emma and I think maybe we ought to come home. What do you think?"

"I think you ought to come home, too. Jesse is a pretty responsible guy. He'll bring her back, I'm sure."

"Yes, you're right. But maybe you ought to alert Deputy Tucker, just in case."

JT's free hand grabbed his hair and he shook his head back and forth. *No, no, no!* He tried to hide his torment by smiling into the phone. "Okay, just in case—but what makes you think—"

"Thank you, honey! I love you!"

JT sat looking at the phone after Heather hung up and muttered. "Of all the people I could have as a sister-in-law…"

※

Rachel shot a glance at her phone. It was vibrating again and it was Heather. "I think I better answer this. I know she has to be worried."

"Rachel? Are you okay?" Heather's voice rang with angst.

"Yes, and before you get upset, I'm with Jesse and we're just talking. I'm perfectly fine."

"You sure you're okay? Just give me the code word if you're not."

Rachel laughed. "Sis, I am just fine. Please believe me and stop worrying."

"Well, Brick is out there, somewhere, you know."

"Yes, I know, and Jesse and I are being super-careful."

"So when are you coming home?"

"Pretty soon. We're out on Dead Cow Road, looking at the cactus blossoms, taking pictures." Rachel then held up her phone and shot a quick photo of the desert through the windshield. "I'm sorry? I didn't hear that last part—I think I'm losing service. We'll be back soon. Love you."

Jesse watched her disconnect. "Man, that was pretty cagy, holding up your phone to take a shot."

"Yeah, you know I can never get away with lying to my sister. And I didn't."

"Technically, no."

"So what are we doing now?"

"We're going to drive back down the road a bit and wait for them to come out. There was a place with a shell of desert varnish that would work. A palo verde tree jutted into the road that would give us some cover, too."

Rachel agreed and, once they were parked, she asked how long they would wait.

"Until they leave. There's no other way out, so they have to come out the way they went in. But my guess is that they'll keep heading west because they'll be going back to LA."

"That makes sense." Rachel pressed the seat release and tilted herself back. "In the meantime, I'm going to relax."

Jesse held the binoculars up to his eyes. "This is good. As soon as I spot them leave, I'll follow the dirt road. My guess is that they may have left something behind."

"Like the missing fourteen-year-old?"

"I don't think so. She's money in the bank. The only liability they have—"

"Is Brick," she said, interrupting. "That makes more sense than anything. He's the only one who can testify against them."

Twenty-five minutes later the black SUV started back up the road and Jesse put down his binoculars. "Yeah, it looks like they are headed back to LA."

"Should we call Deputy Tucker?"

"Not until we check out what they left in the desert." He waited until the Navigator was far enough away before he drove off the desert floor and up the road to the Shark Tooth turn off.

A cloud of dust swelled up from the Porsche as it sped up the washboard road toward the mountain.

Rachel felt every bump. "Isn't this going to wreck your car?"

"It might, but it's not my problem. My brother owns this baby."

"Your brother?"

"That's right. That's why it was such a sweet deal. He needed my truck for a fishing trip and we traded for a week." He looked at the horrified look on Rachel's face. "Oh, don't worry, I'll have it washed and polished before I give it back."

"Okay. Not my circus, not my monkey."

"What?" he asked and laughed.

"It's an old Polish saying a friend used to say."

Before he could comment further, Jesse realized he'd driven a mile already and slowed the Porsche. "Keep your eyes on the side of the road in case they dumped something—or someone."

About another quarter mile later, he slowed to a stop. A flock of turkey vultures took off into the wind. "Well, take a look at this."

Jesse and Rachel got out of the car and took a few steps.

Rachel held out her arm. "Stop. This is a crime scene. We don't want to contaminate it." She inched a little farther and winced at the sight. The bloody, beaten body of Bricknell Krutzer was stretched out on the ground, his wrists and ankles bound to stakes deep in the ground.

"Look, they swept away all their footprints." Jesse said. "Except this one over here." He pointed to a giant shoe print in the loose sand by Brick's foot.

Rachel continued to stare at the scene. Flies had found their way to the blood-soaked man and covered his face, ears, and eyes. A vulture flew down and landed on Brick's chest and pecked at his eye. He barely cried out, a weak, pitiful attempt of a shout.

"Shoo!" Rachel shouted, frightening off the ugly bird.

They both heard a whisper resonate through the quiet. "Heeeeelp. Meeeee."

"Hey, Brick. It's Rachel," she called out to what was left of the man staked to the ground. "How are you doing? Not good, huh? Gee, that's too bad, because we'd like to help you but we can't. We aren't supposed to contaminate a crime scene. I'd overlook that, even, but you've got that restraining order against me."

She looked over at Jesse, who had picked up a rock from the desert floor. He flung it at Brick's face and struck him in cheek, just below his eye.

Brick jerked his heard and barely uttered a moan.

That's for my best friend." Jesse called.

Rachel held her hand up for him to stop and looked down at the bloody man. "Hey, Brick, tell us what you guys did with the fourteen year old girl, and maybe we can help you after all."

A throaty whisper came back before it faded to nothing. "Took herrrrrr."

"They took her to LA?"

"Yeeeeees."

"So she's alive?"

"Yeeeeees."

Rachel took a couple steps back, turned to Jesse, and cocked her head. "Let's talk in the car."

When they were both inside, Jesse cranked up the air conditioner.

Rachel flipped the lever to lean the seat back. "Tucker said it was supposed to be a hundred and ten today," she said conversationally, as if she were merely giving a weather report.

"He won't last long in the heat, if that's what you're saying."

Rachel nodded. "And he's been beaten up pretty badly."

"I'm sure that was one of the reasons they brought the big Russian along."

"Yes, I do believe you're right."

"He's losing a lot of blood from the cut on his face."

"Right. And the ants are going after him, too."

They sat looking at each other for a moment.

"Okay, I guess we stalled long enough," Jesse finally said. "Now what do you want to do?"

"Right now?" She felt a calmness flow ever her and a gentle smile spread across her lips. "Nothing."

"Nothing?"

"Yes, nothing. Let's just sit and wait a few minutes."

"Until he dies?"

"Well, I wouldn't put it that way." She turned her attention back to the man staked out on the sand. "Look. The vultures are back."

Fifteen minutes passed before they went to check on Brick.

Rachel crept as far as her previous footprints went and called out to him. "You still with us, Brick?"

There was no answer. Brick appeared to be breathing and the blood was still seeping from a wound on his face. Rachel looked down at him with ambivalent feelings. "Why do I feel guilty watching that creep die after all the horrible, nightmarish things he's done?"

"Because you're a compassionate human being?"

"Or a fool." She looked down at him again. "Still, he is a human being."

She pulled out her phone and punched in Deputy Tucker's number.

Chapter 21

When the phone rang at the Carpenter's, JT rushed to the phone before Heather could get to it. "I'll take it. It's probably Tucker."

The gravelly voice came loudly over the line. "You busy, JT?"

"No. What's going on?" he said cautiously, hoping he didn't have bad news about Rachel.

"I just got a call from Jesse Albarran. He's out in the desert by the turn off to Shark Tooth Mountain. He said he followed Brick, Shandellan, Hampton, and some other big guy after he saw 'em leave Golden Vista. He followed 'em a while and said they went out Shark Tooth Trail and dropped Brick off about a mile out. They beat him up pretty bad and staked him down in the desert."

"Oh, man. Do you want me to come and help you?"

"Not really. I'm headed out that way now and just wanted to let you know that Rachel is with Jesse."

"Oh, for Pete's sake! I'll be there as fast as I can."

෴

Jesse and Rachel were waiting at the turn-off to Shark Tooth Mountain when Tucker arrived. Jesse talked with the deputy while Rachel decided to remain in the Porsche. Tucker then drove ahead to the site where Brick lay, chased off the vultures, and checked the beaten man's pulse even though he could tell Brick Krutzer was already dead.

The deputy photographed the giant, overlooked footprint by the body and then noted the brush marks around the site before he took shots of the body. After thoroughly checking the site, he drove back to where Jesse and Rachel were.

They all got out of their vehicles and faced each other. The deputy officially pronounced, "He's gone."

"I didn't think he'd last very long after the way he was beaten," Rachel said. "He could barely speak when we arrived."

"His friends did a job on him, that's for sure." He turned to Jesse. "Do you have a description of the big guy?"

Jesse said he did and told Tucker everything he saw. He particularly emphasized the point that he was the one who had called Rachel to ride with him. He also mentioned the jail should have a photograph or security tape of the big Russian because he was the one who actually bailed out Brick.

"Humph," Tucker grunted, a little miffed he hadn't checked back on who finally made the bail. "Well, I got some phone calls to make, so you kids can go on home if you want. I'll get with you both tomorrow if I got any questions."

Jesse and Rachel climbed back into the Porsche and took off down Dead Cow Road. They passed by JT on his way to the meet Tucker and they honked and waved. JT waved back but did not look happy.

Jesse looked over at Rachel. "I think you might be in trouble."

Rachel sighed deeply. "That seems to be the story of my life, Jesse."

೧೨೧

After the medical examiner left and the ambulance took Brick's body away, JT drove on home. Deputy Tucker drove to Yuma. He dreaded having to question Hester about her son's activities, and the thought of him having to arrest her was no happy thought, either. *We'll just have to see how it all pans out. With any luck the old hag will be sedated and won't have to be strapped down.*

When Tucker arrived at the nurses' station, he asked if a nurse could be outside Hester's room in case he needed to call for help. He pictured Hester bolting up out of bed like maniac with a plastic knife ready to do him in. *I'd rather face a nest of rattlesnakes than have to deal with her.*

He was surprised when he walked into her private

room only to see Hester sitting up, happily eating her supper. "Oh!" she said. "I thought you were Brick coming to see me." Her smile changed to a frown and then a sneer. "So what do you want this time, Dewey? Haven't you bothered us enough?"

"I need to ask you a few questions, Hester," he said, pulling up a chair. He pulled a piece of paper and a tape recorder out of his worn leather briefcase.

"Fine. I may or may not answer them, Mr. *Deputy*."

Tucker overlooked the remark and read from the card he pulled out of his pocket: "You are under arrest for murder, conspiracy to commit murder, kidnapping, dispensing drugs to people without a doctor's permission, holding women against their will, and transporting them across state lines for the purposes of prostitution."

Hester's eyebrows shot up in arrogance. "Oh, surely, Dewey, you can do better than that. You know what you're saying is totally absurd."

But Tucker continued on, deaf to her words. "You have the right to remain silent. Anything you say or do can, and will, be used against you in the court of law. You have the right to speak to an attorney. If you cannot afford an attorney, one will be appointed for you. Do you understand these rights as they have been read to you?"

Hester's face slowly changed. Her look of arrogance melted and her eyes narrowed to angry slits filled with venom. Her hatred of him permeated the room like a cloud of noxious gas. She finally spoke very slowly. "I want a lawyer."

"Okay. You're gonna need one. You see, we've already got an all-points out for your buddies Shandellan and Hampton. The CHP should be picking them up any minute. The big Russian was with them, too. You may not know him, but they brought him along this trip for the sole purpose of letting Brick know he better not talk."

The old deputy stood up slowly. "Yep. They made sure of that, too. They beat your son to a pulp and staked him down in the desert to die. It was an agonizing death, too, bein' pecked at by all them buzzards." He turned to walk away.

The look of disbelief that had washed over Heather's face turned to horror. Tucker left the room and her loud screams wailed after him. The nurse rushed into the room, but Tucker heard the screams all the way down the hallway.

Epilogue

Two weeks later the temperature was a hundred and six when Buddy landed on the airstrip at the south edge of Mesquite. He caught up with Rachel and the Carpenters in the Plantation dining room where they were enjoying a bottle of sparkling wine. Rachel poured some into Buddy's glass as he sat next to her.

Dolly came up to the table with a plate of hot appetizers. "Hey, kids. Chef Henri wanted you to try these new Italian treats he made. We're having an Italian mixed platter for a special tonight.

"That looks good," JT said, as Dolly placed the plate in the center of the table.

Rachel took her hand. "That's a lovely ring, Dolly. I've never seen it before."

Dolly blushed and cast her gaze downward. "Uh, it's just a friendship ring."

"A friendship ring? Dolly, is that like a ring you get

before an engagement ring?" she half-way teased.

"I hope so," she giggled, and winked at Rachel. "But I'm not saying *which* friend."

"Oh, you don't have to, I think I already know."

Dolly held her finger up to her lips. "Then don't tell," she whispered, turned, and left the table.

JT smiled his approval after she left. "That Tucker needs to marry that gal."

"Yes, we need to have a wedding here," Heather said and then reached for a piece of calamari. She turned to her "adopted" brother. "Are you going to be able to stay a while this time, Buddy?"

"As long as you need me. I've got things pretty much under control at the office and all the tax late-filers have extensions. Now it's back to regular accounting."

"Doesn't it ever get boring?" Rachel asked.

"Not for me. It's always interesting when we take on millionaires' accounts. Even better when they're billionaires." He made a goofy face at her.

Rachel shook her head. "Well, don't look at me, I failed algebra."

Buddy squeezed her hand. "Yes, but you are so good at other things."

"Yeah, I know—like tracking down murderers. But I want to make it very clear that I've given all that detective business up. I'm taking on a new hobby."

"You are?" JT asked. "Pray tell. I wonder what that could be."

Rachel raised her chin in defiance. "I am learning how to cook. Chef Henri is teaching me. I'm even planning on taking classes over the internet."

Heather looked at her in surprise. "Why, Rachel, how wonderful. I never knew you had a domestic side."

"I guess I never used to. But people grow, you know."

JT nodded. "You're right. And I can see that you have."

"Thank you," she said, nodding in appreciation.

"Yes, we've all come a long way in the last couple of years," he said. "Things have been running along smoothly at the hotel for quite a while now. Maybe too smoothly."

Heather looked at him quizzically. "What do you mean by that?"

"Oh, I don't know. I've been toying around with a couple of other ideas."

"Ideas like what, Mr. Carpenter?" Heather asked with a penetrating gaze.

Everyone turned to look at him. He raised his eyebrows and shrugged at the question. "Well, you know, old Hester Krutzer put her nursing home—" He shot a look at Rachel. "I mean *assisting living home*—up for auction after the Feds shut her down. Not to mention, she needs to raise money for her attorneys."

"Which she's going to need, by the way," Rachel added.

"Yes. So I'm thinking, she may accept a pretty low bid, just to get out from under it."

Heather's voice had an edge to it when she asked, "Are you saying you're going to bid on it?"

"I've considered it." He looked around at the others. "You know, with all the experience we've had running this place, we could handle a business like that. Rosalia could step in as my assistant manager here. She's done so well managing the lounge. I know she could handle the job as assistant."

Rachel raised her glass. "Great idea, JT. The town certainly needs a place like Golden Vista. Miss Emma and Hank can certainly attest to that."

"And if it's run right," Buddy added, "It can be very profitable."

The table turned quiet as everyone considered the idea and delved into the appetizer plate.

Heather pulled off a piece of fried ravioli. "So, any more news on Brick's crew?

Rachel swallowed her sip of wine. "Oh, yeah. Emmet and Tackett still couldn't make bail and are awaiting trial. Shandellan, Hampton, and their Russian buddy, Bogavich, were actually denied bail. They have so many charges against them, they may *never* get back into the free world again."

"Wonderful! So it's a happy ending on *that* story." Heather turned toward her husband. "And a few others."

"Like having Ann Venkman living at the state prison for five to ten years?" JT asked.

Heather responded with a kiss on his cheek.

Rachel turned to both of them. "Just having the truth exposed about our parents' murders made all the difference in the world to me. My whole life has changed. I feel at peace for the first time ever since that happened.

My shrink even allowed me to cut back on my meds." She raised her hand in an oath. "But I will continue to take them until he says I don't have to."

Heather nodded in agreement and then asked sympathetically, "Do you think he ever will?"

"Probably not. Bi-polar illness is a genetic disorder. The neurotransmitters in my brain may always be a little out of sync, but I'm okay with that."

"I think it makes you a little more interesting," Buddy teased.

Rachel laughed and playfully punched him on the shoulder.

Heather looked at JT, as if in confirmation, and then turned to Rachel. "So do you want to come to church with us tomorrow?"

Rachel thought a bit. "Okay. I don't see why not." She turned to Buddy. "Do you want to go?"

"Sure," he said. "We'll need to find *some* place to get married.

"Married?" Rachel asked, surprised. "You haven't even *asked* me yet."

"Only about a dozen times, my dear."

"Oh." She blinked a few times, processing the information. "I thought you were kidding."

Heather giggled.

"But just to make it official…" Buddy pulled a black velvet box out of his pocket and opened it in front of her.

The huge diamond sparkled in the light of the flickering candle and Rachel's eyes widened in surprise.

"So, will you marry me, Rachel Ryan?"

Rachel made him wait a few moments and then smiled at him impishly. "Of course, Buddy! Why do you think I'm taking *cooking* lessons?"

Heather grinned at the two of them and then back at her husband. Filled with delight, she pumped her fist in the air and whooped, "Hallelujah!"

About the Author

Joanne Taylor Moore was born in Massachusetts and enjoyed life on a small, family farm where she learn to love nature and develop her imagination. She has published some of her poems and written newspaper articles, but mystery novels are her favorite genre. Her Blood Mountain series is about life and murder in the Arizona Desert. Moore lives with her husband, Larry, in Yuma, Arizona, and loves to spend her free time reading, designing jewelry, and visiting her four children and eleven grandchildren.